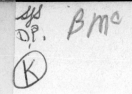

DEATH BY INCHES

It's January in Los Angeles and the city is
experiencing a heatwave. Lieutenant
Mendoza's Homicide Squad has been
shorthanded since the brutal murder of one
of its most dependable members. And now
the number of crimes demanding
Mendoza's attention begins climbing
alongside the temperature gauge . . .

DEATH BY INCHES

Dell Shannon

Chivers Press, Bath, England.
Curley Publishing, Inc.,
Hampton, N.H., U.S.A.

Library of Congress Cataloging-in-Publication Data

Shannon, Dell, 1921–
    Death by inches / by Dell Shannon.—Large print ed.
        p.   cm.—(Atlantic large print)
    ISBN 0–7451–8425–1   (Chivers   Press).—ISBN 0–7451–8430–8
(pbk. : Chivers Press).—ISBN 0–7927–1343–5 (pbk. : Curley Pub.)
    1. Large type books.   I. Title.
[PS3562.I515D37   1992]
813′.54—dc20   92–17552
                                                                         CIP

British Library Cataloguing in Publication Data available

This Large Print edition is published by Chivers Press, England, and
Curley Publishing, Inc, U.S.A. 1992

Published by arrangement with Victor Gollancz Ltd

U.K. Hardback ISBN 0 7451 8425 1
U.K. Softback ISBN 0 7451 8430 8
U.S.A. Softback ISBN 0 7927 1343 5

Photoset, printed and bound in Great Britain by
REDWOOD PRESS LIMITED, Melksham, Wiltshire

Oh, why did God,
Creator wise, that peopled highest Heaven
With spirits masculine, create at last
This novelty on earth, this fair defect
Of nature, and not fill the world at once
With men as angels without feminine,
Or find some other way to generate
Mankind? This mischief had not then befallen.
                          John Milton, *Paradise Lost*

CHAPTER ONE

'Why do I get myself involved in these things, anyway?' asked Alison mournfully.

Mendoza finished his coffee and shoved over his cup for a refill. 'Because you can't bring yourself to be a little rude to people and say "No."'

Alison poured coffee. 'I *know* that. But what a dreary business it—'

'All you have to do, I gather,' said Mendoza, 'is look at all the amateurs' paintings and say which is the best, in your opinion as a professional.'

'Oh, there's more to it than that,' said Alison gloomily. 'They've got hold of Sally Mawson and Tony Lawlor, too—I expect they approached some of the really top local talent and got snubbed, so they were reduced to people like us, who qualify as professionals because we've sold a few pictures. I have a dark suspicion it was Sally steered them onto me ... No, they've managed to get a room in the Arts and Crafts Building up in Barnsdall Park for a week. Today there's going to be a sort of ceremony of hanging all the entries, and then we're supposed to take a week to judge them—I do ask you, Luis! I can just imagine what horrible *daubs*—And then next Saturday there's another little ceremony of

1

announcing the winners. They call themselves,' she added even more gloomily, 'the Hollywood Hobbyists and Amateur Artists. *Artists.*'

Mendoza laughed. 'Cheer up, *cara*—you'll just be bored a little. I'm off, it's nearly eight.' He shoved his chair back and hit Nefertiti, who complained loudly. Bending to pick her up and apologize, he stepped back onto Sheba's tail. Sheba wailed, and Alison got up hurriedly.

'I'll come with you—Señor and Bast are out, and the twins, too.'

'Very maternal afterthought,' said Mendoza. He put Nefertiti down; they slid hastily through the back door before either she or Sheba could slip out. There was no sign of El Señor or Bast, but Master John Luis and Miss Teresa Ann were chasing each other round the wide patio while Mrs. MacTaggart wandered about snipping off dead leaves and keeping an eye on the twins.

Mendoza kissed Alison and put on his hat. Mrs. MacTaggart hurried to corral the twins temporarily. 'What we need around here,' he said, 'is a set of automatic signals, maybe at each end of the drive. Cats out, twins out, extreme caution, or vice versa. Have fun with your art-lovers, *querida*.'

'*So* sympathetic,' said Alison. 'I know, I got myself into it. But I can just *imagine*—Oh, well.'

2

Mendoza started to back the Ferrari out very slowly while Alison paced down the drive beside it watching for cars. Mrs. MacTaggart and the twins waved; he stopped to wave back, reached the street safely, waved at Alison, shoved the *Drive* button, and then slammed on the brakes as El Señor and Bast shot across the street ahead of him. Alison shooed them up the drive and waved again, the sun bright on her red hair.

'Hostages to fortune!' said Mendoza. '*¡Vaya por Dios!*' He took his foot off the brake and stepped on the accelerator.

It was Saturday, January ninth, and as usual sometime in January, L.A. and environs were experiencing a mild heat wave.

When Mendoza got to the Homicide office of the big Central Headquarters building downtown, he found Lieutenant Goldberg chatting with Sergeant Lake at the desk. 'Morning, Saul. What're you doing down here?' Lieutenant Goldberg belonged up in Robbery.

'Some business for you, Luis.'

'Oh? Come on in.' Mendoza went into the inner office. Hackett was leaning on the desk reading a report, a Hackett still burly but considerably trimmer in figure after his hospital siege and only two months back on the job. He glanced up and nodded at Goldberg.

'Teletype in from this one-horse burg in

3

Indiana somewhere, Luis. They think a boy they want might be here.'

'Nice,' said Mendoza. 'As if we haven't enough to keep us busy. Anything new on the Ambler thing?'

'Yeah, but before I forget, has Alison got anything on for next Saturday? I will never,' said Hackett, shaking his sandy head, 'understand females. But never. We don't go to church from one year's end to the next, but here Angel's insisting the baby's got to be officially christened, for God's sake. She's got it set up for next Saturday, the Episcopal church near us. She knows you won't come, but—'

'Well, she'd better check with Alison. I don't know what time the art lovers are going to meet. And I'm not asking how the baby is—just set you off rhapsodizing again. Why the hell any sensible man gets himself embroiled in all these domesticities—What's new on the Ambler job?'

Hackett said with dignity he didn't rhapsodize, that Sheila was just an exceptionally bright and beautiful baby. And Angel hadn't breathed a word about having Mark christened two years back and why she'd suddenly—'All right, all right. Galeano got an anonymous tip over the phone. About five A.M.—funny time. Caller said to take a look at one Joe Tucker, address over on Main, for the Ambler job.' The Ambler job

4

had happened last Tuesday night—Ambler's liquor store on Hill Street held up and Ambler, alone in the place, shot dead. The only thing they knew about it, after four days, was what gun the killer had used—a Colt Woodsman .22. Which was not very enlightening. 'Galeano left it for the day crew, but he had Records look for Tucker. He's there all right, got quite a little pedigree. Heist jobs mostly.'

'Um. Who went out on it?'

'Jase and Palliser, about ten minutes ago. May not find him at home, of course.'

'Jase being on it, they'll fetch him in,' said Mendoza; both he and Hackett laughed.

'Who's that, new boy?' asked Goldberg, blowing his nose.

'*¡Seguramente que sí!*' said Mendoza. He grinned, thinking of Detective Jason Grace.

Bert Dwyer had been shot and killed by the bank robber just three months ago. They were shorthanded as it was, with Scarne having transferred to the lab, but it wasn't until six weeks back they'd been given a new man to replace Dwyer ... Besides the official notification, Mendoza had had a call from Lieutenant Whitney out at the Hollenbeck station, Grace's former superior.

Mendoza was mildly pleased to have a Negro officer join them. There was a large Negro population in Central's territory, and the honest citizens among them (always, thank God, the majority in *any* population) sometimes felt a little easier with a Negro cop. Nobody at Homicide had any funny prejudices, and in any case, Mendoza knew that on this force any man who'd made detective first grade would be a reasonably efficient officer.

That, of course, was before they all found out how unreasonably efficient Detective First Grade Jason Grace was.

'You,' Whitney had said, 'are more than welcome to him, Mendoza. That guy makes me feel so damn inferior, if I could afford it I'd be seeing a head doctor.'

In the last six weeks the boys at Homicide had been finding out what he meant.

One of the first little jobs Detective Grace had been given was that of going to question the hottest suspect in a supermarket heist job, one Hans Borgmann. When Detective Grace had politely announced himself and showed his badge, the hulking Borgmann had turned to his wife and told her in casual German that she'd better back up his alibi of being home all that night or he'd break her neck. Which was a tactical error on Borgmann's part, but just how was he to have guessed that Detective Jason Grace spoke fluent German as well as Spanish and Italian?

Likewise, when Detective Grace came unexpectedly (and alone) face to face with Sonny Lee Endler in the doorway of a pool

6

hall on Second Street, Sonny Lee hadn't been very worried. Sonny Lee was on the Ten Most Wanted list, he could smell cop at fifty feet with the wind in the wrong direction, and he saw that this particular cop had recognized him, but after all, the cop was alone and just a medium-sized cop, while Sonny Lee stood six-four in his stockinged feet and weighed two-forty. So he just reached for the cop before the cop could reach his gun, feeling quite confident—Which was where he made his mistake, but how was Sonny Lee to have known that Detective Jason Grace was a judo expert? He deduced it later on in the prison wing of the General Hospital.

Similarly, Bucky Randall had no hesitation in marching down Broadway in broad daylight, even though his photograph adorned most post offices in the country. It was an old photograph, and since then he'd gained forty pounds, dyed his blond hair black and trimmed his eyebrows, and instead of his customary gaudy sports clothes he was wearing a conservative dark suit and white shirt. Bucky was very surprised when he got neatly collared, but then how could he have known that Detective Jason Grace had trained himself to be a real camera eye, a dick with a long memory for the faces of pro crooks?

Sergeant Rory Farrell, who was a crossword fan, found Detective Grace an invaluable addition to the office: Detective

7

Grace had apparently memorized the dictionary.

His father was one of the staff physicians at the General, so he had a better than average understanding of medicine.

His wife had once been a legal secretary, so he knew a good deal about torts, and so on.

'It's just that I figure,' Grace said in his soft voice, 'you can't ever have too much general knowledge. You just never know when a little bit of it's going to come in handy.' He admitted Hebrew had thrown him—of course it wasn't the sort of thing a detective was apt to find a use for anyway; he was currently taking a night course in the identification of gems and minerals, and in his off time reading anthropology.

Mendoza was still grinning. 'Don't be surprised, Saul, if you drop in here someday and find our new boy sitting at my desk.'

'That'll be the day,' said Hackett. 'Funny, too, Jase'd be insufferable if he wasn't basically a nice guy. But he's got no crystal ball like the boss.'

'So bring out your crystal ball,' said Goldberg. He sneezed, reached for Kleenex, blew his nose, dropped the Kleenex into the wastebasket, and produced a thick sheaf of papers in a cardboard folder. 'I'm very happy to hand this one over, Luis. We've been breaking our hearts over it for nine weeks. Since, in fact, Halloween, which was when

8

the first job got pulled.' He laid the folder on Mendoza's desk with an air of finality. Hackett came over and picked it up.

Mendoza lit a cigarette and leaned back in his chair. 'So what's Homicide got to do with a robbery job? And which?'

Goldberg sneezed and said, 'Damn. The goddamn allergy specialists still telling me to get a different job. Tension, they talk about. Tension, my God. Among everything else we've had to work at, this joker breaking into thirteen places, and for peanuts, and not one single damn lead as to who he is—' He snorted and produced more Kleenex.

Higgins wandered into the office, pulling the knot of his tie loose. 'Morning, Luis. Goldberg. I don't so much like this suicide you chased me out on, Art. That business over on Second. Something about it smells just a little funny.' He mopped his forehead. 'Why the hell isn't the air conditioning on? It's nearly ninety outside.'

'It's January,' said Hackett dryly. 'Who needs air conditioning in January? What about the suicide?'

'Guy cut his throat,' said Higgins, 'apparently. Wife says she found him this morning—What time did the call come in, just as the night crew was going off, wasn't it? So he's there on the living room couch with his throat cut, and an old-fashioned straight razor on the floor across the room. So I

9

suppose he *could* have thrown it there after he did it, in a spasm or something—see what the doctor says—but something about it—'

'Later, later,' said Mendoza. 'One thing at a time. So what's the story, Saul?'

Goldberg sighed. 'So last night our boy pulls Number Thirteen, and it turns out an unlucky number for him all right. This time he kills somebody. So I turn it over to you with my blessing.'

'From the beginning, *por favor*,' said Mendoza. He sat up and emptied the ashtray, lined up blotter and desk tray, straightened the desk clock to a precise angle. Hackett and Higgins exchanged a glance. Higgins had once expressed the private opinion that Mendoza counted the hairs in his neat mustache every morning and trimmed it to come out even, each side matching.

'Sure,' said Goldberg. 'Halloween. An old lady, pensioner, living over on Council Street. Ramshackle old house separated into three apartments. One-story. This guy breaks in, scares the life out of her—about one A.M., it was—knocked her down, ransacked the place, got what was left of her pension money, and *vamos*. Poor old lady's eighty-three, widow without any family. So we start looking, and get nothing. Or almost. He pulled off a screen to get in a window, and we got a couple of prints off the screen which don't belong to the landlord or anybody else who might have had occasion to touch it—but they're not in anybody's files. So we're stymied. We ask around all the stoolies, we get nothing. So then our bird pulls another, November ninth. It's all in there'—he nodded at the file—'all we didn't get. Thirteen of 'em. And last night he hit this woman just a little too hard, cracked her skull. So now it's your baby, and I wish you joy of it.'

'Same M.O., I gather,' said Hackett.

'What else? We know he must case the jobs, because every time he's picked'—Goldberg grimaced—'old people. Poor old people. *In* both senses, if you get me, because it's a cheap neighborhood. That's another funny thing, which you'd think would tell us something—give us some kind of lead, anyway—but so far it hasn't. He's stuck to just this one area. Roughly bounded by Temple and Beverly, Alvarado and Glendale Boulevard.'

'*¿De veras?*' said Mendoza. 'That'd be about a five-by-ten-block square. Does that say he lives somewhere there?'

'Why should it?' Goldberg shrugged. 'He might live in Boyle Heights or Ocean Park, for all we know. Sure, we've been through the area. With, you might put it, the proverbial fine-tooth comb. Four men with pedigrees live in that area. We've got nothing on any of 'em. Their prints don't match the ones we got off the screens. Two other

11

screens as well as the first one. That's how he gets in every time—pulls off screens on back windows. You know those streets, Luis—hardly a house less than fifty years old, the kind of houses the owners haven't the money to keep up. Broken screens, broken windows, leaky plumbing, low rents. He cases the jobs, that much we can guess. He picks, first, the old people—living alone, mostly—who won't or can't put up any physical fight, and second, the places that are easy to break into. We're pretty sure we've got his prints, because we've found the same ones on three different jobs—always on the screens. So that says he's not a pro, he's got no record.'

'Very nice,' said Mendoza wryly. 'Should I thank you? Does he use a weapon of any kind?'

Goldberg shook his head, standing up. 'Just his fists. It's all in there, all the statements, and so on. You'll have fun with it, Luis.'

'I am willing to bet,' said Mendoza. He looked at his cigarette pensively. 'Now why that fairly small area? Just that area?'

'Have a look in your crystal ball,' said Goldberg. 'I've got other things on hand. Let me know if and when you find out anything.' He lifted an amiable hand and ambled out.

'As if we didn't have enough to do,' said Hackett, opening the cardboard file. 'What a

12

hell of an anonymous thing.'

'Ought to be something to get hold of, out of thirteen jobs,' said Higgins. He passed a hand over his ugly rough-hewn face. 'God, it's hot. *January*, my God, doesn't seem fair. It looks to me as if he's got to be connected to that neighborhood somehow. I mean, how else would he know—when he cases the jobs, he'd be spotted as a stranger, wouldn't he?'

'This is a big city, George,' said Mendoza.

'Sure, but even so—Well, a meter reader? A laundry deliveryman? Driver of an ice-cream truck? If he doesn't live right there in that area? Somebody without a record.'

'Saul Goldberg,' said Mendoza, 'has been a cop a good long time, George, and he's a good cop. I wouldn't doubt all those bright ideas occurred to him, too. Well, all we can do is look. I suppose it's early to ask for an autopsy report. Who got killed, by the way?'

Hackett answered without looking up from the page in his hand. 'Woman. Mrs. Marion Stromberg, eighty-six, widow, no family, on the old age pension.'

'Christ,' said Higgins somberly. 'This is a nice guy.'

'So we start looking for him,' said Mendoza. 'Needle in a haystack. So what about the suicide, George?'

'*I* don't know,' said Higgins, shrugging. 'I just don't like it. I left Piggott and Landers there poking around—probably a waste of

13

time. It looks like suicide, for sure. Fellow named Gonzales, about forty. Alfredo Gonzales. Lived with his wife and about seven kids, rented house over on Second Street. Not all his kids, he's the woman's second husband. She says—the wife—he came home drunk last night and fell asleep on the living room couch. She gets up this morning, thinks he's still sleeping it off, gets breakfast for the kids, and so on, and then she goes into the living room and finds him dead like that, his throat cut. Says he's threatened to do it before.'

'Any corroboration on that?'

'I don't know yet. I want to look up any pals he may have been with last night. I just don't like it,' said Higgins.

And like Hackett, Higgins might look like a big dumb cop, but he wasn't—not so dumb, that is.

'Well,' said Mendoza. 'They do keep us busy, don't they? Let's find out things.' He took Goldberg's file and opened it.

In the anteroom, Detective First Grade Jason Grace's deceptively mild voice said, 'Now, Mr. Tucker, let's just take it easy. In here, please—we just want to ask you a few questions.'

CHAPTER TWO

Depressingly, it appeared that Joe Tucker wasn't the boy they wanted for the Ambler job.

He had protested all the way down to headquarters, and he went on protesting as Grace, Sergeant Palliser, Hackett and Mendoza stood around him in the sergeant's office. Eagerly he answered questions before they were asked.

'Sure, sure, I got a little pedigree but I'm clean now, I swear, I been clean since I got out last time, I swear. And I can prove I didn't have nothing to do with that job, I got a good alibi—You did say it was last Tuesday night, din't you? Sure, I got—'

'So let's hear the alibi, Joe,' said Grace mildly. He was a slim man of medium height, and always looked very neat; he favored light gray suits and very plain ties. He had regular features and a hairline mustache as precise as Mendoza's own; his skin was the color of well-creamed coffee and he wore his thick straight black hair unparted off his forehead. His voice was very soft.

'Tuesday night, sure—and I just bet I know what bastard tried to get me into trouble, too! Prob'ly called you and said look at me for that job—prob'ly thought I couldn't

15

prove I never pulled it. Goddamn sorehead. I bet it was Fred, all right. See, I took a little dough off him in a crap game the other night, and he's the goddamnedest sorest loser—I just bet—But anyways, I got an alibi, see, you can check. Honest. I was at a stag party Tuesday night, for a guy gonna get hitched next day, see? That's where I was, till maybe two, three inna morning, and the other guys'll say—'

'Where, Joe?' asked Palliser. 'What guys?'

Tucker rattled off a dozen names readily; both Grace and Palliser wrote them down.

'Any idea where we might find these fellows right now?' asked Palliser.

'Well, gee, let me think—'

Patiently they took notes. Tucker opening up right away, the alibi would probably check out; but it was a murder count after all, so they held Tucker while they checked. It would, they silently agreed, be the hell of a lot of legwork and nothing to show for it at the end but another suspect cleared; but that was routine for you.

Palliser and Grace went out to start checking; Mendoza and Hackett went out on the new job Goldberg had just handed them.

'Do you ever wonder why the hell you joined the force?' asked Palliser as they emerged from the elevators downstairs. He yawned; he'd been out on a date with Roberta Silverman the night before and hadn't got to

16

bed until 1 A.M.

'No, I can't say I ever do,' said Grace seriously. 'You know something, I never wanted to be anything else but a cop. Couldn't say why, exactly.' He grinned. 'I guess you could say I'm one of these dedicated officers all the true-detective magazines talk about.'

'Sometimes—' said Palliser, and yawned again. 'We'll spend the next six hours on this and find the alibi checks and the anonymous tipster was Fred—whoever he is.'

'So we'll know another fellow who didn't do the Ambler job,' said Grace.

'One way to look at it, all right. Look, let's save a little time and divide them up,' said Palliser.

'Anything you say.'

'By what the lieutenant says about this new business, we'll be working round the clock on that. Let's just hope we don't get anything else until we've got at least one of the current jobs straightened out.'

'No bets,' said Grace cheerfully. 'Not down here.'

*   *   *

'As if we hadn't enough on our hands already,' repeated Hackett. 'What's the address?'

'Dawson Street.' Mendoza put the Ferrari

in gear. 'Tucker's probably clean. On the Ambler thing, anyway. Where haven't we checked?'

'Well, it still could be any of a dozen pros we've picked up to question, of course. With no alibis. It could be a first job for somebody; in fact, that's a little bit more likely because experienced elevator men don't often shoot anybody. We're going through the motions—looking at everybody likely out of Records. May still get a lead from one of the pigeons, but—'

'And now George's suicide. And this damn thing. Want to bet we'll get something else dropped in our laps too?' Mendoza braked for a light.

Hackett groaned. 'Damn, I forgot to tell Jimmy to pass that teletype on to Records. The guy was from here originally, they said. Wonder how a big city boy happened to get out in the sticks like that.'

'Where'd you say it was from?'

'Sidalia, Indiana. Chief of Police. I looked it up. Population, nineteen hundred.'

'*Así, así,*' said Mendoza. 'I wonder what it's like, being a cop in a place like that.'

'That's something neither of us'll ever know,' said Hackett with a sigh.

Because homicide in the city got to be a very untidy thing. Probably there weren't many homicides in Sidalia, Indiana, and on the rare occasions when one came along, the

18

Chief of Police and whatever handful of men he had under him were in on it from the start to finish, every step of the way. It would be a nine-day wonder and headlined in the town weekly and everybody in town would probably know just what the cops were doing and thinking. But this was the city, and homicide, untidy anywhere, tended to get even more confused to big-city cops. Take today, for example. It was about par for the course. It was very rare for the Homicide office to be working just one case; on the average, you had one maybe just getting wound up, with a lot of paperwork still to do, and maybe another just begun, and one tough one you'd been working on for some time, and there were usually requests for information and local help in from some other force or forces, and sometimes you were shorthanded because somebody was in court testifying, or on vacation. Somehow Mendoza had to keep all the threads separated, keep an eye on all the various jobs, while doing a little legwork himself on all of them perhaps, and suggest where else to look and question.

Sometimes it got a little rough. And it seemed to be one of the rules, in the big town, that when you had about seventeen things to do already, and several cases bugging you at once, that was just the time somebody was going to decide that this was the right minute to take an ax to his wife, or the guy who took his girl away from him, or the neighbor who argued politics with him, or somebody like that. So you got sirens going and crowds flocking, and after the interns had taken the body away the uniformed cops went peacefully back on tour, but if you were a Homicide cop you had the whole bit to start over again, the questioning, the hunt for evidence, and meanwhile all those other unsolved cases waited.

This one Goldberg had landed them looked like the really tough one. That was what Mendoza and Hackett thought that Saturday, neither of them being clairvoyant and not yet knowing what was going to turn up on Monday. Routine, and/or some whisper from one of the stool pigeons, would in all probability lead them to the Ambler killer sooner or later. Routine, and the doctor's and lab reports, would probably tell them whether Alfredo Gonzales had really committed suicide or not. It probably wouldn't be too much trouble to find out whether the man wanted in Sidalia, Indiana, was here or not. But this one, this X who went around carefully picking out aged people and breaking into their homes to rob them—even when they had his prints, he wasn't going to be easy to catch up to. Not by Goldberg's experience. Prints didn't mean much if you didn't have any to compare them with; and true enough, this X needn't live anywhere near the area where he'd committed his break-ins—and now a murder; and you couldn't fingerprint everybody in the whole damn county.

Mendoza pulled the Ferrari to the curb on Dawson Street and sat looking thoughtfully at the house. And at the street.

It was an old and shabby street. Curiously, although L.A. had slums, all right, they were completely unlike the slums of any other city. And in one way, therefore, they were not really slums. When you thought the word, you thought of tenement buildings, you thought of people crowded close together in dirty streets. This wasn't a street like that. It was a narrow street, its blacktop paving was old and rutted, its curbs were broken, its sidewalk cracked; but it was lined not with apartment buildings, but with old frame houses, large and small, on forty-foot city lots. Most of the houses were painted a uniform khaki color, and most of them were in need of paint. Most of them had been built in the early nineteen hundreds; some of them still bore gingerbread lace around their eaves. Most of the larger ones were now either rooming houses or had been cut up into apartments in a makeshift kind of way, what had been a side door now being somebody's front door. There was grass in front of the houses, but it was brown and dead-looking now and would remain so in summer because landlords here could not afford the water bills to keep lawns green. There were flowers and flowering shrubs against the houses, but the kinds that didn't take much care. There were a few trees along the curb.

There were children playing on the sidewalk farther up the block. The house where Marion Stromberg had been murdered sat on the corner of the street.

Mendoza lit a cigarette, looking at the house. Hackett looked at Mendoza's regular lean profile under the sharp widow's peak. 'Inspiration strike you, *compadre?*'

'*Nada.* But, damn it, Art, the joker's got to have *some* reason for hitting this area. So it doesn't say he lives here—maybe he did once. Maybe there are a good many elderly people living around here? People on pensions. People, even, on relief.'

'Could be,' said Hackett. 'It's a quiet sort of backwater, looks like.'

'Mmh,' said Mendoza. 'I did read the précis on what Saul got on him. He's been seen. A couple of times. In the dark, so it's nothing but a vague description. He's big, at least six feet, and apparently fairly young, by the way he moves.'

'Which figures,' said Hackett impatiently.

'Mmh. We could,' said Mendoza, 'I suppose, find out just how many elderly pensioners live in the area and stake out all those who haven't been hit.'

22

'For the love of God!' said Hackett. 'You forgotten what force we're on, boy? We're the old reliable upstanding L.A.P.D., not New York, with twenty-five thousand boys in blue. New York polices, what, nine million population, and we've got to police about five million with a fifth the force, and who cares how loud the Chief yells for more money? Population going up by a hundred a day, but what the hell, who needs more cops? Where, in other words, are you going to get the men?'

'Very pertinent,' said Mendoza. 'Come on, let's see this landlady.' He tossed his cigarette out the window and opened the car door.

The landlady's name was Mrs. Ethel Brace. She was a woman about fifty who'd once been pretty and was still attractive, a woman who'd kept her figure and was dressed neatly in a flowered cotton house dress. She had graying dark hair and bright brown eyes.

'It's just terrible,' she said. 'Just *terrible*. To think of poor Mrs. Stromberg—in *my* house! I just can't get over it. The things going on around here lately—Why can't you catch this fiend, anyways? After that old man got robbed round on Court Street, I told Mrs. Stromberg, be sure bolt her door ever' night. But it didn't do no good in the end. My daughter says we oughta move. If the neighborhood's getting so things like this happen alla time. It's always been a quiet neighborhood, no trouble; of course there was

23

that Mrs. Pitman's boy downa street, a real tough boy, but they do say you get delinquents, like they call them, even from real respectable familys these days. My daughter says we should move. I've lived here thirty years; it'd be like tearing up roots. But guys *killing* people—I can't hardly believe it yet. Poor Mrs. Stromberg, as never harmed a flea.'

'You told the other officers you saw the man?' asked Mendoza.

'Yes, yes, terrible—just terrible! The middle of the night it was—last night. After one in the morning. Why, Mrs. Stromberg, she's lived here matter o' fifteen years. A nice old lady. She come here after her husband passed away. I don't know what work he done but there wasn't no pension, whatever, and she had the state pension. She didn't need much of a place for herself, one old lady like that—a nice old lady, she was. Polite, and just the little she had—it don't bear thinking of! ... What? ... Yes, yes, that's right, I saw him. I heard her scream, you know. Middle o' the night. I was in bed. I woke right up when I heard her scream, and I got up and went to the window—I didn't rightly know what it was, you know how it is when you're waked up sudden, I didn't rightly know what *had* waked me up—I was in two minds about waking Jim up, didn't seem to be nothing wrong—and then I saw

24

the man. I guess now we know he come out the window there, her apartment, but it's all one floor and I didn't see him till he was in the drive. He was running. He—'

'Can you give us any idea what he looked like, Mrs. Brace?' asked Mendoza.

'Well, I guess not much,' she said dubiously. 'I only saw him for a couple seconds, till he went over the hedge into the Bensons' yard. He was a big guy, six feet, anyways, I'd say, and he had on a white shirt, I saw that—and he didn't have a hat on, I saw his hair, long hair, kind of—'

'Could you see if he was a white man or a Negro?'

'Oh, he was a white man. I'm sure o' that, there was a moon, the light kinda glinted on his face and it was real white. That's all I saw—I couldn't say no more about his face, long nose or what color eyes or like that—it was just a couple seconds, you know, and he was gone. But then I right away thought of that guy been breaking in on old folks, and I woke Jim up, and he give me hell, but I got him to go look because Mrs. Stromberg got the back apartment and the guy came from the back, and like you know, we found—'

'Yes.' The killer had evidently wakened Mrs. Stromberg as he got in the window; she had got out of bed, seen him and screamed, and he had knocked her down. Her head had hit the sharp corner of a chest of drawers, and so now it was murder, now it was their baby. 'Can we see Mrs. Stromberg's apartment, please?'

Marx and Horder were on the way, to print the whole place. Goldberg's men, thankful to hand this one over, hadn't done any work on it.

'Why, sure. Sure. It's just a terrible thing—a *murder*—and my daughter says as we oughta move, neighborhood getting—But we've lived here thirty years and it's always been a quiet—'

They looked at the apartment, so called. A tiny sitting room, a tinier bedroom partitioned off, a minute lavatory with a stall shower, no tub. It was all redolent of age, economically lived, neatly lived. Sparse and shabby furniture. A small stock of canned food on the shelf in the tiny makeshift kitchenette. A few leftovers neatly put away in the small refrigerator. A modest wardrobe of shabby clothes, old-lady clothes, two pairs of shoes, in the little curtained-off closet. The single cot unmade, bedclothes trailing to the floor, where she'd wakened and risen hastily. A fat, old-fashioned-looking Bible on the small table beside the bed. No other books, no magazines.

Drawers had been pulled out and dumped, chair cushions slit, the sugar bowl emptied on the kitchen table.

There was a single just-opened yellow

rosebud, in a dime-store vase, on the little table in the living room, which, when the house was new, had been a bedroom.

'And she wouldn't have had so much, you know—a hundred and nine bucks the pension is now, and she'd paid me the rent—thirty-five that is—and bought some groceries. I don't suppose she'd have had maybe forty, fifty dollars, and to think of somebody *killing*—'

There was a chalked outline where she had fallen and died.

'Thanks very much, Mrs. Brace,' said Mendoza.

Joe Tucker's alibi checked out. He had been at the stag party all right, and quite a party it had been. But Ambler's liquor store had been held up, and Ambler shot, at about nine o'clock—he'd been found by a customer at nine-twenty—and while everybody at the stag party admitted freely that they'd all been well and truly oiled by midnight, the party was just getting under way by nine, and Tucker had definitely been among those present.

'Well, just the way it goes,' said Jason Grace philosophically. 'We look somewhere else.'

'Where?' asked Palliser sourly.

They let Tucker go. It was 2:20 P.M.

Mendoza had studied all the reports in Goldberg's file over lunch. No inspiration had

27

hit him. He handed it over to Hackett, who studied it gloomily and said nothing occurred to him either at the moment.

'Why that one area; is all I come up with.'

'Mmh,' said Mendoza. 'Let's get a breakdown of just how many elderly people do live there. Just for fun. That, by all we can figure, seems to be his criterion—old people, who won't fight back.'

'Yes. I see that. But he's got to be connected to the area in some way.'

'*De veras*,' Mendoza glanced at his watch. Two thirty-five. 'We have to make a start on it somewhere.'

Idly he wondered how Alison had got on with the art lovers.

CHAPTER THREE

'... That everybody should have a hobby of some kind,' said Mrs. Tate firmly, 'and a lot more people than you might think have some creative talent, you know, Miss Weir.'

'Oh, yes,' said Alison. Mrs. Tate was not really a large woman, but she gave that impression with her undoubted authority. She had taken the three local professionals in hand immediately, introducing them to the individual members with a proprietary air. She was, Alison supposed, about fifty. Only a little taller than Alison, not a bad figure if it had thickened slightly at the hips, brown hair which was probably touched up, slightly protuberant blue eyes behind violently upswept plastic-framed glasses, and one of those would-be good plain black crepe dresses that sell for somewhere around eighteen ninety-five, to which she'd added a string of large pearls, pearl earrings, and a big gold costume brooch.

There was a tall, thin old man, Mr. Schubert or Schuman, and a wispy little gray-haired woman—Miss Ames?—with *spinster* practically emblazoned on her forehead, and a woman named Tillinghurst, and another man, blond, with a high tenor voice and a lisp. There were about fifteen other people, all women except for a third man who was apparently dumb.

There were also, of course, the paintings. The paintings already hung with care about the walls of the little room in this new building were about what Alison had expected. She'd exchanged one silent glance with Sally Mawson over them.

'...*And* Mrs. Mawson. Really I think our little group has turned out some very nice things, if I do say so, and we're certainly flattered to get you nice people to come and see our work, Miss Weir. Of course we don't flatter ourselves we're very important—most of us just working people, but we enjoy

29

trying, you know—'

'Well, you might let 'em look at the pictures, May,' said Mr. Schubert a trifle testily. He stared at Alison. 'Therapy,' he added abruptly. 'Doctor suggested it. New interest in life, see? Found it was kind of fun—messin' around with paints, tryin' to draw things right. See? Understand a lot of people do these days, sort of a hobby.'

'Yes,' said Alison. 'Yes, that's so.' Over Mrs. Tate's shoulder she caught a glimpse of Tony Lawlor, that willowy young man, staring with something like consternation at a good-sized canvas upon which was drawn, in very primary oils, with one-dimensional directness, five black-and-white cows in a violent green meadow. The cows' legs looked like sticks, and the black markings on their flanks were geometrically precise. She bit her lip, hoping that Tony would bridle his vitriolic tongue until they were alone. Her first vague impressions of the Amateur Artists were that they were, on the whole, a rather seedy-looking little group, perhaps rather pathetic people—lonely, with few interests— but one couldn't really be rude, it would be too unkind. Although, she reflected, one would have to be *very* rude to penetrate Mrs. May Tate's armor.

'I remember my grandmother telling me how young ladies took up china painting when she was young—' The wispy spinster.

'It really is a very interesting hobby, I've found, and Mr. Coulter—that's the man I work for—says a lot of people have found they had real talent. There was Grandma Moses, you know. Of course I don't suppose *I*—'

'Now we'll just let you have a first teeny look around at all the pictures'—Mrs. Tate recaptured control heartily—'and then we have a little treat for us all, nothing much, a little fruit punch and—'

Alison caught Sally's eye again. Tony was looking even more agitated at the mention of fruit punch.

They toured the paintings solemnly, with a steady running commentary from Mrs. Tate. Mr. Schubert had definite style, they'd notice, and was not afraid of color. (That was the cows.) Miss Ames used her angles interestingly, didn't they think? Mr. Foster leaned a bit toward the symbolic school, as they could see—

The fruit punch and some very hard cookies were duly drunk and eaten. 'I *hope* Miss Archer hasn't spiked the punch for us!' said Mrs. Tate coyly, with a booming laugh. Alison saw a reply trembling on Tony's lips and hastily stepped on his foot...

*　　*　　*

'So that's why you came reeling home,' said

Mendoza.

'I had one Martini, and I can tell you I needed it,' said Alison. 'Tony simply made a beeline for the nearest bar, and Sally and I didn't say no. Poor, pathetic little people. The worst of it is, Tony's going to be difficult. He got to feeling mischievous about it, you know how he does—'

'Mmh? In what way?'

'Well, you *know*,' said Alison, 'we could say eeny, meeny, miney, mo over them, one's as bad as the next, it doesn't really matter, but Tony's insisting on going all solemn over it and really criticizing each one, just for fun. He can be devastatingly funny, but I'm afraid a few of the Hobbyists might be bright enough to see he was being sarcastic. You're not listening.'

'Yes, I am.' Mendoza was stretched out on the sectional with El Señor on his chest.

'Well, anyway, we're going up there again tomorrow to decide. Sally and I can manage Tony, I hope. Then we make the announcements and hand out the ribbons—they've had them made up, you know, with *First Prize*, and so on, in gold—really pathetic, when you—That's next Saturday, and—You're *not* listening.'

Mendoza yawned. 'Sorry, *querida*. It's this damned case. Why just that one area? Granted, it could be coincidence, but—'

Alison considered. 'It could be you're

looking at it wrong, too. You said it's an area about five by ten blocks? That's quite large, really. Whoever it is, *he* might not be thinking of it as an—well, *area*, at all. Maybe he just doesn't go far from home in picking the old people to burglarize. Or maybe—Luis! Maybe it's a milk route, or a postal route. Because a milkman would know about the people on his route—Or there's bottled water, you know how trucks come around, or a water-softening service—'

Mendoza sat up slowly, bringing El Señor with him. El Señor spat to show his opinion of being moved without official leave, and instantly jumped down, to leap on Bast and Sheba comfortably curled in a complicated ball at the other end of the sectional. 'Well, well! A new thought. Thanks very much. I wouldn't think bottled water or a water softener, in that neighborhood. Luxuries. But a milk route—Yes, well, I'll be working tomorrow, too. No rest for the wicked. There's the Ambler thing—'

'That's at ten on Saturday morning,' said Alison, her mind wandering back to the Hobbyists again, 'so I'll be able to get to the christening at two. Luis, *isn't* it funny about Angel wanting Sheila christened? I can't imagine—'

'Mmh,' said Mendoza inattentively. Master John arrived at full speed, clasping a struggling Nefertiti, closely pursued by Mrs.

MacTaggart. Alison leaped up to rescue Nefertiti. Master John broke into a loud wail.

'Now, now, *mo croidhe*,' said Mrs. MacTaggart, and picked him up comfortingly. 'You might just see to Terry, *achara*, I left her in the bath—'

'Domesticities!' said Mendoza.

'—*Or*,' Alison called back as she hurried out, 'it could be a Fuller Brush man or a Helms Bakeries driver—'

*   *   *

He sat in his office on Sunday afternoon and brooded over it. Mostly over that. Detective Grace had brought in another man out of Records on the Ambler job; he and Palliser were questioning him. Sooner or later, probably, they'd drop on that one ... Periodically Mendoza wondered what the hell he was doing here, delving into the sordid and the violent, the dirty stagnation at the bottom of things. Whoever had killed Ambler had got under a hundred bucks out of the register. Ambler's wife said when he'd accumulated more than that he tucked the rest away in a secret cache at the back of the store, and that had been untouched—nearly eight hundred dollars. No useful prints, too many confused prints all over the store. But sooner or later they'd probably get that one. This other thing—

34

Of the thirteen elderly victims, seven had not had time or strength to call out; they hadn't been discovered until the following day, or in one case until two days later. Of the thirteen victims, three were still bedridden from injury and shock; they were all people in their eighties. One of those, an old woman, had suffered a massive stroke as a result of the shock, and was still in the General. Of the thirteen, nine had been subsisting on the state pension, the others on small savings, modest investments, in several cases eked out by the contributions of grown children.

That didn't say much. About the only common denominator in the case was the age of the victims. The youngest had been sixty-nine.

The statements of the victims, others who had seen him, were not much help. In every case it had been dark. Collectively they said that he was big, burly, strong, and wore his hair rather long. No comment on color of hair. One of the victims, Mrs. Velda Stafford, said she'd seen tattoo marks on both his arms. She had struggled with him in her kitchen, and a street light right outside the window, she said, shone in and she'd seen the tattoos, but she couldn't say what they were, just tattoos. Not much help there either—they knew he couldn't be ex-Navy, because nobody anywhere had his prints.

Mendoza had sent out Glasser, Piggott,

35

Landers, and Higgins to ask around the neighborhoods of all the victims about any such man possibly known in the neighborhoods—Postman? Milkman? Door-to-door salesman? But that was at best a forlorn hope. It could pay off unexpectedly, but—

The autopsy report on Marion Stromberg was in. The only thing in it of any interest was that Dr. Bainbridge had found several lightish hairs clenched in her right hand. Not her own. Possibly from her attacker. He had sent them to the lab.

Jason Grace drifted in with Palliser behind him and said, 'Another one clean. I want a search warrant to look at another fellow's room, but I don't figure he's really likely.'

Palliser was looking discouraged. 'I don't think we'll ever drop on him. There just aren't any leads.'

'Or maybe,' said Grace, smiling, 'ten years from now, just before the cyanide drops into the chamber, the guilty man'll say, "By the way, it was me burned that liquor-store owner down in L.A."'

'Maybe,' said Mendoza. 'Either of you know where Art is?'

'He went out looking for that boy Indiana wants,' said Grace. 'Leo Charles Herrick. He's got a little pedigree here—Grand Theft Auto, mostly. He was in the phone book, believe it or not.' He grinned. 'It was me

36

located him—who else'd think of such a simple thing?'

'Like to exercise that brain on this anonymous X, Jase?'

'Thank you, no. Might show up I'm not so damn bright after all. That *is* a thing, Lieutenant. You getting anywhere on it?'

'Early days.'

'Well, let's go get that search warrant,' said Grace. As they went out, Glasser and Piggott came in. It was edging on to five o'clock.

'Brother,' said Glasser, dropping into a chair, 'I am beat. This damn heat, in January. We've got nothing and I don't think we ever will. Asked at every house, just nothing. For one thing, we haven't really got much of a description, and for another, my God, you know how people are. I swear to God I sometimes think the ordinary housewife couldn't give a good description of her own husband. Sure to God nobody we talked to could describe their regular mailman, or the guy they buy bread from off the bakery truck, let alone any recent peddlers have been around. No tattoos, no long hair, nothing. Don't know what Higgins and Tom might have got—more of the same, probably.'

Piggott looked at Mendoza earnestly and said the only thing to do was lay it at the Lord's door. Piggott was a devout Free Methodist. 'The Lord's just biding time,' he said, 'to bring just punishment. I figure we've just got to wait on the Lord.'

Mendoza, looking at him, reminded himself that even detectives came all sorts like other people, and reminded Piggott that it was also said that the Lord helped those who helped themselves. Piggott acknowledged it, looking gloomy.

At five-thirty Tom Landers came in and reported much the same result. 'You know how most people just don't use their eyes. But I did run into a mailman, over on Rockwood Street, and asked him some questions. That area's not all one mail route. One route that covers some of it overlaps onto the other side of Alvarado, and another route takes in most of the area, but also goes over past Glendale Boulevard into the Echo Park district.'

'Helpful,' said Mendoza. 'Where's George?'

Landers grinned. 'At this number, he said to give it to the night sergeant. You need telling what it is?'

Mendoza smiled. '*Claro que no*. I never thought I'd see the day. But of course I was once a confirmed gay bachelor too.'

'You taking any bets on him making it?'

Mendoza swiveled around and looked out the window, into the fast-darkening sky and the city lights coming on. 'No bets,' he said. 'Bert Dwyer was a nice fellow and a good cop.

But even good cops aren't very good insurance risks, are they, Tom? He was thirty-seven. Five slugs in him, on the floor of that bank. You think Mary Dwyer wants to start worrying about another cop?'

'I would guess not,' said Landers with a grimace. It wasn't really very funny, the hard-bitten bachelor Higgins falling for Bert Dwyer's widow. Landers turned away. 'I converted my Army insurance,' he said absently. And after a pause, 'George likes kids, you know. He used to spend a lot of spare time on that Big Brother thing—working with juveniles. I guess he's spending more time on Bert's kids now—the boy's about ten, isn't he? He said something about having to fix Stevie's bike for him.'

'Mmh. You ever meet her?'

'Uh-uh. Pretty?'

'Quite a looker, in a quiet sort of way,' said Mendoza. 'Black hair and gray eyes. About thirty-five.'

'Well, that's another thing. George'd never win any beauty prizes.' Landers looked out the window; it was completely dark now, the sudden dark of all mountain places, and all the lights were on, the advertising signs blinking, the traffic lights, the building lights, the night insignia of the city. 'I guess Mrs. Dwyer wouldn't think so much of that,' he said. 'I guess if she gets married again, Mrs. Dwyer is going to pick somebody who sits at

39

an office desk all day, nine to five, like keeping books or dictating letters, and wouldn't known a Colt .45 from a Hi-Standard .22. I would guess ... Well, I might as well go home. The night crew's coming in.'

'What, upstanding young officer like you, no date?'

'Why, Lieutenant, what nice young lady wants to date a cop? He's liable to get shot out from under you any day,' said Landers. 'No future in that.'

★   ★   ★

On Monday morning Mendoza sat at his desk and did some more brooding. Grace came into the office about nine o'clock and said they'd brought in another one from Records, and did Mendoza want to sit in on the questioning? Fellow seemed very nervous, so it could be—

'He's all yours, Jase. I'm still trying to figure an angle on Goldberg's thing.'

He was poring over a scale city map when Higgins came in. Higgins tossed a couple of stapled sheets on the desk and sat down.

'This is all up in the air,' he said disgustedly. 'I'd be obliged if you'd turn your X-ray eye on it, Luis, and tell me yes or no.'

'What?' Mendoza looked up at him. Undeniably, Higgins would never take any

40

beauty prizes. He was nearly as big as Hackett, at six-three, and built like a heavyweight boxer; he had a boxer's ugly broken nose, too, and his jaw was Neanderthal. Only the deep-set eyes showed the basically shy, kind man under the toughness. Mary Dwyer ... 'What?' said Mendoza.

'This Christ-damned suicide. Gonzales. There's the autopsy report, and it's worth damn all. I saw Bainbridge. What does he give me? Sure, he says, the man could have cut his own throat and then thrown the razor across the room, in a death spasm or something like that. Nothing impossible about it, you die quick of a cut throat but not that quick. So I still don't like it.'

'Why not, George?'

'I don't know.' Higgins passed a hand across his mouth. 'I found a pal of Gonzales' yesterday—before you chased us out on the other new thing—and he tells me this. Gonzales was one of those birds went on a binge about every couple of months. You know. He'd been picked up on D.-and-D. God knows how many times. And every time, when he'd sobered up—we know the type—he'd turn all remorseful, cry, beat his breast, what a lousy rotten husband and father he was, he'd be better dead, and so on. Which never stopped him going on another drunk. Well, all right—so he said he'd be

41

better dead, he never attempted to do anything about it before. *And* there weren't any hesitation cuts at all. Just one nice firm sweep across his jugular vein. Left to right, and he's right-handed—all right. But—'

'This the only friend of his you talked to?'

'So far.'

'Let's find some more.'

'Sure. We'll hear the same tale.'

'Did he have a job?'

'Yes. Laborer. For a big contracting outfit. Reliable except when he went off on a spree, the boss says.'

'Wife?'

'Hell, *I* don't know. I want to see her again. It looks very damn ordinary, Luis, except I smell something funny.'

'So we'd better take a closer look,' said Mendoza, and the inside phone rang. He picked it up. 'Mendoza.'

There was a click as Sergeant Lake plugged in a call, and a deep voice said, 'Homicide? Is that Homicide?'

'Yes, Lieutenant Mendoza speaking.'

'I'm Clark, sir, patrolman over here Echo Park route—I just got called to the Park, sir, it's a body—' The professional calmness slipped a little and excitement slurred the voice. 'The boat guy—I mean the guy rents out the canoes and like that—he called in and we got sent over, Corbett and me—my partner, sir—and—'

'Yes, well?'

Patrolman Clark gulped audibly. 'Sir, it's a body,' he said. 'A dead body. In the lake. I mean, drifted up on shore.'

Something else. Hell. He could have predicted it. Of course, it might be something very simple—straightforward suicide, maybe. He said resignedly, 'All right, stay there until a Homicide crew gets to you. Exactly where about?'

'About fifty yards down from the boathouse, sir. Near that Oriental bridge sort of thing. Sir—'

'All right, I'll—'

'Sir? When I said body—well, that's just what it is.' Patrolman Clark gulped again. 'Just. There's no—no arms or legs, sir—and no head. Just a body.'

'¡Santa María!' said Mendoza. He put the phone down and looked at Higgins. 'Just to save us from boredom, something really interesting now. We haven't had a dismembered corpse for quite a while.'

'For God's sake, where?'

'In the lake at Echo Park. Let's go look at it. Call for a lab crew, will you?' Mendoza reached for his hat.

They met Hackett just coming in, so they took him along.

CHAPTER FOUR

When they got to the park, they found two patrol cars parked double in front of the hydrant at the corner of Echo Park Avenue and Lemoyne. Mendoza left the Ferrari across one of the entrance ramps into the park; crossing the grass, they spotted the little crowd immediately, three uniformed men trying to keep people back from the lake shore. It was a weekday, so there weren't any kids in the park, or, this early, many other people; but the unseasonable heat had brought out some of the elderly people who lived around here, a few housewives dropping into the park on their way to market, perhaps.

Echo Park, which was nearly all Echo Park Lake, was a modest green spot in the midst of an old part of the city, nearly downtown. It lay, a rough rectangle, between Glendale Boulevard and Echo Park Avenue, a strip of lawn, flowers, and tall old trees around the perimeter of the lake. The lake was Y-shaped, and on this side of the Y, where the upper arm curved back on itself, a small Oriental bridge rose abruptly across the little curve. The crowd was just down from there. The boathouse, with its fleet of canoes and small awning-covered motor launches, was almost directly across the lake from where the men from Homicide entered the park.

Not speaking, they hurried across the grass to the crowd.

'Please keep back!' one of the patrolmen was pleading. 'Get back, everybody— Lieutenant? Thank God—We called up another car, but these—'

There were about twenty-five people there, the citizenry, pressing up to stare at a dead body. Sometimes you wondered about the citizenry . . . 'All *right*!' said Mendoza, raising his voice. 'Will all you people step back—we can't have you trampling possible evidence—' Among them they managed to get the crowd back about twenty feet. 'Clark?'

'I'm Corbett, sir.'

'O.K. We're going to have the hell of a traffic jam up there in about five minutes. We're also going to need some more men down here. Will you go up to the road and tell everybody to get their cars off the street as they show up? There'll be the surgeon, and an ambulance, and the lab truck, at least. You'd better call up a few more patrol cars, too. There's never any parking slots free up any of these streets—' The narrow, steep old streets around here were largely lined with small apartment buildings, and also lined perennially with parked cars. 'You'd better tell them to drive inside the park—the walks are wide enough.' Vehicles were not allowed in the park as a rule.

'Yes, sir.' Corbett started off at the double. Perhaps he was happy to get away from the corpse; Mendoza couldn't blame him.

The crowd, immobile now, just stared, fascinated.

'What a hell of a thing,' said Hackett.

The body lay half in and half out of the water, gently lapping the shore. The body swayed a little with the movement of the water. It was the body of a woman, and not, Mendoza thought, a young woman. The arms had been cut off just below the shoulders and the legs just below the hips, and the neck was cut clean through the middle. That had been done some while ago, because the body was bloodless, or at least there was no blood showing in the water. The body was very white—a woman who didn't tan or didn't try to—and a little dumpy, with pockets of fat around the hips. The pubic hair was black. At first glance, there didn't seem to be any marks or scars on the body except one, which looked like an appendectomy scar.

The shore all around the body was trampled and sodden. 'You might know,' said Higgins. 'But I suppose if she was floating whoever spotted her had to pull her in.' He looked up at the crowd. 'Who found her?' he asked, raising his voice.

An old man who stood detached from the crowd stepped forward. 'I did. Pete Silvers is my name. I got charge o' the boats over there, rent 'em out, keep track o' the time, like that. I was linin' them up by the flats over there about half an hour, forty minutes ago, when I happened to just glance up the lake and spotted her. Leastways, didn't know for sure what it was, just somethin' wrong—nobody allowed to swim in the lake, well, you can't, it's dangerous. Weeds. Anyways, there wasn't many people here and I thought maybe somebody was—well, anyways, I hopped into one o' the launches and come over, and there she was.'

'In the lake?'

'Just about like you see her now. I pulled her up a little farther, be sure she didn't slip all the way in, that's all.'

'I don't think she was ever in the lake,' said Mendoza. 'Maybe intended to go all the way in, but somebody botched the job. If she was ever all the way in, say dropped in out there in the middle, she'd never have floated until the gases formed and expanded the body. She hasn't been dead that long.'

'I'll lay you're right, mister,' said Silvers. He came a step farther toward them and looked at the body without expression. 'This lake, she don't let go of bodies just so easy. I know, I worked here nineteen years and some. She ain't very deep, but she's a tricky bitch, this lake. Nor we don't get many people drownded here, acourse. *Acourse* not.

We try to be careful. Got to be, public park. No kids let to take boats out alone, and I allus warn the people rent out canoes, they can be awful damn tricky. But we have had people drownded here. Last one was a college boy. Back in 1951. Canoe turned over on him.' Silvers paused. 'That was in March, and they never got hold of the corpse until June.'

'What?' Mendoza turned, surprised. Echo Park Lane was quite a small body of water, about a third of a mile long and scarcely a quarter mile wide.

'Yep,' said Silvers, as if he took a kind of inverted pride in it. 'Like I said, weeds. We got a lot o' ducks on this lake, and quite a few swans. They eat the weeds, underwater. For all I know, maybe 'twas planted special for 'em. Anyways, whole bottom's all covered over, thick. They couldn't send no diver down, even with these new mouthpiece gadgets they got—weeds'd get him, too, see? Anything gets tangled in 'em stays there. They dragged the whole lake—you guys did, in special boats.' He nodded at Mendoza. 'All they brought up was weeds—about a ton of 'em, day after day. They said like you did, when the body got bloated up it'd float, but it didn't. They had four separate goes, dragging the lake—finally brought him up in June, along with all the weeds that'd held him down.'

'I will be damned,' said Hackett. 'That's a
48

nice outlook. We'll be dragging your lake again, Mr. Silvers.' Because it was, of course, the first obvious place to look for the missing parts of the body.

The doctor arrived, a couple of lab men behind him, and more patrolmen. Hackett and Higgins went over to the crowd and began asking questions. It soon emerged that nobody had noticed anything at all, nobody had been near this part of the park until the uniformed cops had arrived. Then, of course, everybody had hurried over to see what was going on. Trust the citizenry. Hackett said without much hope, 'O.K., you can all go.' They didn't, of course. The patrolmen moved them a little farther back, where they just stood staring.

'Any ideas, Doctor?' asked Mendoza. Bainbridge was squatting over the body.

'A few,' he said without looking up. 'Right off the bat, I'll say she hasn't been dead long. Tell you more after the autopsy, but I'll stick my neck out and say she's been dead, roughly, between thirty-six and seventy-two hours.'

'Any time between Friday night and Saturday night.'

'Um. Have another guess at her age—between forty-five and fifty. She had dark hair, but women these days—head hair could be any color. Tchah. That's all I can tell you here.'

49

'What about the cutting job? Seem to be any knowledge of anatomy involved?'

'Wouldn't say so, no. Certain amount of strength needed, of course. I'll tell you better, have a guess at what might have been used, when I get her to the morgue. Can't do any more here. I'll take her.' He hoisted himself up and beckoned the ambulance attendants.

The crowd muttered excitedly as the body was rolled onto a stretcher, covered, and carried up to the ambulance waiting just inside an entrance to the park. But with the disappearance of the body, the crowd found itself quickly bored. They couldn't hear what the detectives were talking about, and the detectives didn't seem to be doing anything much. In a few minutes the crowd began to disperse.

'Drag the lake,' said Mendoza, 'obviously. I don't suppose we'll get anything if Silvers is right—'

'I'm right,' said the old man at his elbow.

'But we might be lucky. I'll tell you one thing I'm thinking now. If the missing parts are in there, I can see somebody *throwing* them in, you follow me? From the bank here—or another spot. But he couldn't very well throw the body.'

'That's so,' said Hackett, rocking ruminatively back and forth, heel to toe.

Mendoza turned to Silvers. 'What about the boats? Are they locked up somewhere at night?'

'They sure are, mister. Chained to the flats or under the canvas cover, side o' the boathouse, padlocked up. Mainly because we don't want no accidents, like crazy kids coming in at night, you know. That's my job. Jean and Bob, they run the hamburger stand in the boathouse, I take care o' the boats. I work for Parks and Recreation—the hamburger stand's a concession.'

'Mmh. Do you have any regular hours? Open and close certain times?'

'Thought you was a detective, mister,' said Silvers. 'You don't see no fences or gates round the park, do you? We're just a small place—just a plain park, no rides for the kids, like that—just the boats, and benches round under the trees. Anybody can walk in off the street any time o' day or night, any entrance to the park. There's entrances at Echo Park Avenue, and Glendale Boulevard, and Park Avenue, and Bellevue. No regular hours. You take in the summer, hot nights, there'll be people in the park late—ten, eleven o'clock. We do stop rentin' out boats at nine. Longest you can rent a boat for is an hour, see? Mostly everybody'll be out, though, by eleven. We don't get many o' these rowdy young kids here, like teenagers, knock wood, we get the real little kids with their folks, and old folks, and sometimes young folks out on a date, want to boat ride, nice summer night. But

51

this time o' year, mostly we don't get anybody in after dark. I shut down the boats by around five. Acourse we get more people on weekends.'

'What about last night? It's been hot—you have more customers than usual?'

'Over the weekend, sure, a few. Lessee, hot spell started Friday, didn't it? Yeah, but it's cooled off at night, you know, not like real summer. Didn't have a single customer after five last night.'

'Do you get bums using the park to sleep?' asked Higgins.

Silvers looked indignant. 'I should say not. The squad car on this beat, they're supposed to check the park at least twice every night. I guess sometimes they find, you know, kids having petting parties, but not much. We're kind of out of the way down here, middle of town, sure, but—Well, there's a couple lights left on, but all the trees, it'll be dark enough.'

'Anybody sleep on the premises? You?'

'I do not. No facilities for it. Just the boathouse, and that's just the one room, and a couple o' rest rooms, and the hamburger stand. I locked up and went home about six-thirty last night. Wasn't a soul in the park far as I could see.'

'How about Saturday night?'

'About the same. It's cooled off at night, you know. And it's school term and all. I guess I left around the same time on

52

Saturday; there wasn't nobody here except a few people sittin' on the benches. Jean and Bob'd gone by five, no business.'

'Well,' said Mendoza. He looked at Hackett, who was frowning out over the lake, at the hordes of ducks sailing serenely along, and farther up the shore a family of graceful white swans preening themselves. 'You know what sort of job we've got here, don't you? Thank God it isn't Elysian Park—or even MacArthur Park! We're going to search every inch of ground here, but good. Just on the off chance. Particularly right around here. There could be a little something under a bush, or—'

'And meanwhile,' said Hackett, 'somebody's going to go back to base and tell the appropriate office we want to drag the lake.'

'You read my mind, Arturo.'

'You know we'll get nothing.'

'I don't know that at all. Getting assaulted like that turned you pessimist?'

'Weeds,' said Hackett.

'On your way. Pick up anybody at the office and chase them down here.'

Hackett sighed. 'Angel said those special tournedos of beef for dinner.' Hackett's Angel was one of those inspired cooks, and these days, after the hospital siege, Hackett was forgetting about his diet. 'I have a foreboding I'll be calling her not to expect me. O.K., O.K.'

53

Back in the sergeants' room at headquarters, Jason Grace said patiently, 'Now all we want to know, Frank, is where you were last Tuesday night.'

'I wasn't no place,' said Frank Newcome nervously.

'Now that's sort of impossible, isn't it?' said John Palliser. He looked at Newcome tiredly. This was the hell of a tedious thing to work, and he didn't think, privately, they'd ever get anywhere on it—it was too up in the air, no leads at all. But then he realized he'd been feeling like that in general, with good reason, for some time—just low and pessimistic. The hell of it was, it wasn't anybody's fault, there wasn't anybody to take it out on. His mother couldn't help needing the operation, or help having all the complications afterward, and now needing the practical nurse. Only somebody had to pay the bills.

What it all came down to was that he and Roberta couldn't get married this year for pretty sure, all the debts he'd had to get into—God, the surgeon's bill alone—

He tried to put it out of his mind. 'You had to be someplace, Frank. Where?'

Newcome seemed very nervous. He'd pulled one heist job; he was, in fact, only just

54

out of San Quentin. Had he burned Ambler?

'Come on, Frank,' said Grace.

'I—I was with a dame!' Newcome burst out suddenly. 'Look, what the hell, I didn't do nothing, but you guys—Look, for God's sake, she might not even say I *was*, you go 'n' ask her and her husband's there, she's not a goddamn idiot, for God's sake, and he's a gorilla. A gorilla. He finds out about it, and we're both dead, I tell you no lie. But I was *there*. From—from about seven o'clock till maybe midnight. But, for God's sake, would she *say*? Look, he drives a truck, Interstate Shipping, look, you find out when he's not there, see, go 'n' ask her! Look—'

'O.K., Frank,' said Grace gently. He looked amused. 'Who and where?'

'Her name's Darlene Scott. Twenty-two-fifteen St. Andrews in Hollywood. Look—'

Grace and Palliser drifted up the big room. 'What do you think?' asked Grace.

'It sounds plausible. But he's nervous.'

'With good reason,' said Grace, more amused. 'These females. Been leading us astray ever since Eve.'

Females. Roberta sympathetic, Roberta smiling at him, his lovely Roberta with her smooth dark hair and gray eyes—And damn it, he'd turn thirty-three the sixteenth of this month, and it wasn't fair that they couldn't—

'I don't know,' he said. 'Check it. Quietly, with the girl.'

55

'Let him go?'

'Let him go, let him go,' said Palliser. 'It'll probably check out.'

'Probably,' said Grace. He walked back to Newcome and told him he could go. Newcome grabbed his hat and shot out like a scalded cat. 'Gentleman doesn't like us,' said Grace, head on one side. 'Well, just maybe it's once bit, twice shy with Mr. Newcome, and he'll keep out of trouble after this.'

'You believe in miracles?' said Palliser. 'He's got a j.d. record back to age fifteen.'

They came out of the sergeants' room and met Hackett in the hall. 'Anybody else here?' asked Hackett.

'Just us chickens, boss,' said Grace. Hackett grinned. 'Off you go. All hands available down to Echo Park. It—'

'Well, now, I'd enjoy a nice boat ride on the lake, cool off a little,' said Grace. 'That's a nice thought, Sergeant.'

'Anything but. We've got a dismembered corpse down there. We'll be bloodhounding every foot of ground.'

'Holy God,' said Palliser. 'A—On top of everything else—'

'Yeah,' said Hackett. 'We don't get a chance to feel bored around here, at least.'

★　　　★　　　★

Mendoza left an augmented lab crew and six

56

detectives poking around bushes and trees down there, about two o'clock, and came back to the office and called Dr. Bainbridge.

'Well, I can give you this and that,' said Bainbridge. 'I got right to it because I know you want whatever's there as soon as possible. I haven't started any chemical tests—whether she ingested any poisonous substances. That could take weeks, have to look for everything, barbiturates to aspirin, you know. We'll be thorough, Luis, we'll look. Just in case. Just to be sure. But otherwise, unless and until we find she drank some hemlock or swallowed a couple of hundred aspirin, there's not one damn thing to say how she died. Of course, if we had her head, it might be very simple. She could have been shot, or fatally concussed.'

'Yes. Anything else?'

'Sure. You want to find out who she was, don't you? I'll send all this over properly written up, but meanwhile—She was about five-five and a half, give or take an inch, and somewhere between a hundred and forty and a hundred and fifty pounds. Caucasian, fairly light complexion. Between forty-five and fifty, give or take a couple of years. She'd taken care of herself—regular baths, and so on. She'd had her appendix out, no other operation scars. She's not a virgin. She—'

'How many females are by that age?'

'You're a cynic. She'd never borne a child. Natural hair color, brunette. If it isn't dyed,

57

may be turning gray. There are, unfortunately, no birthmarks on the body whatever. She was a little overweight, and if she'd lived longer she'd have had some trouble with her liver.'

'Mmh? A drinker?'

'I don't know. A number of things can cause a liver to give trouble besides alcohol. Her last meal was eaten approximately two hours before her death and consisted of a green salad, pickles, bread, and some kind of cake.'

'You got on the ball, Doctor,' said Mendoza. 'Thanks.'

'Well, we don't often get one like this, do we? Interesting. I'll get on with the other tests. Oh, yes—not much knowledge shown in the dismembering—pretty damn crude job—some fairly sharp tool used. Meat cleaver, ax, something like that.'

'Mmh. Thanks very much, Doctor,' said Mendoza.

He looked at the hasty notes he'd taken.

A cut-up corpse. They hadn't had one of those in quite a while.

He tucked the memo page into his breast pocket and started downstairs to see Lieutenant Carey in Missing Persons.

Five-five and a half, between a hundred and forty and a hundred and fifty pounds, between forty-five and fifty—Hell, she didn't sound very interesting, she didn't sound like

58

anybody any X would have a reason to murder—

But then homicide, apart from the paperbacks, homicide for real, that cops had to cope with, was so seldom glamorous.

CHAPTER FIVE

Higgins looked at Carlota Gonzales exasperatedly. He couldn't get at the woman. And this Gonzales thing was a very little thing compared with what they also had on their hands, but it kept bugging him. There was just something funny about it.

'How long had you been married to him, Mrs. Gonzales?' he asked.

'Seven year.' She faced him stolidly, a woman probably not over thirty-five and looking ten years older; her hands looked sixty, worn with hard work. This shabby living room she had grudgingly let him into was reasonably clean; both the couch where Alfredo Gonzales had died and the carpet he'd bled onto had been taken away, he noticed. She answered questions grudgingly too but he made allowances for that; she was of a class and an economic status which automatically distrusted the law.

'You had children by him?'

'Sí. Three.'

'And the others by your first husband?'
'*Cuatro.*'
'What happened to your first husband?'
'*¿Cómo?* Oh, he iss work in the railroad.
He iss kill by train. *Accidente.*'
'I see.' She had a heavy Spanish accent,
and there was Indian stolidity to her features.
He'd lay a bet she hadn't been born here.
Most native-born Mexican-Americans her
age, these days, spoke unaccented English.
'Well, let's go back. You didn't come into
this room at all, last Saturday morning, until
the children had all gone out? And you
thought your husband was still sleeping.
You—'
'*Si.* He wass drink too much.' Something,
some expression, stirred in her eyes.
'*Malintencionado,*' she muttered. And then, 'I
come in wake him up, he iss dead, blood all
over. I see the erazor on the floor. I remember
how he say, he iss better off dead. He hass cut
his throat.' She shrugged.
'Yes.' Higgins was silent a minute. Damn
it, the inquest was over this morning and the
verdict had been suicide. God knew he had
enough to do; he'd taken his lunch hour to
come and see the woman again, and he still
didn't know why. Crazy. He asked, 'It was
his own razor? He used it for shaving?'
'*Sí.*'
'What will you do now, Mrs. Gonzales? Get
a job? None of the children are old enough to
60

work, are they? The oldest is—'

'Fourteen, María. I got a job. Before, I got a job. Because sometimes he iss not bring home *dinero*. The drink, it wass. Yes, yes!' Suddenly savage light glinted in her eyes. 'I got a job in restaurant. Before. Yes! *La ocasión hace el ladrón.*' She muttered that to herself several times, and repeated, '*Malintencionado.* I tell you this before. It iss over now, yes?' She stood up.

Higgins sighed. 'Yes, I guess so,' he said. 'Thanks very much, Mrs. Gonzales.'

When he got back to the car, he took out his notebook and wrote down phonetically, as best he could, the Spanish words she'd muttered. He wasn't too good at languages, and he didn't know Spanish, he knew the few words of it almost anybody in southern California knew, no more. He sighed again. The heat was still with them; it was Tuesday, and they were getting nowhere fast on both the tough new cases. Shorthanded: Bob Schenke was on sick leave after getting shot up by a heist man last month.

He turned on the ignition and slid out of the parking slot. His question to Mrs. Gonzales made him think of Mary Dwyer. Well, they hadn't got to first names yet, but he always thought of her as Mary. There was a pension, but not enough to raise two kids on—and Steve was a bright boy, probably ought to go to college.

61

But it was a very long chance that she'd ever look twice at George Higgins. She could do a hell of a lot better for herself—if she ever wanted to.

★　　★　　★

There were two women listed as missing who could be the anonymous corpse. Lieutenant Carey had pulled the files for Mendoza.

Mrs. Clara Burton had been reported missing two months ago by her husband. She was forty-six, five feet six, a hundred and forty pounds, and had dark hair. She'd never had a child; she'd had her appendix out about twenty years ago. The husband admitted they'd quarreled because she'd been seeing another man. She'd taken most of her possessions and left while he was at work.

She could have gone to the other man, lived with him all this while, and subsequently been killed by him; or she could have come back to her husband and maybe they quarreled again and he'd killed her; or she could be still with the other man or on her own, alive.

Mrs. LaVerne Hopper had been reported missing by her sister last Thursday. Both sisters were widows, and lived together. LaVerne Hopper was forty-nine, five feet five, weighed a hundred and thirty-five, and had dark hair. She'd never had a child, but

62

had had her appendix removed. She had worked at a Sears Roebuck store as a sales clerk, and had just been promoted to manager of her department, so it didn't look as if the disappearance had been voluntary. The sister, Mrs. Patterson, said they lived a very quiet life, LaVerne didn't have any men friends, and she couldn't imagine where or why she'd gone. She wasn't sure, didn't know, whether LaVerne had taken any clothes with her. It was Mrs. Patterson's house, LaVerne just had a room there, and of course she never pried into LaVerne's things. There didn't, Lieutenant Carey said cautiously, seem to be much of a wardrobe in LaVerne's closet, but on the other hand, a department-store sales clerk probably couldn't afford many clothes.

So, had LaVerne, possibly, recently, met a male friend and gone off with him—or been taken off?

They had, both yesterday and today, dragged the lake. They would probably go on dragging it tomorrow and the next day. All they had succeeded in was (A) attracting a large and interested crowd to flock the lake shores and watch the dragging process, and (B) bringing up about a quarter ton of wet, dripping, dank green weeds from the lake bottom. Surveying the weeds, Mendoza could understand what Pete Silvers meant. The weeds grew like underwater vines, long branches entwined together, and almost

anything that got into them would get
entangled at once and held firmly. In fact, in
the weeds they had dredged up had been all
sorts of things dropped from boats,
unintentionally or not, from sodden
paperback books to wrist watches.

On Tuesday morning Mendoza went to see
LaVerne Hopper's sister. The body, of
course, was still in dissection as Dr.
Bainbridge conducted all his chemical tests;
all Mendoza had to show Mrs. Patterson was
several sharply detailed 8 X 10 photographs
of it. He hoped she wasn't squeamish. He
took Hackett along with him.

The house was an old Spanish stucco,
tucked away at the end of a quiet old street on
the upper side of the Silver Lake Reservoir.
Judging by the living room, it was stuffed
with a lot of old-fashioned furniture, too big
and heavy. Mrs. Patterson obviously never
threw anything away; there was an old
console radio in one corner that must have
been forty years old, and the upright
golden-oak piano was piled with ancient sheet
music. The room smelled faintly of dust,
dead flowers, and peppermint. Mrs.
Patterson was older than her sister by about
five years, Mendoza reckoned. She was a big
woman who moved creakingly; she sucked a
peppermint as she talked to them, and her
voice was deep and slow.

'Mrs. Patterson, I'm sorry to have to ask

64

you to look at these photographs,' said Mendoza. He held the manila envelope in his hand. 'They're not very pleasant to look at. But it is the only way we know of for you to be able to say this is your sister's body or not.'

'The—the one you found down in Echo Park? You said that on the phone. I read about it in the paper this morning.'

'Yes. You understand that the head is missing?'

She nodded. 'I'll look at them. That's all right. But I don't know as I could say. LaVerne—well, let me see them.'

With some misgivings Mendoza took them out of the envelope and handed them over. They had not been taken to flatter a naked, dismembered dead body, but to preserve details; and they did that mercilessly.

The woman's expression showed only slight revulsion, horror, as she looked at them. She handed them back unhurriedly. 'That's a dreadful, dreadful thing to do to a person,' she said. She shook her head. 'I just can't connect LaVerne to a thing like that. I really can't. It must have been some human fiend did a thing like that, and really LaVerne—or I—never knew anybody who might be capable—'

'But do you think it could be your sister's body, Mrs. Patterson?'

She raised her hands and let them fall into

65

her lap. 'I just don't know. It could be. But LaVerne and I—Well, you understand, it isn't as if we'd lived together all our lives. She got married before I did, when she was only seventeen, and her husband worked in San Diego, so they lived there until he got killed in an accident in his car last year. They'd always lived up to the hilt of what he made, and he didn't leave any insurance, nothing but debts. I thought it was only right, and sensible, too, to say she could live here with me—my husband left me comfortably off, you see'—a hint of complacence—'and she's been saving to pay off the debts. But she had her own room, she's used to being independent, and I'm not one to pry. What I'm getting at is, I don't suppose I've seen LaVerne—well, you know, *undressed*—since we were girls together, and that's a long time ago.' She nodded at the envelope. 'But I just can't believe *that* is LaVerne.'

'But it could be, by the general description and size?'

'Oh, it *could* be. But—'

'May we look at her room, Mrs. Patterson?'

'Well, I guess so.' She rose.

It was not a very attractive room. The furniture was old, there was too much of it, the carpet was threadbare. They looked in the closet; Mendoza looked through drawers in the tall old painted chiffonier. Then they thanked Mrs. Patterson and left.

66

'Bright ideas?' asked Hackett as they walked back to the Ferrari.

'A couple,' said Mendoza. 'I don't think it's LaVerne's body at the morgue. You may not be quite as bright as I am, but I expect you noticed that what was there—a little underwear, a few dresses, skirts, two pairs of shoes—was all old. Some of the underwear mended.'

'I noticed.'

'Mmh. *Por consiguiente*, I think LaVerne took off voluntarily. Of course, it could be that she met some—mmh—human fiend who lured her away and then killed her.'

'So you know what we ought to do?' said Hackett. 'Let's find out if she's been to work. Why didn't the sister call and ask?'

'She told Carey she didn't think LaVerne would like being checked up on. LaVerne liked to be independent. Yes, that's the next move, of course. Right now we're going to see Mr. James Burton, whose wife is also missing. Who might also have gone off with a human fiend. If Mr. Burton says maybe about the corpse, I wonder if he knows the name of the man she'd been dating.'

'Yes,' said Hackett. 'Damn, it's after one, let's have some lunch first. I should have sent a teletype off to Sparrow, I forgot.'

'Who the hell is Sparrow?'

'That Chief of Police in Sidalia, Indiana. We're getting quite chummy. This fellow he wants, Leo Charles Herrick. Seems Herrick married a girl from Sidalia, but he's from L.A. and they've been living here—just went back a couple of months ago because the girl's aunt, only living relative, had a stroke and nobody else to take care of her. And while they're there, about ten days back, Herrick hits a guy while he's driving in town, and doesn't stop. The fellow died later, so it's involuntary manslaughter, or whatever they call it in Indiana, but meanwhile—before they positively identified the driver as Herrick—he took off. The Chief naturally thinks maybe he'll head for home—wife doesn't seem to know a thing—so he asks us. And sure enough, the guy's here. Jase thought of the phone book. Well, it's where they were living before—duplex on McCadden in Hollywood—the landlady lives on the other side, and she'd seen him. On Sunday. He'd left a trunk in the garage, came by to pick it up. And she told me he didn't say where he was living now, but he is driving the same car—1951 Dodge sedan—so I checked with the D.M.V. and got the plate number and put it on the hot list. Every squad car in town is looking for it.' Hackett yawned.

'We do go roundabout,' said Mendoza, 'and all to oblige another Chief of Police. Mannings' all right for lunch, or do you want a drink?'

'I could use one, yes. I wish to God this

heat would break.'

'It will. Let's also,' said Mendoza, bypassing the Mannings' coffee shop and heading up Hollywood Boulevard, 'get full press coverage out. Description of body, names of these missing women, et cetera. Might turn up something, you never know.'

'Sure,' said Hackett. He was silent, and then he said, 'You know, I'm still trying to figure Angel and this christening bit. It's not as if she was even brought up very religious. I can't understand it.'

'It is a waste of time, Arturo, to try to understand women. Neither of us is that good a detective.'

★   ★   ★

The Ambler case seemed to have died a natural death. There just wasn't anywhere else to look. About a dozen of the possible men in Records could be the one who'd pulled that job and since got rid of the Colt Woodsman .22, so there was nothing to link him to it. Or it could have been a first job for somebody. There just wasn't anything to say, one way or the other.

At any rate, Grace and Palliser weren't working it any longer. They had joined the minute search of the fortunately not very large (but large enough) area of Echo Park—which had turned up nothing at all that could be linked to the body in the lake—and then they had joined Glasser, Higgins, Piggott, and Landers in asking questions around all the neighborhoods where the elderly victims had been attacked and robbed. So far they hadn't struck any pay dirt.

At the moment, Grace and Palliser were just sitting down at a table at Federico's which was already occupied by Piggott. The waiter came up and Palliser said he'd have a Scotch and water before lunch. Grace said after rumination he'd have a Green Dragon. 'What, sir?' said the waiter.

'Where do you *find* them?' asked Palliser. Piggott merely looked disapproving.

'It's a very interesting subject,' said Grace. 'History of wines and spirits. Fascinating.'

'I thought you were on anthropology.'

'Oh, this is just pleasure reading. Virginia gave me the book for my birthday. It's got this whole index of every known drink at the back—'

'*What* was it, Mr. Grace?' asked the waiter.

'A Green Dragon. You tell the bartender, he'll know—I got talking to him once, he's a good man.'

'So what is it?' asked Palliser.

'Half dry gin, one eighth Kümmel, one quarter Crème de Menthe, an eighth of lemon juice, and four dashes of peach bitters. Very nice,' said Grace, lighting a cigarette.

'God, what a mixture,' said Palliser.

'Very nice ... I'd like to have got that boy,' said Grace. 'Not very often routine doesn't pay off. I just constitutionally don't like to leave a case open like that. You know, one question I keep asking myself is, why the hell did Ambler get shot at all?'

'Well, after all, Jase, it does happen. All the time. The heist man gets a little nervous, or the clerk or whoever's getting held up tries to be a hero—bam, a dead man.'

'Um,' said Grace. 'But I talked to Mrs. Ambler. She said Ambler always told everybody, in case of a holdup, only thing to do is hand over the loot, play it safe. He'd been held up before. Before he got his own store. He wouldn't act cocky, she said, he'd play it straight and safe.'

'All right,' said Palliser. This was flogging a dead horse. 'It was a first job, and/or X got nervous. Thought Ambler *was* going to put up a fight.'

The waiter came with their drinks. Grace's was an exotic-looking green concoction in a frosted cocktail glass. He sniffed it. 'Very nice. Unusual.'

Palliser took a swallow of his drink and felt a little better. Federico's was air-conditioned, thank God.

'I just do wonder,' said Jason Grace, his dark eyes dreamy.

Mr. James Burton shuddered away from the photographs and said, well, it could be Clara. He just couldn't be positive.

Mendoza and Hackett looked at each other. Both of them being husbands, it seemed a little odd to them that a man couldn't definitely recognize the naked body of his wife, even if the head was missing. On the other hand, Mr. James Burton was a rabbity-faced little man with weak pale eyes behind thick glasses, narrow shoulders, a reedy tenor voice, and a job as a department-store window decorator. It could be he hadn't had occasion to see his wife's naked body very often. It could even be that that was why Clara Burton had been dating another man.

'You can't be sure?' said Hackett.

'No, really, I—' Burton touched his glasses nervously. 'You've upset me,' he said. 'Those terrible pictures! No, I can't. It—it *could* be Clara. I just don't know. Without the—the *head*. Awful. Just awful.' He touched his glasses again.

'I'm sorry, Mr. Burton,' said Mendoza. 'You told the other officers that you and your wife quarreled because she'd been going out with another man. Do you happen to know who that was?'

Burton blinked at them. 'Why, yes, of

72

course. Why? Do you think—do you think that *is* Clara you found in the lake? But why would he—'

'Well, we don't know yet, Mr. Burton,' said Mendoza. Possibly they never would know. There was, after all, the still unsolved Black Dahlia case. 'Who was the man?'

'That was just *it*,' said Burton petulantly. 'A vulgar, uneducated common person like that. It was Johnny Orlando. He drives a delivery truck for the store where I work—Clara worked there too, you know—and a man like that, one of those big uncouth fellows, all brawn—' He shook his head.

'Thanks very much, Mr. Burton,' said Mendoza ... In the car, he asked, 'You feel in the mood to see Mr. Johnny Orlando? I have a hunch maybe he knows where Clara Burton is. Or was. I have a hunch Clara got fed up with hubby and got fascinated with Johnny's brawn. Are you with me?'

'You're working yourself right out of possible names for our corpse,' said Hackett. 'I'm with you.'

Mendoza shoved in the cigarette lighter on the dashboard. He hadn't started the engine yet. 'Mmh,' he said reflectively. The lighter jumped out and he hit his cigarette, shoved the lighter back in its slot. 'I have also had a little thought on the other thing. Our burglar who figured out that old people are easy

73

game.'

'What?'

'Because,' said Mendoza, 'they haven't the strength to put up a fight, easy to take. You know what that says to me, Art? A monumental lack of empathy, of any small human feeling.'

'Which is characteristic of a lot of pros,' said Hackett. 'Most of them, in fact.'

'Sure. But even more characteristic of juveniles,' said Mendoza. '*¿Cómo no? ¡Cómo sí!* Just for fun, we're going to take a look at the under-eighteens.'

Hackett looked at him. 'Well, that is a thought.' The under-eighteens, the juveniles—a lot of them full-grown and fairly depraved and vicious juveniles, too—they could take records on *but* couldn't fingerprint, by the laws of the state. Mustn't burden the poor misunderstood youngsters with a police record ... If it was the age of natural rebellion, it was the age of violence, too. Inevitably. In the big city.

'You do have ideas, don't you?' said Hackett thoughtfully.

'I'm a fool,' said Mendoza suddenly. 'Carey will have checked on both those women—Burton and LaVerne Hopper. Let's save ourselves some time.'

CHAPTER SIX

Carey had, he said, seen Johnny Orlando, who admitted he'd dated Clara Burton a few times but said it was nothing serious. Orlando didn't know where she'd gone, so he said, but she'd told him she meant to leave Burton, and who'd blame her? Nothing said whether or not he was telling the truth.

As for LaVerne Hopper, well, they knew how it was, Carey said—there were always about twenty-seven things to do, and he hadn't checked with the Sears store where she worked until Saturday. By phone. He'd got passed around some, but finally learned that she hadn't showed up. So it looked like a real disappearance, since she'd just got promoted. She had a car, a 1960 Rambler, but it was in the garage for major repair; it was promised for delivery next Thursday, and she hadn't been near it.

In fact, right then Mendoza thought that LaVerne Hopper looked much the likeliest prospect for the lady in the lake. She was younger than the sister, and by what the sister said, until LaVerne Hopper had lost her husband she'd probably been leading a good deal gayer life than she had recently, in that dreary cluttered house. It was all too likely that, bored, saving money to pay off debts, she had been fair game for some plausible character.

'Sister doesn't seem to know much about her friends, if any,' said Carey.

'No,' said Mendoza. 'She probably talked to other salesclerks at the store—on coffee breaks, lunch hours, like that. What branch did she work for?'

'Old one over on Santa Monica Boulevard.'

'I know it. I think I'll go up there and see if I can find some of the women who worked with her. Art, you'd better go on up to the office, see if—¡Dios me libre!—anything new has come in, if the boys are getting anywhere on that other thing.'

'Unlikely,' said Hackett. 'Will do.'

Mendoza went out into the heat again—these January heat spells didn't usually last this long, and this one was certainly overstaying its welcome—and drove up to Hollywood. The Sears store he was heading for had been there for years, not quite downtown in Hollywood. It was probably the smallest Sears store in the county. Belatedly, as he went in and took off his hat, he realized he didn't know which department LaVerne Hopper had worked in. He went up to the nearest counter, which happened to be costume jewelry, and asked the clerk where he should go to find the Personnel department.

'Upstairs, second floor, sir.'

76

'Thank you. Did you happen to know a Mrs. Hopper who was employed here until recently?'

The clerk said no. Mendoza climbed stairs, found Personnel, and without introducing himself asked which department Mrs. Hopper had worked in. The girl who'd come up to serve him looked a little doubtful and asked why he wanted to know. Mendoza, who didn't want a lot of people gossiping and making about ninety-four out of two and two before he knew more about this damned case than he knew now, switched on all his charm and said, 'Oh, now, there's nothing very secret about it, is there? I'm an old friend, just thought I'd surprise her, O.K.?' and then cursed himself, because when the woman had walked off the job anybody in Personnel would probably know that.

But the girl didn't seem to. 'Well, you should be a nice surprise, handsome,' she said pertly. 'I'll go look her up.' As she went to the files, she wondered if he was watching her, and swung her hips a little. She really went for that smooth Latin type, mustache and all, even if he was sort of old, maybe pushing forty.

When she came back she gave him a nice smile and said, 'She's in Lamps and Accessories, that's right over on the other side of this floor. Down that aisle.'

'Thanks very much.' Mendoza followed

directions and presently found himself in a forest of floor lamps and table lamps displayed on a maze of tiered counters. He seemed to be the only one there; no customers, no clerks. He wandered around, down several narrow aisles, and finally found a woman putting some extension cords away in a drawer. She straightened and gave him a brisk smile.

'May I help you, sir?'

'Well, I hope so. I understand Mrs. LaVerne Hopper used to work here, in fact has just left.'

Her brow wrinkled. She stared at him. She was quite an attractive woman of about forty-five, with a well-kept figure not looking corseted; she'd taken care of her complexion too, and if her mouth was a bit narrow, her nose a trifle high-bridged, she still gave an impression of smartness, in a neat navy-blue dress with a white collar. 'Just what are you after?' she asked.

'Somebody here who knew LaVerne Hopper, Miss—'

'And just why? And why the past tense?'

Mendoza felt a little surprised. He studied her. 'I don't know if you know it, but Mrs. Hopper seems to be missing. Her sister has reported it. To the police.' Reluctantly he hauled out his badge.

'Well, for the *love* of heaven!' said the woman. 'By that old—by my sister, you said?'

'Your—'

'I'm LaVerne Hopper, mister, and you can just go right back to headquarters or wherever you came from and take my name off your damn missing list. Missing! That old—'

'Well, you seem to have taken off in a hurry without telling anybody,' said Mendoza, feeling as exasperated as he'd ever felt in his life. 'Where have you been, where did you go?'

LaVerne Hopper stared at him. 'If it is any of your business, Sergeant or Captain or whatever—'

'Lieutenant.'

'I suppose *if* you've seen my sister—*and* her house—you won't be too astonished to hear that I hated every second I spent in that—that *hole*. I was down and out, which she probably also told you, and I had to take her offer to live there until I could get rid of some of the debts and begin to get on my feet again. But I never meant to stay one minute longer than I had to—Pauline and I never did get along too well, and *how* she loved lecturing me on how *improvident* Harry was and how much better her husband had been—dreary old man he was, twenty years older than her—at least Harry and I had some fun! When I got my promotion, I knew I could get away, and I tell you, I couldn't get

79

away fast enough! I found myself a little apartment, furnished, and I moved, and that's all about it.'

'Not quite, Mrs. Hopper. We checked with the store on Saturday and it was confirmed that you hadn't showed up.'

'Well, naturally. I don't work Saturdays. I work four nights a week instead.'

Mendoza sighed. Some idiot in Personnel misunderstanding Carey's question. 'And why didn't you tell your sister you were moving, Mrs. Hopper? The reasonable thing to do, after all—instead of leaving her to worry.'

'Worry! A lot of worrying she's been doing! I figured she'd know I'd had as much as I could take. You think she didn't know how I hated her needling me all the time about Harry, how I hated living there? She knew, all right! I naturally figured, when she saw all my things except old stuff were gone, she'd know I'd gone for good, place of my own. I didn't tell her because I didn't want a whole lot of argument. About the only time she ever goes out except to market is every Wednesday night to play cards with some other old biddies. It was bad luck my car being in the garage, but I borrowed Jean's—she works here too—and just packed up all I wanted to take, and got *out*. And that's it. And I'd take a bet,' she added, 'that Pauline made a pretty good guess about it and just wanted to make a little trouble for me, going to you. Missing! For the love of heaven!' She laughed harshly.

'Thanks so much,' said Mendoza. 'We'll be letting your sister know you're not.'

'As if she *didn't* know!' said LaVerne Hopper. 'Old cat!'

Mendoza went back downtown to tell Carey he could take LaVerne Hopper off his list.

Hackett had been down in Records busy on that brain wave Mendoza had had about the under-eighteens. Mendoza wondered if he'd found anything.

He left a note for Nick Galeano, who was sharing night tour with Farrell this month, and went out to find Hackett.

*   *   *

He went home at seven o'clock in a very exasperated frame of mind.

'I tell you what it is,' he said to Alison before he shut the door behind him, 'it's another of those damn things that'll drag on, for years maybe, and we'll never find out any more about it, and every time somebody accuses us of the usual stupidity and brutality, there'll be headlines about it again. "One of the gravest unsolved cases in the police files—" ' It's quite likely, for God's sake, we'll never even find out who she was. Don't tell *me* nobody can drop out of sight

81

and not be missed these days! They—'

'I am not,' said Alison, 'telling you anything, *amante*. You look tired to death. Thank goodness we got the twins to bed early. Come in and sit down, relax. Have you had anything to eat?'

'He has not, can't you tell by listening to the man he's hungry as a bull?' said Mrs. MacTaggart from the doorway. 'I set the stew back in the oven. I'll fetch you a drink, which you'll be needing.'

'Which he does *not* need,' said Alison. 'He's feeling belligerent enough now, and you know what it does to him.'

'I am not,' said Mendoza distinctly, 'feeling belligerent. I am feeling damned exasperated.' He stalked into the living room, stripping off jacket and tie, and Sheba landed on his shoulder from behind, all claws extended. 'Hell take all cats! Missing persons! It's a waste of time, a sheer damned waste of time. *¿Para qué es esto?* Ninety-nine out of a hundred missing persons have taken off voluntarily, and aren't too pleased at being found. About once in a thousand cases it's genuine amnesia—*and* about once in five thousand cases it's something like this. How the hell should we *ever* find out who she was? I don't know if the rest of the body's in the lake, but even if it is, it doesn't seem likely we'll ever get it out.'

'But, Luis, eventually—'

82

'Eventually, eventually! What the hell do you mean, eventually? She'll be missed? *¡No me tomes el pelo!*—don't kid me! So people can't drop out of sight? A nondescript middle-aged female, maybe with no relatives, living in a single room, a cheap apartment, not many belongings, no close friends, an unimportant job—'

'But how do you know—'

'I don't know, damn it! I'm just telling you! A woman like that, who cares? Who notices? She doesn't come back to the room, the apartment—after a while the landlord sells what she had to cover the back rent. Takes it for granted she's gone off of her own volition—'

'Luis—'

Mrs. MacTaggart came back, hotly pursued by the miniature lion El Señor, with a two-ounce shot glass and a saucer. She handed the glass to Mendoza and put the saucer on the floor. El Señor crouched over it and lapped rye whiskey, which he was unaccountably crazy about. 'That unnatural cat!' said Mrs. MacTaggart balefully.

Mendoza poured half the contents of the glass down his throat. 'Thanks, Máiri ... Of her own volition, is he going to get involved with cops over it? She doesn't turn up at her job, they figure she's just walked off—hell, she's a grown woman, presumably in her right mind, are *they* going to take the trouble to—So she's got a few acquaintances, they wonder where she's gone, they talk about it among themselves, but she's a free agent, why shouldn't she move if she wants to? Are *they* going to—¡*Mil rayos!*' He tossed off the rest of the rye.

Mrs. MacTaggart took the glass back, remarked calmly that his dinner would be ready in ten minutes, and marched back to the kitchen.

'Luis—'

'Frightening,' said Mendoza. 'It's frightening, you know, *querida*. There are the hell of a lot of people like that. Women like that. With nobody special. Nobody to notice. They drop out of sight—oh, she got tired of the job, she decided to move, she skipped because she was broke and couldn't pay the back rent—Little people. Little, unimportant people. Especially in any big town. They drop out of one area, they reappear in another. Mostly. But sometimes they don't. Sometimes they turn up next—like this one, in the lake.' Mendoza was silent; she watched him; and then he added violently, '*And* in the police files, from now on—Case Pending! Damnation! She could stay anonymous until the bomb falls a hundred years from now.'

'Luis—you said there were a couple of leads.'

'I always thought Hopper was the best, and she's crossed off now.' He passed a hand across his forehead. 'I don't really think it's Clara Burton. It looks likely that Burton just picked up and went off on her own. It could be she's not even from anywhere around here. Of course, people don't always come in and report somebody missing the day after they take off. It could be that somewhere in the country, right now, a few people are wondering where on earth Mary's got to—and will come to us tomorrow—or next week—to ask. Because that's another thing, of course. A child, a teenager, a young person—somebody like that vanishes, and almost right away there's an anxious family calling the cops. But a middle-aged woman, most probably living alone—'

'You'll get there, darling,' said Alison. 'You usually do, you know.'

Mendoza turned to her. He looked abstracted. 'We usually do, *cara*. But this isn't the usual case.' He smiled wryly.

'Luis, you're tired. It'll look different when—'

'People alone,' he said, and suddenly came to hold her close. 'You are a nuisance, woman,' he said against her hair. 'A wife to tie me down. These noisy twin monsters. But we are not alone, at least.'

Alison tightened her arms around him. '*¿Le sabe mal?* You approve?'

'*Tiene mucha sal esta niña.* No sarcasm, *chica.*'

85

Mrs. MacTaggart considerately waited until he had finished kissing Alison, and said his dinner was waiting.

On Wednesday they went on asking questions of the neighbors of the elderly victims, and got nothing at all for their pains.

A couple of men down in Records, with Piggott to help out, continued pawing through the files kept on the under-eighteens, looking for one who matched the vague general description of the man who had preyed on the elderly victims and murdered Marion Stromberg.

On Wednesday, Mendoza got the lab report on the hairs found clenched in Marion Stromberg's hand. They were, said the report, human head hairs, light sandy-brown in color. That was interesting, but didn't tell them who had originally owned them.

Wednesday was George Higgins' day off. He got up early, fixed himself a large breakfast in his apartment on Bronson Avenue in Hollywood, and then drove over to Mary Dwyer's house in the Silver Lake district. Everybody was gone by the time he got there except Brucie the Scottie, who gruffed at him from the driveway gate and wagged his stub tail. Mary would be at her job—she was an expert photographic retoucher—and the kids, Steve and Laura, at school. But Mary had left the back-door key in the garage; she'd known he was coming, to fix that leaky faucet in the main bathroom.

He didn't know how she felt about him at all. Maybe she thought he just felt sort of obligated to help her out as he could, because he'd liked Bert. Worked with Bert.

Well he had liked Bert.

Mary—

Higgins went into the back yard and found the key in the garage. He spent a few minutes playing with Brucie, patting him. Then he went into the house and fixed the leaky faucet. It was a nice, comfortable house, big rooms, but it wasn't new and it needed keeping up. Higgins thought about the pension. The house payments were a hundred and ten bucks, he knew, she'd let that out in an unguarded moment.

Stevie ought to go to college. About eight years from now. And Laura had cried about having to stop the piano lessons.

As a sergeant, Higgins earned (on this top force) over eight thousand a year.

He'd like to take care of Mary Dwyer and Stevie and Laura—Mary—But of course she'd never look at another cop. Not George Higgins. She thanked him, a little surprised, for the few small things he did, maybe thinking it was because he had liked Bert.

Higgins found Brucie's leash and took him for a walk around the block. He sat in Mary's living room awhile, because it was a nice comfortable homelike room, and feeling very

87

guilty, he went down the hall and looked into her room, with the neat white-covered double bed and the neatly arranged few jars on the dressing table—the one bottle of cologne, *Intimate*.

Intimate, he thought.

He went out into the yard and put the key back in the garage. It was only three months since Bert had died. He really couldn't get up the nerve to ask her to go to dinner with him, or a movie, for a while yet.

The Scottie jumped up against his legs. He bent to pat him. 'Isn't that the hell of a laugh, Brucie?' he said softly. 'Me.' George Higgins, well, he might not be a movie star to look at, but for sure he'd never been very backward with the girls.

But this, of course, was not just any girl. This was Mary.

Higgins patted Brucie again and left. He bought himself lunch at the nearest restaurant, and went home and spent the afternoon looking at an old movie on T.V.

On Thursday they dragged Echo Park Lake again.

They didn't bring up anything useful.

On Thursday, Piggott and a man in Records continued to go through the files on the under-eighteens. In a place like L.A. whatever files you were going through, there were the hell of a lot of them.

Higgins continued, whenever he thought of

it, to feel funny about Alfredo Gonzales' suicide. Sometime he meant to ask Mendoza to translate those Spanish words Mrs. Gonzales had spoken.

Detective Jason Grace continued to brood over Ambler, who had said he would never show fight to a heist man, who had been shot by a heist man. He wondered why Ambler had been shot. Well, it happened. Sure. But he wondered, all the same.

Nothing much happened on Thursday.

Nobody reported anybody else missing. Dr. Bainbridge continued his tedious chemical tests.

★　　★　　★

On Friday morning at nine-twenty Lieutenant Carey called the Homicide office. 'I don't know,' he said, 'it's anything for you. On that body. But this guy just came in to report his sister missing. Stephanie Padgett. From what he said—well, she's got a little pedigree. D.-and-D., shoplifting. He says she's been gone since a week ago yesterday. The description might fit your body, generally speaking.'

'¿Cómo dice? He still there? I'll be right down,' said Mendoza, and slammed down the phone. 'Now what the hell did I do with those photog—'

CHAPTER SEVEN

Fred Evans looked at the photographs, swallowed, and said, 'Jesus, I don't know. I mean, how would I know, anyways? She's my sister, Stephanie, not my girl. Like that. You know. I got to say, I don't know.' He handed the photographs back to Mendoza in a hurry. 'Well, what's the story, Mr. Evans? Why'd you come in?' asked Carey.

Evans was nervous. He sat in a straight chair alongside Carey's desk and fidgeted, moving his feet, twisting his hands together. He was an undersized man about forty, going bald, and shabbily dressed. 'Like, well, see, I know Stephanie's been in trouble before, see. I never been in no trouble, because I got more sense. Sure, so I like a couple of drinks now 'n' then, what's the percentage you go on 'n' get drunk and maybe get picked up 'n' thrown in the tank? This makes sense? Like hell. I got a good job, I'm a barber, assistant manager of the place. But I can't deny Stephanie, she's been in trouble. She always was sort of wild, you know? So I bail her out o' jail, like that. Last thing Ma says to me on her deathbed, she says, you look out for Stephanie. Well, it ain't so easy, you know? I pay the fines, I try to talk some sense into her—she's older 'n me but you'd never know it, way she acts, think anybody 'd learn some sense when they're over forty, but—She leaves Jim Padgett, who was a very nice guy, she takes up with all sorts of oddball characters—'

'Specifically, Mr. Evans?'

Evans blinked. 'Well, I guess that's why I come in. On account of the latest guy she's been traveling around with, he ain't got too good a rep—know what I mean?—and he gets kind of mean when he's high, I understand, and he likes to drink. His name's King Richards. I don't think the King's legit, kind of like a nickname, see? I don't know.'

'Just a minute, Mr. Evans. Your sister lives with you?'

'Well, sort of on and off. When she gets broke she usually does.'

'Does she have a job?'

'Well, on and off. Sort of. She's worked as a waitress, and like that. But I got to tell you the truth, she's just not very reliable, know what I mean?'

'We can guess,' said Carey dryly.

Mendoza leaned forward. 'Has she ever been picked up for prostitution, Mr. Evans?'

Evans looked miserable. He looked down at the floor and mumbled, 'Yeah. I—I don't know if it was a bum rap or not, I mean, I didn't think Stephanie would—But they said—'

'Let's have a look at her pedigree,'

Mendoza suggested to Carey, who nodded and phoned down to Records. 'All right, Mr. Evans, what happened this time?'

Evans took a deep breath. 'Well, she'd been pretty good lately. I got her a job waiting on table at a joint near the shop. And then she picks up with this Richards guy, she brought him home a couple times and I didn't like his looks at all. At all. See? He's a mean-looking bastard, that Richards, and big—about six-four. And I ask around on the q.t., and I get the word he's got a record, for assault or something, *which* don't surprise me none. So then Stephanie takes off—this was a week ago yesterday, she just don't come home, and I figure, hell, she's off on another bat. I go looking, all the bars, you know the routine with a—with a lush. A lush. I guess—I guess she is, all right. Just be foolin' myself, not admit it.' Evans looked at the floor again. 'Well, I don't find her, and now I get to thinking it could be—'

And Bainbridge had said the corpse had a bad liver. Said it wasn't necessarily from alcohol, but—And any woman who might engage in prostitution was about a thousand times as likely to run into a butcher as a woman who wouldn't. There was also King Richards. Carey was already on the phone to Records, asking for his pedigree too.

They got names and addresses from Evans, thanked him for coming in, told him they'd

92

let him know if they found anything definite. He went out as if he was glad to go.

'What do you think?' asked Carey.

'How do I know?' Mendoza shrugged and lit a cigarette. 'Ask around Richards' pals, Stephanie's pals from the bars. One thing—Bainbridge said the woman in the lake had taken care of herself, regular baths, and so on—presumably also meaning face creams, et cetera. That isn't very characteristic of the Stephanies.'

'Well, no, not when they get really on the skids. Maybe she wasn't that far down yet.'

The files from Records arrived; they looked at them.

Stephanie Padgett had been picked up on D.-and-D. counts a good many times. She had been charged three times with shoplifting and twice for soliciting. She'd once served a thirty-day term in the County Jail, on the third shoplifting charge. She was forty-three, five foot six, a hundred and thirty-five pounds, dark hair, blue eyes, appendectomy scar on abdomen.

King Richards did indeed sound like a mean one. He was six-four, two hundred pounds, thirty-nine, black hair and blue eyes, no scars or deformities. His real name was Richard Donato; he had used other aliases. He had served time for armed robbery and mugging, and assault with intent to rape. He had also been charged with, but not convicted of, being one of the attackers in a case where a man was beaten to death. He was currently on parole from San Quentin. He owned a 1961 Ford, plate number such and such. When he worked, he worked on the docks as a stevedore, and he belonged to the Longshoremen's union.

'Well,' said Mendoza. 'So let's go looking for Stephanie, shall we? Until we find her alive, we don't know she isn't the lady in the lake. *Dios*, how I hate these up-in-the-air things!'

'You in your corner and me in mine,' said Carey. 'As long as she might still be alive, she's my job, too.'

Mendoza went back to his own office and brought Hackett up to date on that. Hackett said exasperatedly that he'd almost caught up to Herrick, the boy Indiana wanted. A squad-car driver out in Lawndale had spotted Herrick's car by the plate number and called in—Hackett wasn't taking any chances on a patrolman making the collar, he'd take care of that himself—and by the time Hackett got out there the car was gone. Checking with the manager of the apartment in front of which it had been sitting, he found that Herrick didn't live there but had visited one of the tenants a few times. 'So have we got the men to stake out the place? With all the rest of what we've got to handle? How can I take the chance that this guy Herrick knows there is an honest

94

fellow? Go see him, tell him Herrick's wanted, ask him where Herrick's living now, and nine chances to one he calls Herrick as soon as I leave, tells him we're on his trail, so Herrick runs.'

'Annoying,' agreed Mendoza. 'And not even one of our own jobs.'

'Well. You think this Padgett woman could be—'

'That kind of woman,' said Mendoza, 'always runs a better chance of coming across the sort of character who might murder her and cut her up. Doesn't she? I don't know, Art. We may never know.'

'Now who's being a pessimist?'

Piggott and Landers came in, looking a little excited. 'You and your crystal ball!' said Landers, but there was something like awe in his expression. 'How do you do it?'

'What have I done now?' asked Mendoza. 'Don't tell me something's come unstuck!'

'All those juveniles. God knows how many file cards we've been through. A lot we could eliminate right away, the kids who are colored, or the wrong size, and so on. But we found maybe twenty who correspond to the general description of this guy who goes around bashing grandmothers and grandfathers. And then, just about ten minutes ago, I found this.' Landers laid a couple of file cards on Mendoza's desk. Mendoza picked them up. 'If you haven't got

95

a crystal ball, you've got second sight or something. How the hell did you know to look at the under-eighteens, anyway?'

Mendoza looked at the cards. They contained brief information about one Henry Kinger, then sixteen—the file was two years old—who with two other boys had broken into an empty house, stolen clothing and money, and bashed the owner over the head when he returned unexpectedly. The other two boys had been fifteen. Disposition of the case, psychiatric treatment suggested, two years' probation. 'These damned softheaded judges!' said Mendoza. Henry Kinger had then been five-eleven, a hundred and eighty, brown hair, blue eyes, et cetera; and he might have grown some more after sixteen. But he was only a vague possibility. Why should Landers—'Oh,' said Mendoza. 'Oh, how very interesting.'

At that time Henry Kinger had been living on Welcome Street. Welcome Street was about in the middle of that five-by-ten-block rectangle where the elderly victims had been attacked.

'Just a shot in the dark, Tom,' said Mendoza. 'No crystal ball. But we might just have something here. Let's see, he's still on probation. Let's find out if he's still living there.' He picked up the phone.

⋆　　⋆　　⋆

Henry Kinger had moved. The probation officer said confidently that Henry had responded very well to the psychiatric treatment and seemed to have a clear understanding of his problems. In fact, it looked hopeful that they'd made a cure of Henry, that he wouldn't be getting into trouble again. Mendoza thought, I'll bet, taking the jargon with a liberal amount of salt. Henry's mother, said the officer, had got a better job—she was a receptionist, Henry's father was dead—and they had moved, six months ago, to an address on Catalina Street. Mendoza asked the officer if he'd get in touch with Mrs. Kinger and set up an appointment for him this evening ... Yes, Henry too, please. Just some questions.

'Did you say you're *Homicide?*' asked the officer. 'I don't understand—Yes, of course, but—The psychiatrist said—'

'Just a little routine,' said Mendoza.

He was not, himself, very much inclined necessarily to believe what the psychiatrists said.

He'd seen too many corpses which had become corpses because some psychiatrist had said 'X has made a good adjustment and is suitable for unsupervised release.'

★   ★   ★

At eight o'clock he faced Henry Kinger and Mrs. Helen Kinger and considered them thoughtfully. On the surface Henry looked and sounded good. But a lot of bad ones could sound plausible as hell.

Henry had grown to about six-one and filled out. He wasn't a bad-looking boy, with even white teeth, a cleft chin, a wide brow, big innocent blue eyes. His hair was medium brown, but Mendoza knew that not all the hairs on the same head are quite the same color; conceivably the few sandy-brown hairs clutched in Marion Stromberg's hand could have come from Henry's head.

Mrs. Kinger, rather obviously, would be the psychiatrist's choice for whatever was wrong with Henry. She was a big plump blonde woman with a soft voice which for some reason instantly made Mendoza think of marshmallows. She talked a good deal, in a gentle nonstop flow, when she finally understood what he was talking about. The burden of her talk was all Henry. He was a good boy, the best son in the world, he'd been in that little trouble but the doctor had got him all straightened out now, he'd never get into trouble like that again, he wanted to be an engineer, he was just about to graduate from high school, and he already had a scholarship for college, that would show how good a boy he was—

'Aw, *Mom,*' said Henry, embarrassed.

'Knock it off!' He looked at Mendoza anxiously. 'I—I haven't done anything, honest. I—you know—I got a little off base that time, down there—Well, it just seemed like the smart thing to do at the time, but it sure wasn't very smart, I know that now. I got kind of straightened out. Honest. That's the only bad thing I ever did. Like Mom says, I got this scholarship—well, it's only five hundred bucks, but I'm going to get a job after I graduate from high, and save some more money for college in September. I don't know 'why you think I did something else bad—'

He sounded very plausible. Mendoza wondered. Coincidence, Welcome Street? 'Do you remember where you were all evening, Henry, a week ago tonight? That was the eighth. A Friday.'

'Why? What—'

'A week ago tonight, of course,' said Mrs. Kinger instantly. 'I remember, Officer. Friday night. Of *course* you remember, Henry. You were going to take Sue to a movie—Sue Mappin, she's a very nice girl, not at all *fast* like so many teenage girls these days,' she added to Mendoza parenthetically. 'And then she called while we were having dinner and said she couldn't go, her mother'd been taken sick. So you were home here all evening, you didn't go anywhere.'

'Oh, yeah, that's right,' said Henry.

99

'So you see, Officer, whatever funny idea you may have had about Henry, it's not so. If you were thinking he did something last Friday night, something bad, it just couldn't be.'

'Was anyone else here except you, Mrs. Kinger?'

'Well, no. But I *was* here, all the time, and I can tell you that Henry was here all evening—'

And Mendoza didn't like it. Not one damned bit. Possessive, doting mother—mother widowed when Henry was just a baby—Henry all she had. Love, so they said, was blind. And also often amoral, thought Mendoza. Henry, maybe, sounded just a bit too damned good. He had hit a man over the head with a hammer and damned near killed him. So adolescence is a difficult period. Could the psychiatrists really say with such confidence—

And so maybe Mrs. Kinger hadn't been here all that Friday evening, maybe she was just backing Henry blindly because she knew her boy couldn't do anything bad—

Which left it all up in the air. Like the other damned thing. Well, he wasn't going to get her to change her story by looking at her.

Bring Henry in alone, lean on him a little? He was over eighteen now.

And Henry, confident of his alibi, looking innocent and honest with his baby-blue eyes

100

and saying, 'Me, sir? I never did anything wrong, sir, not since that one time, honest. I've got a scholarship—'

Hell.

Everything up in the air.

★　　★　　★

'I still think,' said Sally Mawson, 'we should have given first prize to the cows. Mr. Schubert's a lamb. I brought Andy up here on purpose to see Mr. Schubert's cows, and he blenched. I never knew what blenching was before, but he did.'

Considering that Andrew Mawson had been mentioned in a recent review as 'one of America's most gifted young painters,' Alison could understand the blenching. Mr. Schubert's cows—well.

'How on earth did these—these people ever rate a free room here for a week?' wondered Tony Lawlor, running a hand through his hair.

'It's supposed to be a sort of art center for the public,' said Alison.

'God,' said Tony. He stopped before the canvas they'd doubtfully agreed on as being the least awful of the twenty-odd. It was a rankly bad attempt at a landscape, obviously patterned after Corot, oils laid on heavily with the knife in messily muted colors. It had been executed—the exact word for it, thought

Alison—by one Margaret Beamish.

'God,' said Tony. 'These—'

'Ssh,' said Alison, 'there's some of them coming.'

Mr. Schubert was the first arrival, with little Miss Ames in tow. The Archer woman followed. It was ten o'clock on Saturday morning, and the professional judges were about to make their official pronouncements about the prizes to the Amateur Artists. Most of whom were there by the stroke of the hour, standing about awkwardly and looking, Alison thought, pathetic, anxious and eager at once, and dreadfully apprehensive.

Thank heaven it would be over in half an hour or so. And then the christening this afternoon. Really very odd, Angel wanting the baby christened. It wasn't as if—A very sweet baby, and nice to name her for Art's mother—

'Is everyone here?' Tony spoke up charmingly in his pleasant deep voice—she and Sally had finally convinced him to be nice, but he was impatient to get the thing over with. 'Let's just—'

'Oh, May Tate's not here,' said Miss Ames.

'But it's a quarter past ten,' said Mrs. Archer. 'How very odd. She's usually quite punctual.'

Somebody in the little crowd muttered, '*Too* punctual.'

'Hear, hear,' said another voice.

102

'Well, I know she's very interested in the competition, she certainly meant to be here. Maybe her car broke down or—'

'That's no never mind,' said Mr. Schubert in a loud voice. 'May knew what time we're supposed to meet. She doesn't get here in time, that's just too bad. I vote—'

'Oh, but, Mr. Schubert, she probably meant to get here in good time! I mean, I know she would have. She does *mean* so well,' said Miss Ames earnestly, 'it'd be a dreadful shame to—Let's wait a few minutes more, I'm sure she'll—'

'Bossy females,' said the rather too beautiful young man named Foster. 'I find Mrs. Tate obnoxious. Obnoxious. And I will say so *to* her face.'

'Oh, really, Brian, that's—'

Alison realized what she had missed from the little crowd: Mrs. Tate's firm, loud-voiced authority.

'Oh, Lord,' said Sally, *sotto voce*, 'are we going to waste the whole morning hanging around here because that damned woman had a flat tire or something?'

'It is twenty-three minutes past ten,' said the beautiful young man, 'and if Mrs. Tate cannot be punctual it's her own—'

'But maybe she's had an accident!' said Miss Ames. 'You *know* how interested she is in the competition! She wouldn't miss being here if she could *possibly* help it—I'm sure

103

she'll—Please let's just wait a little longer—er—if the judges don't mind—'

'Oh, for God's sake,' said Tony to Alison. 'Well, I don't see what else we can do—'

'Put it to a vote. After all, we can't expect the judges—'

And of course Alison would never have thought of it if she hadn't happened to be married to a cop—and the cop on that case downtown, the cut-up corpse in Echo Park Lake. But suddenly she found herself thinking, by what she'd seen of Mrs. May Tate last Saturday, she considered herself, did Mrs. Tate, the guiding light of the Amateur Artists. She *wouldn't* miss the prize-giving today if she could possibly help it. And she was now thirty-five minutes late. It was crazy, it was impossible, of course—her car had had a flat tire or a run-down battery, that was all. But in a kind of way Mrs. May Tate did correspond to the general description of the cut-up corpse. Didn't she? Forty-five to fifty, about a hundred and fifty pounds, dark-haired—

Ridiculous, thought Alison. Because the woman was late.

But she'd been very interested in this little competition. She could have taken a cab if her car—

Alison began to feel a little excited. If it *was* possible—She stepped forward before she knew she meant to, and raised her voice.

104

'Please! Have any of you seen Mrs. Tate since last Saturday?' Because the times fit, too, if—

Silence for a moment, and then confused replies. No, none of them would have occasion to—There hadn't been a regular meeting scheduled—They didn't meet at each other's homes, of course, anyway, it was only—No, none of them had spoken to Mrs. Tate on the telephone, but what—

'Try to take over the whole club!' said somebody indignantly. 'Nice peaceful little group, she comes in and starts organizing! Can't stand the woman myself. So she's not here, so what? Her own lookout. I vote we get on with it, she knew what time she was supposed to be here!'

It was ten-fifty.

'Does anyone know where she lives?' asked Alison. Because, just *suppose*. Just suppose it was—wilder things had happened, and she could tell Luis who the corpse was—It was crazy, but *maybe*. And just in case—

Miss Ames said in a bewildered tone, 'Why, yes, I know—but why—Yes, I have her phone number somewhere—' She began to fumble in her bag.

CHAPTER EIGHT

Mendoza was sitting at his desk brooding over Henry Kinger when Sergeant Lake put his head in the doorway and said, 'Your wife's on the phone.'

'Um,' said Mendoza, and reached for the phone. He had about decided to bring Henry in—alone—for some intensive questioning. It couldn't be let just to lie, the way it was now: so Mrs. Kinger had been there, how nice, alibi for Henry. Not with Welcome Street in the picture. 'Hello, *cara*.' After all, Henry had known that area; how long had they lived there? He'd probably known some of those old people—known of them, anyway ... 'What? One of your art lovers hasn't showed up. How disappointing ... *¿Cómo dices?* ... My darling, I'm Homicide, I haven't anything to do with ... And why the hell should I—What?'

'If you'd listen,' said Alison at the other end of the wire, 'that's all I ask. Look, I'm telling you that this Mrs. Tate just could be your corpse. She—'

'Because she didn't show up at your prize-giving? Now, I'd appreciate any help on that one, *querida*, but I'm the detective in the family and I really don't think—'

'If you'd just *listen*,' said Alison. 'First, she

106

fits the general description of the body. Yes, I know quite a lot of middle-aged women do, but there's more. Of course, I only met her once, last Saturday, but she was obviously very interested in this—this competition. I know I was awfully surprised when she didn't turn up this morning, but now I get from the art lovers that the whole thing was her idea—most of the rest of them felt a little diffident about asking—well, what they call real artists to look at their things. Apparently when Mrs. Tate joined the group, she tried to take the whole thing over, in various ways, and none of them seem to have liked her very well. All right. That makes it even odder that she hasn't showed up, *¿conforme?*'

'My dear addlepate, the woman could have been suddenly called to a deathbed—or her car broke down—or—'

'We thought of all that. If she'd had a telegram or something like that, she'd have let one of the others know. And she'd have intended to be here by ten, so she's had nearly two hours to get here in a cab. None of the others has seen her since last Saturday—'

'Which doesn't say nobody else has,' Mendoza pointed out.

'Well, all I'm saying is, it just *could* be, and I don't suppose it'd take you half an hour to check it out. Whether she's been at work this week—she works at Robinson's, the one on Wilshire.'

'Presumably someone would have missed her before—'

'Not so necessarily, by what the other art lovers tell me. Only two of them knew where she lived—Just a minute, I've got the address—yes, here it is, Winona Boulevard in Hollywood. She lived alone, she's a widow. So you see—And you said yourself, just the other night, that if somebody just walked off a job, no employer would start actively looking for her. They'd just think she'd quit without telling them. All I'm saying is, it's a *chance*, and you could check it without much trouble.'

From force of habit Mendoza had copied down the address on his memo pad. 'I'll say this,' Alison's voice went on in his ear, 'if she was working for me, I'd be quite happy to see her walk out, Luis. Just from meeting her once. One of those loud-voiced women with a gimlet eye, who wants to take over everything—you know the kind. But the point is, this was a pet project of hers, she was terribly interested in it, and if something had come up to prevent her being here, she'd not only have let someone know, she'd probably have made all new arrangements so she could be here when we announced the prizes.'

'Yes, I do see that. That is a little funny.'

'So I think you ought to call the store and find out if she has been at work this week. Of course I realize there could be another explanation—she could have had a heart attack or a stroke and be in the hospital, or even lying dead in her own bedroom—but if that's so, well, you ought to find that out, too, hadn't you?'

'*Claro que sí.* Well, we'll check on her, but—What did you say her name is?'

'Mrs. May Tate. Have you got the address?'

'I've got it.'

'You'll probably forget all about it,' said Alison suspiciously. 'You don't think it says anything at all. Of course Miss Ames is practically in hysterics—she's convinced that Mrs. Tate has been murdered in her bed—I don't know why it should be so much worse to be murdered in your bed than murdered *per se*—And Tony is convinced I'm quite right, she *is* your cut-up corpse, and he's itching to rush up to her address and start detecting.'

'All of you keep away,' said Mendoza. 'If by a millionth chance you are right, which I very much doubt, I don't want a horde of civilians trampling all over possible evidence.'

'I think,' said Alison meditatively, 'he's convinced because he took such a dislike to the woman. She stood right over him, you know, and made him drink that awful punch—he'd been just about to tip it into a potted plant. He says she was the sort of woman anybody might be proud to murder. You will check on her?'

'Yes, yes.'

'And call me back to let me know? Because I'm *terribly* curious as to why she didn't turn up, if she *hasn't* been murdered.'

'Where are you? Still at Barnsdall Park?'

'Oh, no, we're—Just a minute—' Alison vanished from the line and could be heard asking where they were. 'Gigi's. It's on Sunset Boulevard. We finally announced the prizes, and then we stood around talking about Mrs. Tate, and a couple of the art lovers, as I say, were all for going out to her place and seeing if anything serious *was* wrong, but I said I'd call you—everybody was *most* interested to hear I was married to a cop—so they finally dispersed, still talking. We were spared the punch this time. Sally had a lunch date, but Tony and I are getting more curious all the time, we stopped in here for lunch and to talk about it. But,' said Alison, 'there's the christening, it'll take me at least twenty minutes to drive to Angel's, so after about one twenty I'll be on my way there. If you call after that, we'll be back at Angel's by three.'

'Listen, is that long-haired Greek profile buying you lunch? I don't like the idea of my wife lunching with another man.'

'Don't be ridiculous,' said Alison. 'At the moment, Tony's trying to re-enact the crime.

110

He's figured out that it was Mr. Schubert who murdered her, and he's working out how he got her down to Echo Park.'

'¡*Maravilloso!*' said Mendoza. 'Thanks very much for the new lead, *amante.*' He hung up and almost went back to brooding over Henry Kinger, but looking at the memo pad, reflected that sometimes the unlikeliest leads turned out to be useful.

He hauled out the appropriate phone book, looked up that branch of Robinson's, and in a few minutes was talking to someone in Personnel. He was passed on to someone else, and then someone else again, and finally found himself talking to a man named Paulsen, who seemed on the ball.

'You're asking about a Mrs. May Tate?'

'Yes, please. Which department—'

'Did you say you're *police?*'

'That's right, Mr. Paulsen. We'd like to—'

'Has something *happened* to Mrs. Tate?'

'Well, we don't know, Mr. Paulsen. What I called to ask is, has she been working as usual this week?'

'Oh,' said Paulsen. He sounded surprised and uneasy. 'Well, I most certainly hope we haven't been unfair to Mrs. Tate. If something has happened to her, so she couldn't—No, she hasn't, sir, did you say Lieutenant?'

'Yes.' Mendoza frowned at the desk blotter. *Caray*, he thought, was Alison going

111

to turn out to have a crystal ball of her own? Still—

'No, she hasn't been here all the week. She's always been prompt and efficient, and her immediate superior couldn't understand it, frankly. It seemed odd and—er—unlike Mrs. Tate that she wouldn't call to explain, if she were ill or—you understand. *Has something happened to her?*'

'Well, we're just checking, Mr. Paulsen. How was she employed in the store, as a salesclerk or—'

'Yes, that's right, in our Little Frocks. She was, as a matter of fact, assistant buyer for that department. I say *was*, well, Mrs. Maynard was most upset about it. She tried calling Mrs. Tate at home on Monday, when she hadn't come in by noon, and then on Tuesday, when the woman again didn't show up, she came in and reported it to me, very properly. I told her to let me know when and if Mrs. Tate did come in. After all, we try to give our patrons the best service, you know, and when just one clerk is unexpectedly off duty, it makes things difficult for the others. I tried to call Mrs. Tate, too, at her home number, but I didn't get any answer. On Wednesday, Mrs. Maynard came in again and reported that Mrs. Tate had not been in at all, and so I marked her card as Discharged. I thought it odd at the time, she had—has—an excellent record with us, never tardy, always

112

efficient, and so on—never took more than her allowed days of sick leave—and she'd been with us for nine years. But we really can't have our schedule of service impaired, and when an employee turns irresponsible like that—'

'Yes. Has anyone at the store made any further effort to get in touch with Mrs. Tate?' asked Mendoza.

'Certainly not, to my knowledge.'

Just as he had said. *De veras.* Robinson's was no hole-in-the-wall junkshop, but one of the best and most expensive department stores in the city, and its employees would be superior ones, and carefully chosen. Yet when a woman who had been a satisfactory employee for nine years suddenly failed to come to work, without explanation, nothing was done about it except to discharge her officially. Of course, that said also that probably she hadn't had any friends among the other clerks, otherwise they might have done some unofficial investigating. And just as he'd said to Alison, a mature woman presumed to be in possession of all her faculties had a right to come and go as she pleased.

'Well, thanks very much, Mr. Paulsen,' he said.

'Will you let us know if something has happened to her, please? We do try to be fair—and there's a health insurance plan—'

'Yes, certainly. Thanks again.' Mendoza hung up and went out to the anteroom. Sergeant Lake was reading a paperback novel. Mendoza thrust his head into the sergeants' room and found Jason Grace and Higgins sitting at their respective desks.

'I had heard of that one,' Higgins was saying.

'And then a thing called a Fall River,' said Grace. 'Do you suppose it goes all the way back to the Borden case? I haven't tried that one yet—it sounds pretty damn lethal. One third gin, one third brandy, one sixth white Crème de Menthe, and one sixth maraschino.'

'God,' said Higgins in simple comment.

'I tell you,' said Grace, 'drinks you never heard of. It's a very interesting book.'

'Is this what you're paid for, boys?' asked Mendoza.

Grace and Higgins both grinned.

He filled them in on Mrs. Tate. 'Look, it's a wild-goose chase,' he said. 'It's nothing—I think. The woman may have just walked off—but she could also be lying in her living room with a broken leg, *or* she could be—at long odds—the lady we're looking for. So trot up there and do a little snooping, mmh? It ought to be checked out.'

'O.K.,' said Higgins. 'We'll get on it.'

'Here's the address. It's one of those little side streets off Vermont, up above Hollywood Boulevard.' Mendoza went back to his office, and instead of thinking about Henry Kinger, he was thinking, *One of those little side streets off Vermont—*

A while ago a girl who lived on one of those streets had got raped and murdered, and they'd got the wrong man for it, and that had turned out to be quite a thing . . . One way and another. If it hadn't been for that girl getting murdered, Luis Rodolfo Vicente Mendoza might never have found out—well, that for every man there is just one important woman. He might not have Alison now—or, of course, the twin monsters . . .

       ★   ★   ★

It was a modest street, lined with old trees. Except for a four-family apartment at the corner, it was a street of houses, mostly old frame California bungalows, comfortable-looking, kept up fairly well. At this time of year even watered lawns were brownish, but the houses were framed by cared-for flowering shrubs, rose bushes, climbing bougainvillaea.

This was rental-zoned, and at least half the houses, in old southern California custom, had a second, smaller house built at the rear of their deep lots.

The address they wanted was one like that. They were in Grace's car, a middle-aged Buick; Grace pulled up to the curb in front of

115

the house and cut the motor. 'People in the front house away somewhere,' he said interestedly.

'Looks as if,' agreed Higgins. The Venetian blinds were pulled shut on the front windows of the bungalow and an accumulation of rolled newspapers littered the lawn and front porch. 'What goddamned fools people are,' he added. 'They remembered to tell the post office about mail, and then go off leaving the blinds pulled and papers to collect. An open invitation to burglars, for God's sake. And if burglars come, then they say why in hell aren't the police doing their job. People!'

'Human nature, human nature,' said Grace tolerantly. 'If people were all sensible, we wouldn't have jobs, you know.' He got out of the car. 'The address is five fifty-two and a half, which says it's the rear house.'

They walked down the drive. It was, as usual in a neighborhood like this, two strips of cracked cement with grass growing between. The sprawling old bungalow was good-sized. There was a kitchen door giving on the drive, with an empty clean garbage can sitting at the foot of the steps, and there was a chain-link fence around the entire back yard. The gate across the driveway had a firm bolt driven home, but no padlock.

'Dog,' said Grace, 'maybe?'

Inside the fence there was another house at the very rear of the lot. It was a neat small

116

frame house, probably of about four rooms, painted white with green trim. There was a double garage attached to it. In this neighborhood it would probably rent for somewhere around eighty a month, and offer more privacy in a way than an apartment: a bargain.

The dog appeared suddenly. It was a medium-sized dog óf stunning appearance, with sharp pricked ears, a foxy face, and a thick coat of shining silver-white hair, with a great plume of tail carried curled over its back. The dog had shining black eyes, beautiful against the silver coat. The dog said, 'Woof,' in a low voice.

'Damn,' said Higgins.

'Quite all right, Sergeant,' said Grace.

'What the hell you mean, all right? The minute we open that gate, the damn dog'll—'

'Not this dog,' said Grace, pulling back the bolt.

'Hey, watch out—'

'Woof,' said the dog happily, and rose up on his hind legs to greet humans. Grace bent and patted him. The dog enthusiastically swiped Grace's cheek with a long pink tongue.

'What the hell kind of watchdog is that?' asked Higgins, thinking of Brucie, who would raise seven kinds of hell if a stranger came into *his* back yard.

'This,' said Grace, 'is about the nicest kind

117

of dog there is. He's a Sammy—Samoyed, Sergeant. Funny how so many people think the Eskimo dogs are all fierce—they're the only dogs that've never in all their history ever been trained to hunt or attack, see. They just like everybody. Especially the Sammies.' The dog was washing his face happily. 'Hey, boy, you get down now. Pretty lonesome, hah?'

Higgins came into the yard and shut the gate behind him. The dog jumped up on him. Quite clearly, the dog was very pleased at having company. He followed at their heels up to the front door of the little rear house. Grace pushed the doorbell. They listened to its empty buzz.

'Nobody home.' Higgins went round to the closed garage and pulled back the doors. One side was empty. In the other space there sat a 1954 two-door Ford.

The dog whined plaintively. Grace patted the smooth head, fondled the thick ruff of silver hair around his throat. 'Nice dogs. I'd like one of these myself.' He turned and surveyed the back yard.

There was a good expanse of lawn, and tended flowering shrubs in neat beds against the fence, against the house—lantana, and well-grown camellias, a climbing rose, hibiscus, oleander. The garden hose, bright-green plastic, had been left improvidently snaked out across the grass, and whoever had last used it had been careless about turning off the faucet—it still dribbled a trickle of water onto the lawn. Up near the back of the house a few scraps of paper blew about untidily.

'Well, what do we do next?' asked Higgins. The dog whined again, worriedly.

'No search warrant,' said Grace, 'but the woman just could be in there, dead of a stroke or something. Sort of a duty to find out, isn't it? Poor lone widow.' There wasn't any screen door; he tried the knob. The door opened quietly.

The dog followed them in, wagging his full plume of a tail.

There was nobody in the little house. There was a small living room, a smaller bedroom, a neat tiled bathroom, a tiny kitchen. A row of ceramic planters on the kitchen window sill, with drooping, untended plants in them. Nothing seemed out of place in the house; the unremarkable furniture stood tidily in place. A portable TV was on a chest of drawers in the bedroom; the single bed was neatly made up.

The dog went straight into the kitchen, stood on his hind legs against the small refrigerator, and barked.

'Now you know,' said Grace, looking at the dog, 'that Tate woman, she was dog-sitting.'

'Come again?' said Higgins.

'The people in the front house, they own

119

the dog. Probably. Nice dog,' said Grace, and the dog barked again. 'They're away—vacation or whatever. And Mrs. Tate was looking after the dog for them. And that dog's hungry.' He took out a handkerchief and pulled the refrigerator door open. The dog whined.

'Oh,' said Higgins. 'I follow you.'

'I don't guess,' said Grace to the dog, 'it'd be safe to give you this hamburger, fellow.' He sniffed it cautiously. 'No knowing how long it's been here. Let's just see.' He opened the cupboard above the sink. 'Here's something.' He took down a package of dry kibbled dog food and spilled a generous amount on the floor. The dog began to eat greedily. 'Yes,' said Grace thoughtfully, 'that dog is hungry.'

Higgins wandered into the little bedroom. It was neat and reasonably clean. 'Why the hell would she just take off? And without her car?' He pulled open a drawer. It was full of feminine underwear. There was a portable plywood wardrobe in one corner; using his handkerchief, he slid back one door. The wardrobe was full of women's clothes, dresses, skirts, blouses, a wool coat, a raincoat.

Grace spilled more dog food on the kitchen floor. The dog looked up from eating to say, 'Woof,' in a gratified tone. 'Nice dog,' said Grace. He went into the bathroom again.

'You know, Sergeant—'

'What?' Higgins came in, crowding the little room. They stared at the bathtub.

It was one of the new, almost-square bathtubs, intended for cramped situations. It was pink, fitted neatly into a corner. And it was not—contrasting with the rest of the house—very clean. All over its bottom, and especially around the water outlet, was a thin, spotty, reddish-brown scum.

'I wonder—' said Grace. He turned and went out to the kitchen. The dog was eating steadily. Grace pulled open drawers. At the third one he paused.

In the drawer was a meat cleaver. Delicately Higgins reached in with a handkerchief and nudged it out onto the tile drainboard. They looked at it.

In the minute crevice where the blade fitted into the handle with the naked eye they could see darkish-red stains, dried. A couple of stains on the blade, too.

'Well, I will be damned,' said Higgins. 'This looks too good to be true.'

Grace said yes absently. The dog barked. Grace went out into the kitchen, and the dog had golloped down all the kibbled food, so he spilled some more on the floor.

'I think,' he said, 'maybe we'd better call the Lieutenant, hah?'

CHAPTER NINE

They went back downtown and got a search warrant. Everybody in the office came up to Hollywood with them—Mendoza, Palliser, Landers, Hackett. A mobile lab unit trailed them. They turned the lab men loose in the house and stood around waiting for them to finish. By that time it was nearly three o'clock, and as it was Saturday and most people were home, a good many of the neighbors came out to stare and speculate. The lab truck was, of course, prominently labeled for what it was.

The lab men took up all the plentiful sediment in the bathtub carefully. One man began scraping up stains from the cracks of the tile floor. A couple of the others went over the kitchen and finally cut out some sections of the linoleum there.

The men from Homicide stood around. The dog was delighted to have so much unexpected company. The lab men came and went from the truck; one of them stopped long enough to say to Mendoza, 'Well, it's blood. Human blood, all right. Haven't typed it yet, do that downtown.'

Another man had crawled under the house, after shutting off the water main, and was disconnecting the length of pipe which led to the bathtub. The contents would be thoroughly examined.

'I'll never hear the end of it,' said Mendoza. 'And who would have believed it?'

'This all doesn't say that the Tate woman is also the corpse in Echo Park Lake,' said Hackett.

'No. But even in L.A. we don't get cut-up corpses just so often, do we? And the chances of getting two at once are damned astronomical, Art. The way things are shaping up, though it's early to say, it looks as if something certainly happened to somebody in this house. The woman's missing. And by all that sediment and blood in the tub—well, it's the handiest place to use if you're dismembering a body.'

The tow car arrived, to tow the Ford in for examination. The Ford was registered to May Tate at this address. It had been dusted for prints, and they had, of course, looked in the trunk. They had been gratified to find several good-sized stains on the floor of the trunk. The lab would tell them what the stains were; they were all ready to go out on a limb and say blood. The keys were in the car; on the same ring was the key to the house.

'Used her own car to transport the body,' said Hackett. 'Or parts of same.' The dog was pressing against his knee. He looked around the back yard. 'God, whoever owns this place is going to have a fit. Don't you think we

123

ought to start asking some questions, Luis? God knows there seem to be enough people out there to talk to.'

What looked to be every resident of the block was standing around out there, in little groups, crowding up to the closed driveway gate, where Palliser had stationed himself to keep them out.

'Yes, we'd better.' Mendoza dropped his cigarette and stepped on it, and went over to the gate. Just outside it a stout middle-aged man was peering intently at all the activity; an equally stout woman pressed up beside him, with others behind them. 'Are you neighbors?' asked Mendoza, producing his badge. 'Do you know who lives in the front house?'

'Why the hell are you fellows nosing around? What's happened? What's all the excitement, anyway? Nobody could make out—Has something happened to Joe and Vera? ... Yes, yes, we live right next door, lived there ten years now, we—'

'Joe and Vera who, Mr.—?'

'Bailey, my name's Bailey. What's your name?'

'Lieutenant Mendoza, Mr. Bailey. This is Sergeant Hackett—Sergeant Higgins.' Mendoza opened the gate and they all came out; Hackett and Higgins pressed past into the little crowd, to find more neighbors.

'Jesus, you get big bastards,' said Bailey

resentfully.

'Language,' said the stout woman. 'What's happened to Joe and Vera, Officer? Were they in an accident?'

'Joe and Vera who? Do they own the front house?'

'Yes, sure. The Bessemers. Joe and Vera Bessemer. Why, for goodness' sake, those men are cutting up the kitchen linoleum—great big piece out of it. Look, I remember when Vera had it put in new, only two years ago. How come you can bull your way in and destroy property like—'

'Evidence, Mrs.—it is Mrs. Bailey? Do you know where the Bessemers are?'

'They'll be back tomorrow. Vera'll have a *fit*. They went up to Fresno, his mother just died and they went up for the funeral and, you know, settle up her affairs. They left a week ago Friday. But what's *happened*? Why—'

Conscious of other listening, avidly curious people, Mendoza said, 'It's Mrs. Tate, in the rear house, something seems to have happened to her. Do you know her? Anybody here?'

'Why, yes, acourse,' said the Baileys in unison; other voices joined in. 'What's happened to her?' asked Mrs. Bailey. 'Is she dead? Is she—'

'We don't know,' said Mendoza. 'But apparently she's missing, at least. When did

125

you see her last, Mrs. Bailey, do you remember?'

'May Tate? Now just fancy! Well, let me see—it'd have been last week sometime. You see, she works, and she gets up kinda early, she's got a little ways to drive to work, I guess. I usually hear her car go out about quarter past seven, just about as we're getting up. And our kitchen's over the other side o' the house, so—'

'Did you hear her car go out any time this week?'

'Why, no, come to think of it,' she said slowly. 'No, I didn't. I didn't think much about it, sometimes I hear it and sometimes I don't. Let me see—I didn't know her awful well, you know, nobody did but maybe Vera and Joe—she's rented the place, oh, how long, Jack?'

''Bout two years. She's a working woman, Officer, like the wife says, she's gone early and about the time she's getting home from work everybody's sittin' down to dinner. I don't guess anybody around here knows very much about her. A widow, I understand. She—'

'Is she dead in there? Did she have a heart attack? How'd you find out?' asked another woman in the crowd.

'No, nobody's in there now. What about weekends and during her vacations?'

'She didn't stay home much.' The girl who

edged forward was a pretty blonde in blue shorts and a white blouse. She had very good legs, which the men all eyed in academic appreciation. 'I'm Cynthia Rogers—we live next door, the other side I mean—in the back. We rent from the Vosses, they're in the front house. I'm out in the yard a lot, nice weather, I kind of like to mess around the garden and take sun baths, and so on. I knew Mrs. Tate to see, sure, but she wasn't home much at all. Well, a woman alone like that, it's a drag, you know? I didn't blame her. I didn't like her much but I had to hand it to her, she kept up, like they say, an interest in life. You know what I mean. She was one of these amateur artists, she had this easel thing that folded up and a big box of paints and all, she'd go out on the weekends, I guess finding things to paint. Landscapes and like that.'

'That's right,' said Mrs. Bailey. 'I've seen her with that. She'd be polite enough when you spoke, but like Cynthia says, she just sort of used this place to eat and sleep, kind of. What I gathered. So nobody really knows much about her, around here. Unless Vera and Joe—and Vera never said anything but that she's a widow, and has this job—some store, I forget—'

'Did she have visitors coming here to see her very often?'

'I think so, sometimes,' said Mrs. Bailey. 'Car out in front, like that, but acourse we

127

wouldn't know were the people coming to her place or the Bessemers'. Well, for heaven's sake, you gonna take the *furniture*, too?' A couple of the lab men came toward the gate carrying the coffee table from the living room.

'Just get back, please, let them by.' Mendoza wondered why the coffee table: stains on it? 'You can't tell me about any specific person who came to see Mrs. Tate? I realize that at this time of year it's dark early, you wouldn't see visitors arriving in the evening, but you said she's lived here for two years. Last summer, for instance—'

'Yeah, there was some women came,' said Bailey. 'I'd see them when I was working around the yard after supper. A couple different women. I'd see 'em come up the drive, ring the bell. I never paid much notice, all I could say was they looked about her age. One of 'em always had on a fancy hat—dressed pretty fancy.'

'Can you remember when you saw her last, Mrs. Bailey?'

'I've been thinking. Vera's going to be awful mad, about what all those men are doing. For the Lord's sake, they tearing out the pipes, too? I just don't—Yes, yes, I do remember. It was when Vera came over on Friday morning, that's a week ago yesterday, to give me the key to the house. While they were away. In case of a fire or something, see.

128

It was real early because they wanted to miss the early-morning traffic. Matter of fact, she got me up. She apologized, said she'd meant to come over the evening before but what with packing in a hurry and like that she'd forgot. Anyway, as she handed me the key that Tate woman was just backing out the drive. She waved at us. It was about seven o'clock. And I can't recall seeing her since. I didn't much anyway—didn't think about it.'

'Thanks very much,' said Mendoza. The Baileys seemed to be incurious neighbors. The young housewife, Mrs. Rogers, would have her own concerns, and be uninterested in a much older woman, but—He turned to her. 'When did you see her last?'

'Gee, I don't know. I didn't pay much attention to her, you know, her being older and all. Besides I work too. At a bank. Sometimes we'd be getting home about the same time. But even though we both lived in the rear houses, you see, ours is on the other side of that lot and she wasn't out in the yard much.'

The dog was having a lovely time in all this crowd; he wandered about happily, licking faces and hands. The lab men kept coming and going. 'You hadn't ought to let Nicky out like that,' said Bailey disapprovingly. 'He's a valuable animal, pedigreed dog. Some fancy breed. Joe never lets him out except on a leash. Here, Nicky, Nicky!' He stared at

129

Mendoza; he seemed to be more disenchanted with the cops by the minute. 'Jesus, talk about high-handed! You walk in here and bust up Joe's property and walk off with the furniture and—You got a warrant? What's it all about?'

'We've got a warrant,' said Mendoza. Hackett and Higgins came back with a small nervous-looking man who said he knew Mrs. Tate very slightly. They had both shopped at the same market over on Vermont—'I'm a widower, Parker's my name, I rent a room from Mrs. Broadman down at the end of the block—and sometimes Mrs. Tate and I got talking. In the market. She wanted me to join this artists' club she belongs to—they're all amateurs, you know—said it was such a jolly little group—but I'm not much of a joiner, I guess. I like to read. I go to the library twice a week.' He looked nervously at Mendoza, at the two hulking detectives flanking him. 'What's happened to Mrs. Tate?'

'We don't know. When—'

'He says he saw her Saturday morning, a week ago today, Luis,' said Hackett.

'Yes, that's right, I did,' said Parker. 'At the market. No, that's a lie, I'm sorry, it was at the bakery. There's a very good bakery right next to the market, it's a Danish bakery, I'm quite partial to pastry and I do miss my wife's, she was a very good cook, but really this bakery is—'

'You met Mrs. Tate there? What time?'

'Oh, it was about eleven-thirty. I would estimate. She was buying some fancy little cakes. Those petit-fours things, you know? ... Yes, we spoke. I—she was rather an—an overwhelming woman. Rather a loud laugh, and—and a loud voice. She was ahead of me, she was just opening her purse—And she said she had to get something special because she was expecting a friend for lunch. That was all. She left before I did.'

A friend for lunch. Well, well. Mendoza glanced over the crowd pressing close, eager and interested. 'How many of you were home at, say, between eleven-thirty and one? Anybody see a car drive up here?'

'I was at the market,' said Mrs. Bailey. 'I had to walk because of Jack leaving that fool old movie on TV. I left about then—eleven—and after I'd shopped I met Mrs. Horst and we went to the drugstore and had a sandwich together. I guess it was on to one before I got home. I don't recall a car in front of the Bessemers', but there coulda been. Lotsa cars parked up and down the street, on and off, all day.'

'Mrs. Rogers?'

'Oh, well we went to the beach on Saturday. Don and I. We left about nine, and it was after dark when we got home.'

'What about your landlord—did you say Voss?'

131

A big beefy bull-shouldered man in a violently patterned sports shirt, who'd been silently listening, said in a hoarse voice, 'I'm Voss. We weren't home either. Went to the wife's sister's for lunch, and it's in Compton; we were gone by ten o'clock.'

Mendoza looked around the crowd. Nobody else spoke up.

'Does anyone remember seeing a car in front of the Bessemers' house on Saturday? At any time?' Even in such an incurious neighborhood, he thought, X would have had to wait for darkness before removing the body. If, of course, there had been a body by then.

Shrugs answered him. He looked at Hackett. Higgins was already taking out his notebook. Routine, it always went back to routine. Get the names and addresses of everybody on the block, go back and back for individual questioning, eventually some little useful thing might come out.

He thought about Mrs. Tate's luncheon guest. They would, of course, now want to find out everything about Mrs. May Tate they possibly could, they'd be asking questions at the store where she'd worked, they'd be questioning all the art lovers—by what Alison said, she hadn't been too well loved there—and they'd be questioning everybody listed in her address book, if she'd had one—But as far as they'd gone now, Mendoza just wondered if maybe Mrs. Tate's mode of life had robbed her of a little common sense and led her into danger. As such women had been led into danger countless times before—see some of the classic cases.

A widow. Not young, not good-looking. Working, and not at a very high salary—department stores didn't pay salesclerks very high salaries. All she was qualified for? Evidently her husband hadn't left her much, if anything. He just wondered whether Mrs. Tate hadn't been eager and anxious to acquire another husband, and had maybe, somehow, on the prowl for a man, got involved with some nut. A woman of her age and looks couldn't be too particular, in fact any man who showed interest in her, probably, would be encouraged—

A nut. Because you really didn't get the dismemberment business very often. But on the other hand, when it was done it was usually done in the hope of preventing identification. Well, that worked out all right—X would be afraid he could be connected with her in some way.

'What *is* it all about, anyway?' asked Bailey.

'O.K., Lieutenant, it's all yours,' said one of the lab men, trudging past. 'We'll send up reports on everything.'

The mobile unit took off.

Mendoza and the other detectives went up

to the house. The dog came along, wagging his tail.

Detective Grace looked at the dog and said, 'Nicky boy, I surely do wish you could talk English. Probably tell us all about it.'

'Woof,' said Nicky amiably.

★　　★　　★

'You don't mean to tell me it *was*,' said Alison. She looked awed. 'I didn't really believe it myself. In a place this size. Out of eight million—You think she *was* the woman in Echo Park?'

'Well, let's just wait for all the lab reports,' said Mendoza, shrugging off his jacket. 'But there seems to have been a good deal of blood spilled in that house—and the butchers do usually use the bathtub—and there's the blood in the car. For pretty damn sure. Something funny happened there, anyway. We checked with Robinson's again—got some names and addresses to check tomorrow, other employees—so far as we know now, this Parker is the one who saw her last, at the bakery that Saturday morning. She was expecting a luncheon guest. My money's on him for X. I think she was cut up that night and put in the park Sunday night, and your guess is as good as mine as to whether the rest of the body's still in the lake or somewhere else.'

'For heaven's *sake*,' said Alison. 'Why? She was a—one of those bossy women, a woman who'd bore you to death or—exasperate you, but—just a very ordinary sort of woman, Luis. Why should anybody—'

'I'll tell you one place I'm going to check,' said Mendoza. He looked down at her, at her clear hazel-green eyes raised to his, her blazing copper hair, a little untidy because she'd just been playing with the twins; he smiled. '*Allá va*, reminds me I haven't kissed you yet,' and he remedied the omission rather thoroughly.

'*¡Vaya con el mozo!* Mmh—yes—you were saying?'

'The lonely hearts clubs,' said Mendoza. 'I think Mrs. Tate could have been on the make.'

'*Mrs. Tate?*'

'*Amante*, a lonely poor widow, not very young, not very good-looking, isn't necessarily interested in that old devil sex when she's on the make. What she's interested in is a modest bank balance. Yes, have to see her bank, too, I suppose. And those clubs have to be licensed, sure, they screen their members, but—'

'Oh,' said Alison. 'I see what you mean. You know something else, Luis? There's this dancing-lesson racket. There was something in the paper just the other day—The laws on the books don't seem to cover it. Even the

135

famous-name ones, because they haven't anything to do with how individual managers operate. And the unscrupulous ones make a play for people like that—The lonely widows—and she might have met somebody at such a place—It must have been a lunatic of some sort.'

'Fifty-fifty,' said Mendoza. 'Could be. Or it could be a very sane and logical motive. We've got a lot of places to look. And, damnation, I'd like to get the rest of the body—as it is, we haven't got a real identification. Well, I know—pending the lab tests, it probably *is* her—but then again—'

'I don't believe it yet,' said Alison. 'It was just a long off chance, really. And such an *ordinary* woman—'

'Most of the people,' said Mendoza, 'who get mixed up in homicide are ordinary. Just people. Which is what differentiates homicide in real life from the paperbacks.'

★　　★　　★

The lab reports began to come in about noon on Sunday; there was priority on this one. They couldn't start to do much about it until they had seen the lab reports.

The sediment in Mrs. May Tate's bathtub was all human blood and a little human tissue. There was a good deal more human tissue, bits of flesh, and a few pieces of

136

human bone in the waste pipe of the tub and the trap below. There was human blood on the meat cleaver from Mrs. Tate's kitchen and on four knives from the same drawer. There was human blood in the trunk of Mrs. Tate's Ford.

The blood was all Type O.

It was a somewhat academic point since they hadn't yet found the missing arms (presumably with hands intact) of the corpse, but they had queried the FBI about Mrs. May Tate. She had never been fingerprinted, at least not under that name.

Robinson's had turned over what they had on Mrs. May Tate. She had applied for a job in the store in April of 1956. She had stated on the application form that she was aged forty, a widow, with no former experience of working, that she was Protestant, that she had graduated from high school (no mention of where), that she was resident of an address on DeLongpre Avenue.

On Sunday afternoon, after they'd seen the first lab reports, they began to work the routine as best they could. Mendoza had a couple of the art lovers' names from Alison; those would give them the rest. They didn't find any of the art lovers home. Out practicing art, maybe.

In a forlorn hope, they had the experts drag Echo Park Lake again.

They didn't get anything out of the lake

but a lot more of the lake-bottom weeds.

Mendoza went out to the DeLongpre Avenue address where Mrs. Tate had formerly lived. It was a dreary-looking old court of ten units. The present manager had been there only a year and had never laid eyes on Mrs. Tate. None of the tenants had either, or said they hadn't. None of them had been living there more than two years.

Another lab report came in about four o'clock. The solid marble-topped coffee table from Mrs. Tate's little house had borne bloodstains on (A) one corner of the top and (B) the short leg below that corner. The stains were Type O.

Which was, of course, the commonest type.

★   ★   ★

At 1:45 A.M. on Sunday night, or technically on Monday morning the eighteenth of January, somebody invaded the three-room apartment of Mr. Paul Coleman on Lakeshore Terrace. Which was within that chosen area where somebody was choosing elderly victims. Mr. Coleman woke up, got out of bed, and grappled with the intruder.

Mr. Coleman was seventy-nine years old, and besides being a diabetic, had a heart condition. Presumably in the course of the struggle he suffered a heart attack. At any rate, he was dead on the floor of his

138

apartment when the landlord investigated the disturbance.

Mendoza heard about that when he got to the office at eight-ten on Monday morning. He said to Hackett imperatively, 'Go and bring in Henry Kinger, *pronto!*'

CHAPTER TEN

Hackett found Henry Kinger virtuously at school. The vice-principal was astonished and indignant to hear that the cops wanted Henry for questioning; the boy had a perfectly good record with him, and he most certainly had not known that Henry was still on probation. That news changed his outlook slightly; he sent for Henry and handed him over to Hackett, and Hackett drove him downtown.

He and Palliser joined Mendoza in questioning Henry. The simple weight of numbers sometimes paid off in questioning; and having questions fired at him from different directions could often muddle a suspect sufficiently to come out inadvertently with the truth.

'Were you out last night, Henry?' asked Mendoza.

The boy looked bewildered and frightened. 'No, I wasn't. What's this all about? That big guy wouldn't tell me. What am I supposed to have done? I didn't do anything!'

'Was your mother out last evening?' Palliser.

'No, she wasn't.'

'Anybody come to see you?' Hackett.

'No. What—'

'What time did you both go to bed?' Mendoza.

'I don't know, ten, ten-thirty. Mom went a little later, maybe eleven. Listen, what—'

'Do you have a key to the apartment, Henry?' Hackett.

Henry looked from Mendoza to Hackett. 'Yes, I got a key. I got to get in after school, don't I? What am I supposed—'

'Ever sneak out at night after your mother's asleep? Just for fun?' Mendoza.

'No, I never. Why should I? Listen, I got in that trouble before, it was really Dave's idea but I was a fool kid then and I went along. We never meant to hurt anybody. I was just scared when I hit that man. So I learn my lesson about it, I'll never do anything like that again. Honest. I *haven't* done anything. Why you think I have?'

'Because you used to live on Welcome Street, Henry,' said Hackett, 'and somebody has been busy down there burglarizing a lot of old men and women, right around your old stamping ground.'

'Well, it isn't me,' said Henry. 'I wouldn't do a thing like that. A lot of other people still
140

live down there.'

'You did once. Let's see what you've got on you.'

A little sullenly the boy emptied his pockets on Hackett's desk. It was the usual collection of miscellany an eighteen-year-old might carry: a couple of ball point pens, a cheap wallet with a little under three dollars in it, a book of school bus-passes, nothing unusual or incriminating. He had brought his school notebook with him; they looked through that, and it was all ordinary papers, not even any mildly pornographic drawings.

'He's too good to be true,' said Hackett to Mendoza.

'*Puede ser*. And he's got a point that he doesn't live down there any longer and a lot of other people do. I don't know, Art. Another thing is, among the very few details on our description is the long hair. Several witnesses mentioned it. Well, it occurs to me belatedly that when it was dark, and so forth, the man's hair must be very noticeably long for anybody to have noticed it. Henry's isn't.'

'All right. We haven't got any statements from last night's witnesses to long hair, and Henry could have had his cut in the meantime.'

'I don't think I like that. Anybody we asked who knew him could say, "Why, yes, his hair used to be—" And what high school kid would, Art? You know how conventional

141

most kids are. No, I know Henry looked pretty hot as a suspect, but I'm thinking now, from what we've seen of him, that he's quite a bit immature for his age. Hell, look at that notebook—not one drawing of a girl, anything like that. Quite possibly one of those fifteen-year-olds was the ringleader in that little caper two years ago—Henry just following along. He isn't acting like eighteen now. Mother kept him a bit of a baby? Anyway, we haven't a damn thing to hold him on.'

'Go on questioning him, might break him down.'

'Sure,' said Mendoza. 'Ask him all the questions twenty times over again, try to get him confused. I want to get this one, and it *could* be Henry, he looked like the best bet until ten minutes ago. Now I don't think so. So you carry on with the questioning, and I'll try to come up with an idea where else to look.'

Because the Tate thing was important, all right—it was still making minor headlines and would get back on the front page again when they told the press they'd made a tentative identification—but this other business was maybe more important. The Tate thing was the offbeat thing, the kind you didn't get very often, while the burglar and incidental killer was the perennial crime, the chronic crime, the run-of-the-mill business that cropped up monotonously, in only slightly different forms, this year, next year, forever.

Whoever had killed Mrs. Tate had most probably never killed anybody else—unless it was a lunatic, and even then it was possible that was his first kill. But whoever was pulling the break-ins had all the earmarks of a psychopathic criminal, and that kind they wanted to find out about right away.

Piggott and Glasser were out questioning the landlord and other tenants of the place where Coleman had died last night. Higgins and Landers and Grace were out contacting the art lovers and the people whose names had been in Mrs. Tate's small address book, and the people at Robinson's with whom she had worked. When they finished with Henry, whatever the result, Hackett and Palliser would go out to join them at that.

Now Mendoza left the office and drove out Wilshire to the store. He wanted to talk to Mrs. Tate's recent superior himself.

*　　*　　*

'Well, I wouldn't say she was a likable woman,' said Mrs. Grace Maynard doubtfully. She was a tall, buxom woman with a smoothly coiffed head of pure white hair, a magnificent complexion, and mild brown eyes. 'She was efficient, though. She

143

caught right onto things when she was transferred up here six months ago. She had been over in Better Dresses up to then. I could see right away—well, I've been working here nearly twenty years—Mrs. Tate was the kind you had to sit on once in a while, if you know what I mean.' She raised her brows. 'But I just can't believe that—you think she's been *murdered*? I can't get over it! Do you know who did it?'

'Not yet.' She'd get the more sensational news that Mrs. Tate was very probably the cut-up corpse in Echo Park, in tonight's headlines. 'I know it's not a thing one expects to happen, but it does. Did you—mmh—have to sit on her?'

'She was that kind. I shouldn't be talking about the poor thing now she's dead, I suppose. I did feel sorry for her, because she never would be very much liked, but there it is. And then, too,' added Mrs. Maynard, 'that kind of person never really knows people don't like them.'

'Thick-skinned, as they say. Did—'

'There is one thing I think you ought to hear about, Lieutenant.' They were talking here in the privacy of the small stock room behind the dressing rooms, standing. 'In fact, I've been wondering about it ever since, and while I don't see what possible bearing it could have on her—her death—you know I still can't take that in, murder!—well, it

144

seemed funny. Funny in both senses,' said Mrs. Maynard. 'This was last Wednesday—a week ago Wednesday, that is, the Wednesday before she—didn't come in. There was a little lull in customers along about ten-thirty, there usually is on weekdays, and both Madeleine and Lois, our two younger clerks, had gone out on a coffee break. I could see that Mrs. Tate was just dying to tell me something, and she could hardly wait to get it out. She was'—Mrs. Maynard paused—'heavy-handed in conversation, if that's clear—she led up to it by saying that she was surprised Madeleine had captured a man, homely as she is. Madeleine's just got engaged, you see—she may not be a beauty but she's a nice reliable pleasant girl, and I said so. Not trying to start an argument, just saying so.'

Mendoza nodded. 'And?'

'And—now let me get it straight, what she actually said. She put her head on one side, trying to look—oh, coy, arch, like that—and said, sort of demurely, "Well, if it comes to that, *I* may be having an interesting announcement to make soon." Which I took to mean that she was planning to remarry, and I did just wonder what man—Well, not to speak ill of the poor woman, but she wouldn't be everybody's choice.'

¡*Helo por aquí*! said Mendoza to himself. Jackpot. Maybe. He had wondered if she was man-hunting. All this gave her more reason to

145

be looking for somebody, somebody with a good job and/or savings, so she could quit an uncongenial job. It would have been difficult if not impossible for Mrs. Tate, at her age, to quit this job and find another possibly more congenial; she'd been lucky to get this one at forty, nine years ago, when she'd never worked before. (Married straight from high school? Would it be worthwhile to dig up her past at all?) Now it seemed she had found somebody.

'Did she mention any name?' he asked urgently.

'No, that was all she said. I had to say something, and I just said, Oh, that was interesting, something like that. I knew if I encouraged her, she'd have talked and talked, and—'

'*¡Mil rayos!*' muttered Mendoza. 'If you only had! Because it might very well be—' He let that trail off. No, Mrs. Tate couldn't have afforded to be overparticular. And just where might she have met such a man? Lonely hearts? Dancing lessons? 'Do you know whether she belonged to any clubs? A church?'

'I don't think she went to church, no. I really don't know, because I never let her get talking much about herself. She was the kind who'd just run on and on, you know, always thinking you're as interested in themselves as they are. And then of course we really hadn't

146

much time for personal—'

Mendoza had a presentiment that he would come across a number of people who had politely choked off May Tate from garrulous personal accounts. Damn.

And where the hell was the rest of the body? In the lake? By what the old boatkeeper said about that, persistence could pay off. On the other hand, why bother to cut up the body into six pieces if you meant to put them all in one place?

When you came to think about it, he thought suddenly, just why was the body dismembered at all? It was a difficult and messy job.

Pure blood lust? The lunatic? Sheer hatred, even when the woman was dead? Or why?

★　　★　　★

At about the same time Alison was putting on a new jade-green silk shirtmaker and arguing with Mrs. MacTaggart. The twins, who were seventeen months old and as active as most that age, had just discovered that they could make a race-track circle of the house, from entrance hall through living room, out to the kitchen, down the long hall, swooping into all the rooms there alternately, and thence back to the entrance hall; and consequently Alison and Mrs. MacTaggart were talking at the tops of their voices, as the twins were using theirs lustily.

'. . . A perfectly reasonable sort of thing to do,' said Alison, buttoning the dress.

'The Lieutenant won't like it at all, you getting mixed into a murder case.'

'The Lieutenant will like it,' said Alison, putting on the emerald earrings, 'if I get him some information he doesn't have. And a few of those art lovers like Miss Ames would probably turn dumb to a real detective and say as little as they could get away with. I—Johnny! Terry! *¡Bastante!* Quiet down! *¡Vaya despacio!*'

'You'll have those two not knowing at all what language they are talking,' said Mrs. MacTaggart, shaking her neat gray head.

Alison laughed. 'Including the Gaelic you use on them, Máiri! But I picked up Spanish before English—Dad working in Mexico, you know, and having to keep me with him—and I don't seem to have been harmed by it. Besides, the advantage—'

'The Lieutenant,' said Mrs. MacTaggart, reverting to the first argument, 'is not going to like it. You interfering in a case.'

'All I'm going to do is invite the woman to lunch,' said Alison, fastening on her watch. 'After all, in a sort of way, it's my case too. If I hadn't had that hunch—And I might get something the men wouldn't, you know. And anyway, any time I let the Lieutenant tell me what to do—'

148

'Ah, that'll be the McCann in you,' said Mrs. MacTaggart gloomily. 'As well, I can't deny, as the Weir. Isn't it truthfully said, "Biting and scarting is Scots folks' wooing." And the Irish worse. I've said my last word on it. The poor man'—Mrs. MacTaggart had formed a romantic attachment to her gallant Spanish man since she first joined the household—'being worried to death with all these murderers running around, and why he had to burden himself with the daughter of a Glasga' Irishwoman in the first place, and red-haired with it—thinking up new ways to bother him—'

'Yes, Máiri,' said Alison, stepping into her shoes. 'Let him swear. It'll be done when he hears about it.'

'I'll be out to pick up a fresh bottle of rye for the man.'

There was no doubt that Alison had got infected by detective fever. This was, in a kind of way, her very own murder; why shouldn't she take an active interest in it?

She backed out the Facel-Vega Mendoza had given her as a wedding present, careful for cats, and drove down the hill to Hollywood, to Sunset Boulevard, where Miss Leona Ames was secretary to an architect named Coulter. It was a quarter to twelve when she parked the car and went into the building.

Miss Ames was, she realized, seeing her in

149

her workday setting, probably the perfect secretary: the mousy little woman in the background, neat and unnoticeable, who was the only one who understood the filing system, and lived for the office. Probably had been in love with the boss, mutely, all her working life. One of those.

Miss Ames was fluttered and flattered to be invited out to lunch. That Alison should remember her, single her out—'Such a smart dress, Miss Weir—Oh, do pardon me, you did say it's Mrs. Mendoza. Well, really—let me see, I suppose I *could*—'

When Alison had her settled in a booth at Frascati's on the Strip, and supplied with a drink—'Oh, but I *never*—I really don't think—well, if it's only *wine*, did you say sherry?'—she confessed that she was awfully curious about Mrs. Tate, and would Miss Ames tell her anything at all she could about the woman? There was a spate of exclaiming over Mrs. Tate's mysterious disappearance (the murder hadn't come out as yet, officially) before anything definite emerged. Just as well, reflected Alison, that the murder wasn't out, because (although the unaccustomed sherry had loosened Miss Ames's tongue a little) had she known the woman was dead, she probably wouldn't have said all she did say.

And what she did say didn't really add up to much. Apparently the Amateur Artists
150

hadn't been a real club until Mrs. Tate got into it. Just a little social group, people who knew each other from church or residential proximity, all about the same age group, people with hobbies—not all amateur painters. But then Mrs. Tate had got into it, and organized it. Said they should hold regular meetings, and have dues so they could serve refreshments. She'd got the use of the Arts and Lecture Room, every second Wednesday night, at the public library on Santa Monica Boulevard, for their meetings. 'And really, it was quite difficult for some of us to *get* to meetings, we don't all drive—and she put up notices about the club, inviting the public to join, and a couple of very *peculiar* new people did—like that young man named Foster—she *means* so well, but—perhaps just a tiny bit tactless, and wanting all the *say*, you know. Of course I didn't *say* all this to the detective who came to the office this morning.'

'Oh,' said Alison. *So there*, she thought.

'Yes. A *black* man, he was. Well, there was a white officer with him, quite a handsome young man, very tall and dark.'

Jason Grace and John Palliser, thought Alison. 'Yes. Did you ever hear Mrs. Tate speak of a—a man friend she had? Not in the club, I mean someone who took her to dinner or—'

Miss Ames looked astonished. 'Oh, no, of

151

course not. Why, she was older than me,' she said, the sherry working on her grammar.

Well, though, Alison. To Miss Ames, that certainly clinched it. As far as Miss Ames was concerned, in her never-to-be-doubted virginity, that old devil sex just didn't figure on the horizon of anybody, say, over thirty-five. Which was a somewhat unrealistic attitude, if you knew a bit more about human nature. And Luis Mendoza, who was certainly over thirty-five but—mmh, well, reflected Alison, could hardly be complained about on *that* score—might take the cynical outlook that Mrs. Tate had been more concerned about a bank balance in hunting a second husband; but Alison wasn't convinced. After all, the woman had had a husband, and when you were accustomed to having a man around—

What she was vaguely thinking about was some handsome, professionally charming con-man who might—But they really didn't often turn violent. Some good-looking young man, say an instructor at one of those dancing schools, who might have got hold of Mrs. Tate and conned her out of some money and then—

'Do you know if she belonged to any other organizations?' she asked. 'I was thinking, she must have been a lonely person. Sometimes people like that fall for these lonely hearts social clubs, or the course of

152

dancing lessons—you've probably heard—'

'Oh, I'm quite sure she didn't,' said Miss Ames earnestly. 'No, because I remember her saying something about that—at our last regular meeting I think it was, yes—' She paused with a forkful of the herb omelette they do so well at Frascati's uplifted. 'There'd been something in the papers about those dancing courses, and she said any woman who was fool enough to fall for such a racket deserved all she got. She was really quite outspoken about it. She said any woman over forty who let herself be—er—"conned," I think was the word she used—by a stranger, just because he was smooth-talking and flattered her, she should—well, she said, have her head examined.'

'Oh, really,' said Alison. A hardheaded, common-sensible woman, Mrs. May Tate. 'Then she probably wouldn't have been taken in by a man like that.'

'Indeed no. She was quite—well, *frank* about it.' Miss Ames turned a little pink. 'She said she wanted to get married again, she didn't like living alone, but she'd never marry a man she'd only just met, she'd want some man she *knew* about.'

¡Cómo! thought Alison. But, ¿pues y qué? That was what she had said. It might be a different story, with the hardest-headed female, if a personable strange male showed up and turned on the charm.

153

But why should anybody make up to Mrs. Tate? She hadn't had any money.

Well, all that might say something...

CHAPTER ELEVEN

Grace and Palliser stood on the front porch of a neat, newly painted frame house on Juanita Avenue in Hollywood. Palliser had just rung the bell.

'That Ambler thing still annoys me,' said Grace. 'He told everybody he'd never put up a fight against a holdup man. Most pro heist men don't shoot people—the whole object of the exercise is money, not murder. It could have been a first job—maybe a juvenile—but I still don't like it.'

'It's dead, anyway,' said Palliser, thinking about Roberta and his mother.

'Constitutionally I don't like to file cases away open,' said Grace.

'Who does?' Palliser pressed the bell again and the door opened suddenly.

'Yais?' The woman was scraggly and scrawny, in her sixties; she held a broom in one hand, and her head was bound up gypsylike in a red scarf.

'Does a Mr. George Barrington live here?' It was a name out of Mrs. Tate's address book.

154

'Yais?'

'We'd like to speak to him, please,' said Palliser.

'He's not here.'

'Are you Mrs. Barrington, ma'am?' asked Grace.

She drew herself up. 'I am not,' she said. 'I come in to clean. He's not married. Now. Had three wives, I believe, but he's not married now. Not all at once, I don't mean, he's not a Mormon.'

'Well, would you know where we might—'

'He's gone off,' said the woman. 'Over to Las Vegas, most likely. You know what he does?'

'No, ma'am, we—'

'He's a steelworker. That man's seventy-two years old, he still climbs up and walks along them girders and all, never turn a hair. Up twelve stories, never turn a hair. Doctor says he's more like a man forty-five. He fell off a scaffold three stories high last year when a rope broke, day in hospital and he's good as new. Imagine. He earns good wages. Union. Went on Social Security and got bored, so he went off and went back to work. Seventy-two. You wouldn't think it.'

'Would you know where—' began Palliser.

'Las Vegas, likeliest. He's got a lot of money, he's a gambler by nature. A lucky gambler. My first husband, he was a gambler too, but not a lucky one. Most aren't. Mr.

155

Barrington is. Shrewd. Lord knows how much money that man's got, and he only went to school about four years. He gets off a job, he takes off over to Nevada—play the tables, or maybe prospectin', anywhere in the desert.'

'Well,' said Palliser. 'Do you know when he'll be back?'

'Nope. In his own good time. When he gets bored.'

'Well, thanks,' said Palliser.

'Welcome.' She shut the door.

'Who's next?'

Grace riffled through the address book; they had the original; they'd copied down names for the other men to check. 'Woman named Brown—Janet Brown. Over on Fountain Avenue. It's getting on for one, you feel like stopping for lunch first?'

'O.K.,' said Palliser. They were walking back toward the car when Grace stopped.

'Hey,' he said.

'What?'

Grace held out the book. It was an ordinary small cheap address book, the kind meant to be carried in pocket or handbag, with the pages held in by a spiral metal fastener. It measured about two by four inches. There were three pages for each letter of the alphabet, Grace pointed out; but under V there were only two. The third page had been neatly removed, but not neatly enough; one minute fragment was left clinging to the metal spiral.

'Now that's a funny thing,' said Palliser. 'Was X's name listed there?'

'Just very possibly,' said Grace in a thoughtful tone. 'Just very possibly.'

*　　*　　*

The Bessemers hadn't been home at nine o'clock last night. At about noon Higgins went back there to see if they'd arrived, and found them both very indignant at the wanton destruction of their property by a stupid, inefficient, and probably corrupt police force.

'Everything will be put back as it was,' said Higgins. 'Mr. Bessemer, when a case comes up we like to get on it right away. We had a warrant, you know. We had to—'

'Are you going to pay for new linoleum?' demanded Mrs. Bessemer. They were people in their sixties, the man big and still well built, she a sparrowlike little thing. 'I must say—'

'Mrs. Bessemer, you've probably seen the papers by now. We think Mrs. Tate's body is the one found down in Echo Park. We like to get on a thing like that right away.'

'Yes, I saw that. I can't hardly believe it! How'd a nice quiet woman like that come to get murdered? And in *our* place! Do you

157

mean—you mean whoever it was *cut her up* there—right out back in *our* place?' She looked delightedly horrified.

'Well, that's how it looks right now,' said Higgins cautiously. 'You see, that's why we had to examine the linoleum and the pipes, and so forth.'

'Oh,' said Bessemer. 'My God, who'd do a thing like that to that poor woman?'

'Well, I'd like to ask you a few questions. What you knew about her, and so on. Did you know her before she rented the place from you?'

Bessemer settled back; he looked a little more friendly now. 'No, first time we laid eyes on her was when she come to rent the house. From an ad in the paper. We had an old lady renting it, but she got so she couldn't live alone and her son took her and put her in a rest home. So we put an ad in the paper, and Mrs. Tate was the first to answer it.'

'Did you ask references or anything like that?'

'Mister, I figure between us we can size up a person well enough. She told us where she worked, seemed like a decent woman. Matter of fact—'

The woman carried on for him. 'Matter of fact, she was all businesslike right off. She said she supposed we wanted to know about her, and told she was a widow and worked at Robinson's and said as she was out a good deal and hardly ever had visitors. And like that. I could see she'd be a nice quiet tenant, and so she was. Rent on the dot first of every month—'

'Do you mind telling me how much it was, Mrs. Bessemer?'

'Eighty-five,' said the man. He had a pipe lit by now. 'Eighty for the house and five for the garage.'

'Did she tell you much about herself?'

'Well, I can't say as I recall anything else,' said the woman. 'She was out a lot. And then I don't encourage tenants to get all so friendly. Not after some experiences we had. You do that, nice as they might seem at first, and first thing you know they're barging in any old time, and wanting to borrow cream or eggs or flour, or just to chat. I'm not so crazy about that, so when a tenant starts getting all chummy I act sort of cool, and they soon get the idea. I kind of think Mrs. Tate was the sort who'd talk the hind leg off a donkey, you give her any encouragement, so I certainly didn't. She did tell me once her husband'd lost all his money and didn't leave her a cent, reason she had to work.'

Higgins stayed on for half an hour and asked more questions, but that was the substance of what the Bessemers had to tell. He wondered what the other boys were getting from Tate's friends.

Now he had a quick lunch and went back

to the office, found Mendoza there, and told him about the Bessemers. 'I've still got to see this Tillinghurst woman—member of that Amateur Artists thing.'

Mendoza was inattentively swiveled around staring out the window. By the grace of God, the heat had gone away yesterday: a strong cool steady wind had swept it away and along with it the smog, and today, as was seldom the case, from this high window they had a panoramic view over the city, right up the folds and hollows and heights of the Hollywood foothills, behind which lay the San Fernando Valley. The sky was a clear blue with no clouds, and the sun was strong. 'Hey!' said Higgins. 'Wake up. You in a trance.'

'I heard you, I heard you.'

'So I thought—' Higgins paused; he had had his notebook open to give Mendoza what he had from the Bessemers, and as he went to flip it shut, a page slid over exposing a few words. 'Oh, by the way, there was something I wanted to ask you, Luis. When I saw that Gonzales woman the other day, you know the one where her husband committed suicide—maybe and maybe not, too—she said a couple of things in Spanish. I put them down as best I could, how they sounded. Here—What's it translate to, if you can make it out?'

Mendoza took the book from him. '*Caray*,'

he said, 'didn't they teach you to write a legible hand in school? Wait a minute, what's this, an *L*? "*Lah oh-kass-ee-own*—" You know, it's not at all a difficult language to learn, George, and in southern California it's an advantage to know it.'

'I'm no good at languages,' said Higgins. 'I'm the only person in the state of California ever graduated from high school without taking at least two years of a foreign language. That's compulsory, you know.'

'Yes, well,' said Mendoza, 'what your Mrs. Gonzales said was, *La ocasión hace el ladrón*, which is an old proverb, not confined to Spanish-speakers, meaning that the opportunity creates the thief. That is, exposed to temptation, the weak person may succumb. Seems a funny thing to say about a suicided husband.'

'She hadn't been talking about her husband,' said Higgins slowly. 'She'd been talking about—let me think—the first time she said it, she'd been talking about having got a job herself, before he did it, because he was unreliable.'

'Oh. Still seems peculiar.'

'What's the other phrase mean?'

'It's not a phrase, it's all one word.'

'My God. Well, what's it mean?'

'*Malintencionado*. Oh, evil-minded, having wicked thoughts.'

'I'll be damned,' said Higgins. 'She said

161

that directly about her husband.'

'Oh? It seems rather a strong word to use about the man—he seems to have been just a more or less harmless weakling, doesn't he? What you got. But then I suppose, too,' said Mendoza, 'she's a devout Catholic, and of course the Church's view of suicide—maybe she was thinking about that.' He smiled; Mendoza didn't think much of any church's attitude on anything.

'Maybe. It's dead now, I guess.' Higgins put his notebook away. 'What were you daydreaming over? Had one of those brilliant flashes of inspiration you're famous for?'

'It just could be I have, George,' said Mendoza. 'It just could be. The long hair on our break-in artist. Hair long enough to be noticeable in dim light. Of course, a couple of the witnesses felt it in a struggle. Long hair on a man—that long hair—is a little unusual.'

'Beatniks,' said Higgins.

'Yes—but not all of those. You know what just occurred to me? There was Mary Ann Sheldon, after all, a couple of years back.'

Higgins stared at him. Mary Ann Sheldon was a big mannish-looking woman with an aggressive disposition who had pulled a number of heist jobs, always at liquor stores, before Saul Goldberg caught up to her; at the moment she was stashed away in Tehachapi. Everybody had been surprised to discover her sex. She'd been described as male by all her

162

victims and several witnesses.

'For Christ's sake,' said Higgins, 'where out in left field did you pick that one? And at that, you could be right.'

'Mmh. Let's go back to Records and see if they've got any females like that in the files besides Mary Ann. At least we know she couldn't have done it.'

'Yeah. A butch?'

Mendoza shrugged. 'Look in the sex files, too.'

'Well, you want to come and see this Tillinghurst woman with me?'

All Mrs. Tillinghurst could tell them was a little interesting, but not of much help. She admitted frankly she hadn't liked Mrs. Tate much—they hadn't found anyone who had. 'Terribly aggressive, you know, and one of those nonstop talkers.' She knew about Mrs. Tate's husband; Mrs. Tate had been very bitter and resentful about that. The husband had been an accountant at a brokerage in Pasadena, one Edwin Tate. They'd been married twenty-one years, never had any children. 'She didn't mind that—she said she didn't really like children, never wanted any.' Mrs. Tillinghurst shook her head. 'She wasn't really a very nice woman.'

Higgins thought about Stevie Dwyer, who ought to go to college, and eight-year-old Laura, who had really liked the piano lessons and cried about stopping them. People who

163

didn't like children, he thought suddenly, were the people who were saying 'No' to life. And then he thought of Mary Dwyer, with her silver-gray eyes, and forced his mind back to Mrs. Tillinghurst.

Instead, for one brief shocking moment which still held pain, it showed him Bert Dwyer dead on the marble bank floor with five slugs in him, a pond of blood widening around him.

Tate had, Mrs. Tillinghurst said, put everything he had into a business his brother had started, and then the brother went bankrupt, so when Tate died of a heart attack not long after, he'd left her nothing. She'd had to go to work, and she'd been lucky, in Mrs. Tillinghurst's opinion, to get any work, inexperienced as she was and that age, but she'd grumbled about it.

Mrs. Tate had been, she added, an excellent cook. And yes, she'd admitted she wanted to get married again, but Mrs. Tillinghurst didn't know at all whether she had any male friends, except for a Mr. Barrington she'd mentioned and a Frederick Weller. She didn't know anything about either of them.

★   ★   ★

They would probably get the autopsy report on Paul Coleman sometime tomorrow. To

164

find out whether that was legally accidental death or murder by the break-in artist. Another murder.

Dr. Bainbridge was still patiently conducting all his tests on the cut-up body, to find out whether the body contained anything toxic. As he said, that could take weeks. Privately he had expressed the opinion that if they ever came across the head belonging to the body, they'd have the cause of death *pronto*. Considering the stains on the coffee table, she could have sustained a fatal concussion; or she could, of course, have been shot.

Where the hell were the arms and legs and head? Well, there was a lot of empty territory around here. If X had, say, driven out into the desert somewhere and buried the missing parts, they might never find them. Before the coyotes.

Why dismember the body? Why pick Echo Park?

A lot of whys.

Higgins was still pondering that suicide. *The opportunity creates the thief.* And, *evil-minded.* Why had Mrs. Gonzales said those things?

Detective Jason Grace, who was as tidy-minded as Mendoza, still wondered about the Ambler job. He had had one rather offbeat idea about it, which he intended sometime to check out—if he ever had a spare moment to do it. You got kept busy at Central H.Q., he'd found.

Hackett still hadn't caught up to the fellow Sidalia, Indiana, was after. Squad cars all over town were keeping an eye out for Leo Charles Herrick's plate number. Well, involuntary manslaughter—or whatever Indiana called it legally—wasn't too important: he'd probably, when he'd been picked up and sent back there under extradition, get six months, something like that. All the same, Hackett hoped he'd be spotted soon. The L.A.P.D. had a reputation, and he wouldn't like the small-town Chief of Police Sparrow to think it was undeserved.

Mendoza and Higgins left Mrs. Tillinghurst and sought the nearest drugstore, where they looked in the phone book. There was a Frederick Weller listed on Melrose Avenue in Hollywood.

'Go and see him now?' asked Higgins. He had ordered a Coke; he looked at the last half of it and added, 'I could use a drink. I ran into Palliser and Jase at lunch, at Federico's. Jase was awfully damned pleased, he'd just found a cocktail in that fool book of his called Grace's Delight. Said he'd make it his specialty. God. What a concoction.'

'What goes into it?'

'A good deal of whiskey—I forget proportions—and dry vermouth, and

166

framboise, whatever that is, and orange juice, and orange bitters, and cinnamon and nutmeg and juniper berries. God.'

Mendoza laughed. 'Two hours of the working day left. So-called. I think I'll do some prowling around our break-in boy's area tonight. See what it looks like. Meanwhile, let's go see Mr. Weller.'

'Thank God the heat wave's broken,' said Higgins.

CHAPTER TWELVE

Mr. Weller, when they found him behind the counter of his small grocery store, had to think to remember Mrs. May Tate, and finally said, 'Oh, that one.' He'd met her a while back, introduced by someone, he forgot who. Hadn't seen her recently. It did beat all, he said, how those biddies would chase the men. They'd be surprised if they knew the trouble he'd had since his wife died. He was sure no great shakes to look at, which he knew—Mr. Weller was a short spare man about fifty-five, with a bald head—but some of these middle-aged widows, *nothing* in pants was safe from them. Any man that looked like a good meal ticket and reliable, they chased the hell out of him. But Mr. Weller for one didn't intend to get caught, no, sir. Man was a fool to get married again after fifty, never knew what you might get.

'Wasted trip,' said Higgins, back at the car. Mendoza grunted and slid under the wheel of the Ferrari.

'He's genuine, all right.'

When they got back to the office, he called Alison and told her not to expect him for dinner. Alison said resignedly that as a cop's wife she'd discovered this happened every now and then.

'Are you still burning to help us out by questioning all the art lovers?'

'Well—' said Alison.

'Because we're shorthanded, but not that much,' said Mendoza.

He took himself out to dinner and even had a drink beforehand—thinking of Jase's Grace's Special with a small shudder. In the dusk, he made some inquiries of Traffic, drove down to Alvarado Street, parked the car in a lot, and flagged down the black-and-white squad car due to hit that corner about then. 'Like some company for the evening, boys?' He introduced himself. 'I'd like to get the feel of this area at night. Your tour takes it all in and then some.'

'Sure, Lieutenant,' said the driver. 'Oh, you mean that guy's been breaking in on the old people. That's a bastard, isn't it? We get this and that, but it's not a real rough tour like over on Main or east L.A. somewhere.

We picked up most of those calls first.'

'You can't place any likely one for it out of this area?'

The other uniformed man in the front seat turned to speak over his shoulder. 'It's not like walking a beat. Excuse me, sir, you know that. My dad was a cop on the New York force for thirty years. He says in the days he was beat-walking he knew every kid in the area, every shopkeeper, and who argued with his wife and all like that. So something happened, he could maybe point a finger right off.' He laughed. 'He says we're all lazy these days. But a ten-block beat in New York is the hell of a lot different from a tour like this.'

'I know,' said Mendoza.

'I ask you, how can we get any idea of individual people? We tour from way out on Beverly to almost the Civic Center. Sure, we keep an eye on the trouble spots, we know *them*, a couple bars, a few other places. But mostly we just cruise and hand out tickets. Or hunt prowlers.'

'I know,' said Mendoza again.

He rode with the men for three hours. It was a quiet night; they wrote a few tickets, answered three calls to check for prowlers, picked up a couple of drunks. The area Mendoza was interested in was not well lighted; old trees shaded the streets. But it seemed quiet tonight, hardly anyone on foot

169

down there.

Sometime tomorrow Records should have something for him on the possible females. Was that a brain storm or wasn't it?

He left the squad car at the same corner at eleven o'clock, redeemed the Ferrari, and drove home.

*　　*　　*

On Tuesday morning he went with Landers to the bank where Mrs. Tate had had an account. It was the Bank of America on the corner of Hollywood Boulevard and Vermont, not far from where she'd lived.

The assistant vice-president was cooperative. 'I knew you'd be in,' he said. 'I had the whole file set aside for you. It was a very simple little account—you can see the whole picture at once. No, I never had any dealings with the woman personally—but what a thing! We're all following it closely in the papers, one of *our* clients murdered and dismembered!' He laughed a jolly laugh.

The account had been, as he said, a very simple one. Mrs. Tate had been paid a hundred and forty-four dollars take home pay every two weeks, and had regularly deposited the checks, each time paying varied amounts out of them into a small savings account. That had never climbed over three hundred dollars. There was forty-nine-sixty in it now, and a hundred and two dollars in her checking account. Each time she had deposited a check, she took twenty dollars in cash. And once a month there was a check made out to Bessemer for eighty-five dollars.

Well, she had to live pretty close to the bone on three hundred a month.

On the Friday before she had vanished, she had come into the bank just before its six-o'clock closing time and withdrawn practically all of her savings account, two hundred and fifty dollars. That was the only unusual thing in the file. 'I wonder why,' said Mendoza. The current file went back to the first of the year and she'd never taken any money out of that account, but been building it up. Maybe for some special purpose.

'Let's find the teller,' said Landers.

The teller was identified, a tired-looking middle-aged man, named Purcell, who examined the withdrawal slip and said, 'Oh, yes, I remember. In fact, I especially asked Mr. Byrd to let me know when any officers came to ask questions—but I see he's stepped out. I knew you'd be interested.' He gazed at them with mild wonder as if they were Martians—men who dealt with corpses and criminals, so far apart from the quiet bank. 'My goodness, that woman killed like that. I remember her from years back. Ordinary sort of woman. I suppose it was some lunatic—' He shook his head. 'Well, I don't know if you

171

will be interested at all, but she told me what this money was for.'

'Oh, she did! That's a little unusual, isn't it? What did she say?'

'Well, when she handed over the withdrawal slip and her book, I said—in a joking way, you know, most of our regular clients pass a pleasant word or two—I said we didn't encourage savings withdrawals, she'd be missing a lot of interest. And I'm afraid she took offense—thought I was questioning her right to take out the money—anyway, she rather—er—snapped at me. She said *if* it was any of my business, anybody who lived in this horrible metropolis needed a decent car, and as she couldn't afford a new one she was getting the best secondhand one she could afford. That was all. I gave her the money and she went out.'

'It was cash? Not a certified check?'

'It was cash. I gave her four fifties, two twenties, and a ten.'

'Well, now, why cash? Why not a certified check? She didn't, of course, say who she was buying the car from?'

'Well, no.'

'*Naturalmente*,' said Mendoza resignedly. He thought. There was, however, the eager interest of these bank people: that was a factor. In an offbeat homicide like this, which was getting publicity, he thought that any used-car dealer (or new-car dealer with a

172

secondhand lot, which most had) who had had any dealing with Mrs. Tate would have come in and said so by now. In a thing like this usually the citizenry was eager to get in on the act. And Mrs. Tate had withdrawn cash to buy the car. Why? Maybe she hadn't known about certified checks, but she seemed to have been a pretty efficient businesswoman.

Was it possible that the seller, for some reason, had *asked* for cash? Why? And if so, that ruled out a public lot.

Everything had been left intact in the house, and the door was sealed; they knew they'd probably want to go over it again. Bessemer had grumbled, but he'd had January's rent. Mendoza said to Landers, 'You stay here and get them to show you the microfilms of the back files. I'll be back in an hour or so.'

He drove up to the Bessemer house, was greeted happily by the big white dog Nicky and peered at from a window by Mrs. Bessemer. He broke the seal on the door, went in, and looked around. There weren't any newspapers lying around, but in a bottom kitchen cupboard he found a two-week-old Sunday *Times*. She'd taken only a Sunday paper, to save money. And now he was wondering about the Ford she had had. She'd told Mrs. Tillinghurst when her husband died she'd have to give up the car. Possibly she hadn't had this one very long. He separated the enormous classified-ad section from the rest of the paper and began looking at it from the back page; automobiles were the last classification. Under Used Cars, he concentrated on the individual small ads, and was rewarded by finding three of them ringed decisively in pencil. The first read, '1955 2-dr. Ford white stick shift good cond. $500.' The second one read, '1955 Chevy 4-dr. gearshift $450 or best offer or part swap.' The third one read, '1956 Pont. 4-dr. blue clean autom. $550 or will trade.' All three had phone numbers appended.

But she hadn't actually bought her car, after withdrawing the cash. Maybe the seller worked, and the deal had been set up for that Sunday? That could be. Mendoza used the phone to call Sergeant Lake, read the ads and phone numbers to him, asked him to check. Then he drove back to the bank and met Landers.

There wasn't anything at all unusual in Mrs. Tate's bank records back to when she'd first become a client nine years ago. One thing showed up: she had bought the Ford only eighteen months ago, paying two hundred and ninety-five dollars for it to a dealer; and that had been a certified check.

★　　★　　★

'Small steak as usual, Adam,' he said to the waiter at Federico's.

Hackett said he'd have a Scotch and water and the grilled T-bone. Yes, of course French-fried potatoes. He leaned back in his chair, said, 'Ahhhh,' and lit a cigarette.

Mendoza wondered academically just how often he and Art had sat at a table here talking a case out over lunch. Sometimes like this, or with one of the other men in the office—often, with Bert. When Adam came back with Hackett's drink he said, 'I'll have one too, Adam. Break a precedent.'

'Yes, sir. Rye straight.'

'I wish they'd spot that Herrick,' said Hackett. 'I know it's a big town, but—'

'I wish we had anywhere to go on Tate,' said Mendoza. 'Let's take a good hard look at it, what do you think?'

'The way it shapes up, I don't think it was anybody she knew,' said Hackett. 'I don't see how it could have been, do you?'

'No. Nothing shows up in her private life to give us any sane motive for wanting her dead. The people she knew look like just ordinary people. She hadn't any money, or none to speak of, and so far as we know no relations, so no expectations.' Mrs. Tillinghurst had said she remembered her mentioning a sister, but had the vague impression the sister was dead. 'Well, we don't know that, she presumably has this

175

brother-in-law, if he's still alive—not so funny he hasn't come in, he probably didn't like her any better than she did him—but we ought to find out who he is, the city'll come down on him for burial costs. We don't even know where she came from. Mrs. Tillinghurst thought somewhere back East, but isn't sure. There weren't any addresses out of the state in her address book, none out of the county. But then again, if she kept up any correspondence with a sister or an aunt or someone, maybe she knew the address so well she didn't bother to put it down.'

'Yes,' said Hackett, 'and we can see what mail continues to come for her, if any—George said the Bessemers told him she hardly ever got much mail—but if you're casting around for some logical motive for somebody to murder her, and saying maybe a relative from way back East somewhere killed her so he'd inherit all Aunt Bessie's money instead, I don't buy it, Luis. A dandy plot for a paperback mystery, but this is real life.'

'Oh, I wasn't suggesting it seriously.'

'How you'd love to have it that complicated. The complicated one's always easier to see through.' Hackett, complacently back to a hundred and ninety pounds, swallowed calories of Scotch. 'No, this looks like the anonymous kill. Same sort of thing I always thought that Black Dahlia thing was. A pervert, a nut. Wanting to kill, and picking a woman at random.'

'And could be, not at random,' said Mendoza, 'or not exactly. She was before the public all day. Somebody like that could have seen her in the store, or wherever she went for lunch, and maybe she reminded him of his mean old grandmother, something like that. And he followed her home.'

'And she let him walk right in with her?'

'I've had second thoughts on that one, Art. We don't know when she was killed. It could have been on the Sunday. I thought about Saturday's lunch guest and I'm still thinking. But the more we know about her, the more it looks like the anonymous thing. So suppose the guest was just somebody she knew we haven't talked to yet. I would guess that the whole population of the state has heard about our cut-up corpse by now, but just possibly somebody hasn't. Who haven't we seen yet?'

Hackett thought. 'Woman named Janet Brown—Jase has gone there once, she wasn't home, but he talked to the manager of the apartment building, who told him she works at a florist shop, so he was going to try to catch her there. I don't know whether he has or not, probably sometime today. Then there's a Mrs. Edna Manning—I went to her place once, and John did, too, later, but she wasn't home. The manager of that building says she doesn't work, she's a widow living on a pension of some sort, so we ought to find

177

her home sometime. Then I think there's another woman—'

'Helen Anderson,' said Higgins, taking the third chair at the table. 'I saw her a while ago. She wasn't the lunch guest, hadn't much to offer but "Wasn't it terrible?"'

'Well, there you are, two possibles,' said Mendoza. 'The way it shapes up, it's almost got to be an anonymous kill, damn it. Nobody liked the woman much, but that's no reason to murder her. I don't like it, but I think we're looking for almost anybody, boys—a special somebody in that he's got a blood lust, and if we don't get him he'll probably do it again—and the worst of that is that it could be a psycho we don't know about. Might be somebody in the sex files, little things, Peeping Tom, stealing underwear off clotheslines—we all know how they start—who suddenly went berserk. Could be somebody who's never so much as spit on the sidewalk who suddenly went berserk.'

'Yes,' said Hackett, finishing his drink, 'and have you also thought that it could be—our anonymous somebody—from right around close to where she lived? If he marked her in the store he could also have spotted her doing her marketing, in the drugstore, at that bakery.'

'Could even be little Mr. Parker,' said Higgins as the waiter came up. 'Oh, a Scotch and soda, and I guess the Salisbury steak with mushroom sauce. After all, he's the last man we know saw her.'

'And those little meek-looking fellows sometimes—Yes, and another thing,' said Mendoza, 'somebody could have marked her simply as a woman living alone. Have we found anybody who saw her on Sunday?'

'No,' said Hackett and Higgins in unison. 'What,' asked Hackett, 'was your second thought about her letting X in?'

'Well, it's pure speculation, but count out the lunch guest. Say that was one of these women we haven't seen, and they haven't heard about the murder yet—or say it was somebody who isn't sure we know about a lunch guest and doesn't want to get mixed up in it in any way. There are people like that. All right. Now we know, from what Alison heard from the Ames woman'—Mendoza grinned; he hadn't, to Mrs. MacTaggart's disappointment, minded that at all—'that Tate was a common-sensible female who at least said she wouldn't be taken in by a plausible stranger. But, first, that little house is fairly isolated back there, and the dog doesn't mind strangers—in fact, loves them. If somebody rang her doorbell she'd open the door, wouldn't she? And there's no screen door, he could push right in.'

'The dog,' said Higgins suddenly. 'Wait a minute. How would a stranger know the dog
179

wouldn't raise a fuss? Most dogs would.'

'Mmh,' said Mendoza. 'There is that. Maybe you've got something with your somebody in the neighborhood, Art.'

'The dog—' said Higgins again. 'Something about the dog—No, I don't know, I can't put a finger on it. It doesn't look as if it could have been the personal thing, no.'

'But I,' said Mendoza, 'have turned up another lead.' He told them about her intended purchase of the car. 'Jimmy should have contacted all three by now, with any luck.'

'I don't see—Oh, I suppose it could be,' said Hackett doubtfully.

'It could. Nuts and perverts have cars as well as other people. The D.M.V. tries to screen drivers, but in a place where you've almost got to have a car or stay home all the time, it's difficult. So say she has a deal set up to buy a car. Maybe he's taking her old one and the two-fifty, or maybe some other way; anyway, he's going to come Sunday with the car. She'd let him in, too, somebody she'd just met but on a business deal. And he goes berserk. Front house empty, nobody hears anything. Because, you know, that money isn't in the house. So what became of it, when she's still got her old car sitting in the garage?'

'Oh,' said Hackett. 'Yes, indeed. How I do

not like these random things. Of course, any X could also have taken the money.'

'True.'

'So take a closer look at the neighborhood, too?' asked Higgins.

'I think so.'

'I'll say one thing,' said Higgins, taking a long swallow of his drink, 'I'll lay a bet she was chasing hell out of that old codger, George Barrington. Jase said so too. He hasn't come home yet, but from that cleaning woman, he's one of those shrewd old fellows with quite a bit salted away. From this other woman in the address book—Mrs. Garnett—I got that Barrington had been in the picture some time. Both Mrs. Garnett and Tate had known his latest wife. He's evidently an eccentric old coot, but Tate wouldn't have cared about that if she could have got him to make her Number Four.'

'And so what?' asked Mendoza. 'Probably a very canny old coot where females are concerned, with no intention of being caught.'

'I just mentioned it,' said Higgins mildly.

* * *

When Mendoza got back to the office, he found a note on his desk from Records. Records informed him that the only likely female pro to match his vague description was

181

one Clarissa Jones. Clarissa was the girl friend of a pro heist man named Robert Lord, and had participated in several jobs with him. She was at present on parole from Tehachapi, on a three-to-five for a heist job pulled alone. She was five-ten, a hundred and seventy, Caucasian, blonde hair, blue eyes, no scars or tattoos. Address in Montebello.

Mendoza put out a pick-up-and-hold on Clarissa.

There was also the autopsy report on Paul Coleman. He had died a natural death—heart attack. So the break-in artist was still liable for only one death, that of Marion Stromberg.

Damn, thought Mendoza. The anonymous thing. It so often was. When you started working it, it might be anybody in the city, and most of the time routine eventually narrowed it down, you went through the files, you hauled in the pros for questioning, and because the pros were never very smart, eventually you found the answer. But all cops hated the lunatic things because they were the toughest kind to work; and if it was the first time the lunatic had showed his lunacy—the first time a potential psychopath had broken the law—and he wasn't in Records and nobody knew about him, just how in hell did you start to look for him?

Mrs. Tate's neighborhood. That other neighborhood down there. Hell.

Mendoza looked up from the autopsy

report as the door opened. Jason Grace, wearing a pleased smile, and Palliser, looking excited, came in with an anemic-looking dishwater blonde dressed badly in a skirt that sagged and a rayon blouse that was untidily half out of the skirt band. She wore an indifferent expression, as if she wasn't much interested at being hauled down to Central Police Headquarters.

'We thought you ought to hear this,' said Grace.

'It could be a real something,' said Palliser. 'This is Mrs. Janet Brown. Lieutenant Mendoza, Mrs. Brown.'

'Pleased to meet ya,' she said indifferently. 'I don't know it's so important, but they seem to think—'

'Just tell the Lieutenant the way you told us, please.'

*   *   *

Higgins didn't hear about that before he went home. He'd been out to see if George Barrington had got home yet (he hadn't) and then to the Manning woman's place; she wasn't there either. And then he'd taken the rest of the afternoon, feeling guilty, on a private project; but he thought he'd solved a problem. It remained to be seen whether he was a good enough actor to carry it off. He thought about it, and he had a Scotch

183

straight, and at seven-thirty he dialed Mary Dwyer's number . . .

'. . . Well, you see, this woman is interested in talented children. She gives very cheap lessons to a certain number of children who are talented.' He hadn't dared say free lessons. He'd found the piano teacher in the classified ads, and asked around; she seemed to be a very good teacher. He'd gone to see her this afternoon; she was a nice-looking thirtyish woman who'd been amused but understood him instantly, and agreed to conspire with him . . . 'No, I happened to come across her in a case—just coincidence, but I thought—Well, you know how Laura *minded* quitting, and if she qualified—'

'Oh. Well, that's very nice of you, Sergeant,' said Mary Dwyer in her cool voice. 'Do you think she would? How much does she charge?'

'Well, I thought,' said Higgins, gripping the phone so hard his knuckles whitened, 'I might drop by and give you her name and address? I—I've got to be over that way, anyway.'

'That's very kind of you. I suppose there's a test of some sort? Oh, it would be wonderful, if she could . . . Yes, that's fine, Sergeant.'

Higgins put the phone down, feeling mildly intoxicated. It was going to work. He had got the piano teacher to tell Mary Dwyer it was

184

only a dollar a lesson (she'd think she could afford that, surely?) and let him make up the rest.

The only thing that worried him was, suppose Mary should find out?

Well, you had to do what you could.

He sighed deeply, and got up and reached for his hat. He'd be seeing her a little while, anyway.

Mendoza was bringing Alison up to date on her very own murder when the telephone rang.

'Mendoza.'

'Farrell,' said the telephone. 'Say. I finally reached that number Jimmy couldn't get. The guy with the Chevy for sale. On Tate. He sounded very damn nervous, Lieutenant. You know the other two checked out clean—Glasser saw them—she'd called both of them, but no deal. This guy finally hung up on me. I didn't like the sound of him, so I routed out the classified people with an ad, even if it doesn't go in—and he's a William Heflin out on Euclid Avenue. You want to do anything on it?'

'*¡Pues sí!*' said Mendoza. 'I'm on my way. Send a squad car out to back me up, O.K.? What's the address?'

⋆　　⋆　　⋆

Detective Jason Grace was doing some

spare-time work too. 'It's just,' he said to his wife, 'I don't like loose ends.'

'No, darling,' said Virginia.

'And it just *could* be—'

'You do have an imagination,' said Virginia.

Grace grinned. 'I suppose. But the man did say he'd never put up a fight. I can make guesses, can't I? As a supposedly trained detective?'

'Talk about the wild blue yonder,' said Virginia.

Grace laughed and kissed her.

Twenty minutes later a door opened to him and he said politely, 'Mrs. Ambler, I wonder if I can bother you again?'

CHAPTER THIRTEEN

Hackett was still in the office at seven-forty when Mendoza came in with William Heflin. Galeano was there too, bored on night duty; they both looked up. 'Something?' said Hackett.

Mendoza told Heflin to sit down. 'Maybe,' he said. Heflin looked as terrified as if he'd got into a den of snakes, he never took his eyes off Mendoza until he and Hackett walked up to where Heflin was sitting, and then it was only to take in Hackett and look even more terrified.

'I haven't done anything,' he said in a shaking voice.

'Well, let's sort it out,' said Mendoza. 'You put an ad in the paper to sell a 1955 Chevy four-door?'

Heflin nodded. He was about twenty-one, a slim medium-sized kid, not quite a man, something immature about him. He was wearing a pair of old stained slacks and a white shirt with no tie. He had long-lashed brown eyes in a white face, and his dark hair was smoothed back with hair cream. He kept clasping and unclasping his hands.

'And a Mrs. Tate called you to make an offer for the car?'

Heflin nodded again. Hackett exchanged a look with Mendoza; Heflin didn't look a very likely subject to go berserk and do murder and then chop up the body, but you never did know. 'Well, what happened?' asked Mendoza. 'We don't bite, boy. What did she say?'

'Offered me three hundred.' Heflin had an unexpectedly deep voice.

'And what did you say?'

'I said—I said did she have a car to swap with maybe a little extra. I told you. She had a Ford. We made a deal. She—she was gonna give me the Ford and two-fifty, and she gets the Chevy. That's it. I never laid eyes on the woman. I never did, I swear by God. She

187

never showed.'

'Didn't you take a look at the Ford?' asked Hackett.

Heflin shook his head.

'Why not?' Mendoza sounded surprised. 'You're buying a car—well, getting it in a trade—you don't even look it over to see what shape it's in?'

'She said it was runnin'. I'm a pretty good mechanic, they taught me at St. John's, I figure I can—'

'Where's that?'

'St. John's. The Lutheran Orphanage of St. John.'

'That's here?'

Heflin nodded, keeping his head down. 'Long Beach. I never met that Tate woman. She was supposed to come Sunday, hand over the car and the cash, but she never showed. I—'

'The *cash*,' said Hackett. 'Did you ask her for cash?'

Heflin was scared green; he hadn't meant to say that. 'I—'

'Why did you want cash?'

'I—No reason. I just thought it'd be easier, I haven't got a bank account. Pastor Luke said as I ought to try to save, but I—It's not so easy, you don't know, I'm a good mechanic but not union, like, I'd 'a' joined, but they said I couldn't take a job for ninety days. I had to eat. You gotta eat and have a

188

place to sleep, for God's sake. I'm sorry, I shouldn't 'a' said that, it's not good to go swearing. But I only get forty a week at the gas station and I got to pay ten for just the one room and—' He went silent suddenly.

'Well, didn't you plan to put the two-fifty in the bank, start an account? Where'd you get the Chevy to sell?'

'I—' said Heflin. 'I got it with the money left. When I got out of St. John's. I only got it five months ago—the car, I mean—when I turned twenty-one. But it's nice to have a car. I always wanted one. I *did* save that money, I was savin' it to get a car. It was five hundred dollars.'

'Where'd it come from?' asked Hackett.

Heflin blinked up at him almost as if he was crying. 'Why, it was what my grandfather left for me. Honest. My mother and father, they got killed in an accident when I was just a little kid, and my grandfather died pretty soon after but he put it in a paper I'm to go to St. John's and have that money when I leave.'

'All right, why'd you want to change cars so soon?'

'I—I—No reason.'

'You must have had some reason. Why? Why didn't you bother to go and check over the Ford before you agreed to buy it?'

'I—Well, I could see it when she brought it.'

189

'Yes, with the deal already closed. You just took a strange woman's word that the Ford was in running shape?'

'I didn't have nothing to do with her!' said Heflin desperately. 'I never!'

'Did you go to see her where she lived?'

'No, I never!'

'Have you ever been in trouble with the law, Heflin?'

'No, no—and I swear I'm never gonna be!' blurted Heflin. 'Listen, I tell you the truth, I get to feelin' desperate. I'm a good mechanic, so I can't join a union they don't let me take a job. I got a nice girl, we want to get married, but her folks can't help and forty a week don't hardly—I was gonna—I was gonna pull a stick-up, see, I had it all thought out, the store owner's got insurance so he don't really get hurt, and I pretend I got a gun and—I wanted another car, a car everybody'd know wasn't mine. I just thought—But that woman never showed, and honest, I swear I won't get into any trouble like that now! Honest to God! I just didn't know how it'd be, feelin' so guilty like—And it's no ways to do anyway, I swear to God—'

'No, it's not,' said Mendoza. 'You learned better than that at the orphanage. Maybe you've been lucky, Bill—they call you Bill?'

Heflin nodded. A great weight seemed to have dropped from him. 'I was just feelin' kind of desperate, you know. Seems like

190

whatever I do, it's no good, I can't—But I'm not gonna do anything wrong now, honest. And I never saw that woman. When I saw in the papers how she'd got murdered, I—gee—'

'Well.' Mendoza looked down at him. This one had petered out fast. 'Where were you on Saturday and Sunday the ninth and tenth of this month, you remember?'

'Yeah, yeah, I do!' Heflin smiled uncertainly. 'I do remember, on account when I saw in the papers about that woman I figured back, and I was with Sally—my girl—that day. We went to the beach all day with another couple, they'll say. And next day I went to church, acourse, in the morning, and Sally and her folks go there too, it's the Lutheran church on Lorena, and I went back and had Sunday dinner with them, so—'

'Well,' said Mendoza again. It was very gratifying that a combination of circumstances had probably prevented William Heflin from embarking on a life of crime, but it left them right where they had been with Mrs. Tate.

'O.K., what's the names?' Hackett was asking resignedly.

'Behrens. Mr. and Mrs. Stanley Behrens. They'll tell you.' Heflin sighed a long deep sigh. 'Is that all you want to ask me? Can I go now?'

'We'll have a car drive you home,' said Mendoza.

'Well, gee, that's nice of you,' said Heflin, sounding very surprised.

When he had gone, Hackett said, 'So she was killed on Sunday?'

'Or on Saturday. We don't even narrow it down that much.'

'Yeah,' said Hackett. 'You know we probably never will get this one. Look at the Black Dahlia, how we worked that.' He meant the L.A.P.D.; he'd still been a rookie and Mendoza riding a squad car then.

'That was the hell of a lot more complex case,' said Mendoza. 'They should have got that one.'

'Just like we ought to get this one,' said Hackett, 'and I ask you how?'

'There are still a lot of places to look.'

'Too damned many places,' said Hackett.

*　　*　　*

He went home and told Angel the time hadn't been wasted, they'd set a potential criminal on the upward path. 'Though I don't think he'd have actually done it, come to that. Brought up too religious.'

'Oh?' said Angel. 'For goodness' sake, Art, don't go in to moon over the baby, I only just got her to sleep.'

'Well—' said Hackett. He looked at her,

192

brown head bent over some sewing. 'Why in—well, why *did* you want her christened, anyway?'

Angel looked up vaguely. 'I really couldn't tell you,' she said. 'I just felt it was the proper thing to do somehow.'

Hackett decided Mendoza was right, women were simply not to be understood. He didn't think they understood themselves half the time.

★   ★   ★

Mendoza went home and was pounced on by Alison, who had been waiting for him. 'To start a story and then walk off when you'd just got to the interesting part! What did this Janet Brown *say*? I can see your latest lead hasn't led to anything—'

'False alarm, yes.' Mendoza stripped off his jacket and went down the hall to the bedroom to hang it up. Alison followed him.

'What did she *say*?'

'Where'd I got to? Well, Jase and John thought it was interesting enough to bring her in to make a statement on it. And it might turn out to be something, at that.' Mendoza wandered out to the kitchen, where a steady crunching noise from the service porch informed them that one or more of the cats was supplementing dinner with the kibbled dry cereal left out for them. 'Funny sort of woman—no life in her. Said wasn't it awful about Mrs. Tate, but not much expression when she said it. I think she must be anemic or something. Máiri's getting careless,' he added, reaching to a half-open cupboard door. It opened wider and the slit-eyed blond mask of El Señor appeared around it. 'It's a good thing I'm not a nervous sort of fellow,' Mendoza told him. 'What are you up to in there, *¿cómo?*'

'That,' said Alison, 'is where we keep the rye.'

'So it is.' Mendoza lifted El Señor out, and then the bottle. El Señor spoke in the piercing loud voice he'd inherited from his Siamese father. Mendoza filled a shot glass and dribbled an ounce of rye into a saucer. 'Prrrrneeyoww!' said El Señor, and crouched over it.

'Go *on!*'

'She'd known Tate for some time, since before her husband died. They lost their husbands about the same time—Brown was killed in an accident—and both had to go back to work. She works in a florist's shop on Western Avenue. Anyway, she said that she and Tate used to meet and go out to dinner together on the average of once a week. And that they liked this big kosher place not far from the florist's, so Tate used to meet her at the florist's. And she went on to say—I'm separating the wheat from the chaff—that

194

about the last six months this man has been regularly dropping into the shop about twice a week, and she thinks he's a very odd sort of man. He says funny things, she said. We pressed her for an example, of course, but all she could remember was that he quoted poetry about flowers, and just seemed funny.'

'Staring eyes or something?'

'*No sé*, she's not very articulate. He's just funny. She gave us a vague description. Well, he always comes in very late, about six, when she goes off. And at least twice, she says, when Mrs. Tate came to meet her at the shop, he was there—and once, she thinks about a month ago, she went to the back to get her coat and when she came out Mrs. Tate had been talking to him. Janet told Mrs. Tate later she thought there was something funny about him, but Tate disagreed. Said he seemed a very pleasant man.'

'Aha!' said Alison. 'Very, very interesting. Maybe they got better acquainted than Janet Brown suspected. Maybe he is very peculiar. Maybe—'

'You read so much into it,' said Mendoza. 'He could be peculiar just in Janet Brown's imagination—though I admit she doesn't look as if she had much. Anyway, she's agreed to call us next time he comes in, and try to stall him.'

'It still seems to me that it was very funny for Mrs. Tate to get murdered at all. She just

195

wasn't the sort of woman.'

'*Querida*, when you get a lunatic with a blood lust, which is what it looks like, any sort of woman can get murdered.' Mendoza finished the rye.

'Well, I suppose. But one thing that seems funny to me, Luis, she was a fairly big, strong woman. Wouldn't she have put up a fight when he attacked her? You said the house was perfectly neat, no signs of a struggle.'

'Two answers. No, she wouldn't if he attacked her from behind, or suddenly, and she was knocked out right away. And also he could have tidied up afterward, though I think the lab boys would have spotted that.'

'Well, anyway, the fact that she got into casual conversation with this strange man says that what she told Miss Ames wasn't necessarily so. And another thing, Luis—if he attacked her from behind, it must have been somebody she trusted. Somebody she knew.'

'You do jump to conclusions. If we knew what time she'd been killed—but it could have been broad daylight. She wouldn't have hesitated to open the door if he'd said he had a parcel or a telegram for her—Y-e-s,' said Mendoza slowly. 'I think I like the idea that our lunatic had marked her, which doesn't necessarily say she knew him, of course. Very probably marked her because she lived alone. And we are going to take a long hard look at the surrounding neighborhood, because she

196

could also have been picked out because the Bessemers in the front house were away. This could wind up turning out to be one of those juveniles—God knows they come along—some psycho-kid everyone knows is odd but nothing's been done about. Because there's also the dog, isn't there? The very friendly dog. Of course, an outsider could have, mmh, cased the place and found out about the dog.'

'Well, you can talk about your anonymous lunatics all you please,' said Alison. 'I don't believe it. I've been thinking it over, and when an ordinary woman like that got murdered so—so violently, I think there's got to be some motive for it. *I* think it was the lunch guest.'

'All logical like the detective stories?' Mendoza laughed. 'Sad to say, *cara*, mostly the violence is at random.'

Wednesday morning, and Higgins' day off. He'd fixed Steve's bike, but he hadn't anything particular to do, so after breakfast he drove up to Mary Dwyer's house. She hadn't expected him, so there'd be no key left. He took Brucie for a walk, and was slightly cheered to discover that the latch on the garage door was loose. Bert had kept a few tools in the garage; Higgins fixed the latch.

She'd fallen for the piano-teacher thing, said she'd call her right away. About all she had left was the kids, and the way she looked sometimes, what she said, he guessed she'd do anything to get the best for them. Well, mothers were like—

All of a sudden something slid into his mind and out. It had something to do with Mrs. Gonzales, but he couldn't think what. Funny. He still didn't like that business much. What had he been thinking of just then, when—

Mothers—

★   ★   ★

Sergeant Lake said Jase had been in and said he and Palliser were going out on a wild-goose chase, apologize to the Lieutenant. 'He didn't say what, but John was saying he ought to set up as a fortune teller instead of a cop.'

'Oh? Well, time will tell,' said Mendoza. Nobody else was in the office. There were several reports waiting for him; he sat down, lit a cigarette, and began to go through them.

At ten-fifteen he heard sounds in the anteroom and went out. Detective Jason Grace and Palliser, flanking a big florid man, were just turning into the sergeant's room. '*¿Qué es esto?*' asked Mendoza.

Grace turned a gentle brown beam on him. '*Es hermoso sin pero*, Lieutenant. You like to hear a nice clear-cut case?' He shoved the man into a chair and looked at him pleasedly.

Mendoza followed them in. Palliser was

198

looking a trifle dazed. 'Maybe he's borrowed your crystal ball,' he said.

'I just got to wondering,' said Grace. 'This is Joseph Tolliver, Lieutenant.'

'I know,' said Mendoza. 'We had him in to question on Ambler. He could have done it, but there wasn't a thing—' He stopped, conscious of being overheard by a suspect.

'It was *dead*, for God's sake,' said Palliser.

'I don't like loose ends,' said Grace amiably. 'Now, Joe. You—'

'Mr. Tolliver to you, nigger!'

'Now, Joe, let's just look at the record,' said Grace, smiling. 'You've been in twice for heist jobs. Only times we caught up to you, hah? The one I'm interested in is the second time you got caught. You held up a liquor store called DeFore's Liquors, up on Beverly Boulevard, on June sixth, 1955. Didn't you?'

'You know so damned much—'

'Well, you did. There was just one clerk in the store, and he didn't show you any fight, it all went just as you planned it, nice and easy. You got a total of three hundred and seventy-eight bucks, Joe, and you walked out with no trouble. But we caught up to you pretty soon, because the clerk picked out your mug shot right down here at Records.' Grace shook his head. 'You're not just so very smart, are you, Joe?'

'You go to hell! All right, so what, I done the time, I'm clean now!'

'Well, I don't think so,' said Grace. 'I did just wonder why Ambler got shot at all when he always said he'd put up no fight to a heist man. And I remembered the first time I talked to his wife, she mentioned he'd been held up before, before he had his own store, when he was just a clerk. So you see, Joe, I went to see her again last night, and I asked her what store that had been and when it had happened, and had we got the boy pulled the job. And—'

'You lousy black son of a bitch—'

'And what *do* you know, Joe, it turns out Mr. Ambler was clerking at DeFore's Liquors on Beverly, and it was June of 1955, and Mrs. Ambler remembers we did get the boy who pulled the job, and guess who it was, Joe?'

'I done the time, I done the time, so all right, damn it, I'm clean—'

'I don't think so, Joe,' said Grace, and suddenly his voice went hard and very cold. 'Look at me! You walked into Ambler's store that Tuesday night and he recognized you, didn't he? Didn't he? You'd cased the job but you didn't know Ambler was the owner, did you? The same man you'd held up before? And you saw he recognized you, didn't you? *Didn't you?* You got a five-to-ten on that one, you're only eighteen months out of Quentin. You weren't about to go back, were you? Answer me, Tolliver!' Grace reached down

200

and yanked the man's head up, to face him. 'You shot him in cold blood, when he wasn't putting up any fight, because you knew he knew you. *Didn't you?*'

'Goddamn you, I wasn't nowhere near—'

'*Didn't you?* You don't need to answer, boy.' Grace grinned at him and let him go. 'We found that Colt Woodsman .22 under that loose floor board in your bedroom. We really should have got to that first time around. Ballistics is going to tell us it's the equalizer killed Ambler. What do you say, Joe?'

'Goddamn you, goddamn you—all right, all right, all *right*, so I wasn't about to go back! You ever sit there have the walls come down on you like to crush you straight to hell? I couldn't take—I couldn't stand—I like to go crazy, I couldn't—Like you can't breathe, there's—like on your lungs, you can't—So he knew me, I had to—I had to—I saw he knew me—All the crazy goddamn bad luck, the same guy, the same—I had to, I had to, because they'd take and shut me in again and I couldn't, I couldn't, I couldn't—' Tolliver lunged out of the chair and flailed wildly at Grace; Palliser stepped in and they got a firm hold on him.

'Well, now, I'm just afraid they will shut you in, Joe,' said Grace softly. 'For a little while, anyway.'

201

'Guesses!' said Palliser. They had sent Tolliver under adequate guard over to the new jail a few blocks away. They would get a statement from him later—maybe. In any case, it was wrapped up tight, with the gun found. 'You reached out so far—'

'Just imagining how it could be,' said Grace. 'That's all.' He was very pleased to have Ambler off his mind. 'So now we've kind of cleared the deck to concentrate on Tate.'

'Oh, yes?' said Mendoza. 'I'd also very much like to get something on that break-in boy down there. I don't know about my brain wave that that could be a female. You like to turn your X-ray eye on it, Jase?'

Grace shook his head. 'That is a thing. When and if we had the men to spare, my only idea is, stake out a couple of the old people's places.'

'Mmh. I had the same idea. Art sat on it. Where in hell are that many men?'

'Well,' said Palliser, 'the publicity the Tate thing is getting the sooner we—Hackett said something about checking the neighborhood where she lived—'

'*Pues sí*. Next on the agenda. ¡*Porvida!*' said Mendoza suddenly, violently. 'Where *do* we look? It could be the random thing, it could be somebody from the neighborhood, it

202

could be, for God's sake, little Mr. Parker—'

'So we keep on looking,' said Grace tranquilly. He sat down and lit a cigarette. He said in a meditative tone, 'You know, that dog—'

'What about the dog?' Hackett came in. 'Understand from Jimmy we've cleared up something, anyway. Congratulations. I had a thought about that dog. That very friendly dog. It—'

'Could have been somebody in the neighborhood who knew about the dog, yes,' said Grace. 'But what I thought about the dog is, whoever X is, he likes dogs. Because of that hose.'

'*Hose?*' said Palliser.

'Um-hum. If the dog got very hungry he'd bark and raise a fuss, and the neighbors would take notice. Investigate, and so forth. See the dog was taken care of. You know. As a matter of fact, he could have left a lot of that kibbled dry food around, that doesn't deteriorate, enough to last the dog until his people came home. The dog wouldn't starve to death, even so, before that happened— before Tate was missed, who was supposed to be looking after the dog. But there was that heat wave, you know.' Grace contemplated his cigarette. 'Damned hot, it was. So X—whoever—left the hose turned on, just a little bit, so the dog would have water at least. I kind of wondered about that at the time.'

'Be damned,' said Hackett. 'I never—but that could be—'

'Woman like the Tate,' said Grace, 'probably very efficient about turning off faucets. Just occurred to me.'

'I think I'll go home,' said Mendoza. 'Jase can run things.'

Grace grinned at him. 'Just occurred to me.'

'Things seem to,' said Palliser dryly.

Sergeant Lake stuck his head in the door. 'Art?'

'Hmmm?'

'Squad car just called in. They've spotted Herrick's car. Eleven hundred block on Grand Avenue. They checked—he's registered at a hotel there, the Royal Arms. He's in. You want to—'

'I'm on my way!' said Hackett, and was.

CHAPTER FOURTEEN

Five minutes after Hackett had left, the other three men were still sitting around smoking and talking, when the inside phone rang and Sergeant Lake said, 'Say, I've got a long-distance call for Art, you want to take it? It's that Chief of Police—Bird or Pigeon or something—back in Indiana.'

'Sparrow,' said Mendoza. 'I'll take it.

Wonder why a phone call?'

'They've found they don't want Herrick after all,' said Palliser.

There was a lot of clicking on the line, and then a voice said, 'Sergeant Hackett? Is that Sergeant—'

'Sergeant Hackett isn't here, this is Lieutenant Mendoza. Chief Sparrow? I know about your case, and Hackett's just—'

'Well, now, Lieutenant, there's a little bit more just come to light, and you better tell Sergeant Hackett about it pretty quick.' It was an elderly voice over the wire, but still alert, and Mendoza formed a mental vision of a neat spare gray-haired fellow, not very big, sitting on the edge of his chair—for some reason the voice suggested that.

'Well, he's just gone out to—'

'Because, now, well, it's like this, sir. You know about the case? Well, it seems, like I told the sergeant, we thought Herrick's wife didn't know anything about it—seems he'd took off before we got there to question her—'

'Yes?' Mendoza idly drew a very modernistic cat on the memo pad and began to shade in El Señor's markings.

'Well, Mrs. Herrick—Betty Jo Taylor she was, from right here—see, Mrs. Taylor's farm, where they were, it's a little nearer to Cedarbrook than Sidalia, and she always did most of her shopping in there.' Chief Sparrow was breathing rather heavily over the wire; it was a very clear connection. Mendoza wondered why on earth Chief Sparrow thought Hackett would be interested in where Mrs. Herrick did her shopping. He said 'Yes' again. 'Well, we had Mrs. Christensen in here this morning, 'long about two hours ago—and she says she's awful worried about Mrs. Taylor and Betty Jo. Mrs. Taylor's an old friend o' hers. It's not a working farm, I should say, Mrs. Taylor's—they just live there. She tells me she can't find anybody who's seen Betty Jo here or in Cedarbrook either, since three weeks back about, and she never did like that husband o' Betty Jo's anyway. I ask her some questions, and the first thing comes out it—I should say, the Christensen place isn't far away from Mrs. Taylor's—'

Mendoza reflected that it was Sidalia, Indiana's money which was paying for the call, and sat back resignedly. He put some long whiskers on the cat.

'First thing comes out, that Herrick fellow, he was still around there when Betty Jo lied to us and said he'd took off. She was covering for him, see. And before that, Mrs. Christensen said Betty Jo'd told her she was kinda scared of him. Well, now, Mrs. Christensen, she's had four in the family down sick with some kind of flu, had her hands full, see, but she tells me when she's

206

got a minute to spare she runs over to see Mrs. Taylor, just this morning, and she can't raise nobody at the house and the car's still there so Betty Jo isn't in town. I guess everybody in Cedarbrook figured she was shopping in Sidalia and t'other way around. What I'm getting at, I come right back to town in a hurry to contact Sergeant Hackett, because a couple of us went out to Mrs. Taylor's then and broke in, and my God, there the two of 'em was—Mrs. Taylor and Betty Jo, my God, those two poor women, shot dead three weeks back it must be—a .38, looks like—both of 'em shot four, five times, so might be he's got two guns—and I thought the sergeant ought to know—'

'¡Qué demonio—Santa María!' said Mendoza. He slammed the phone down, yanked open the top drawer and snatched out the Police Positive .38, got up and ran for the door. 'Come on—Art could be heading for a double killer—' and thinking he was just going out to meet a careless driver, for God's sake—

'What's up?' Grace and Palliser came up behind him. He started down the stairs on the double—they were nearly ten minutes behind Hackett now and he hadn't far to go. The Royal Arms on Grand, about sixteen blocks uptown—and they didn't dare take a squad car, use the siren to alert Herrick—

Hackett asked the desk clerk, 'What's his room number?' The original squad car which had spotted Herrick's car had, of course, gone back on tour; he wouldn't need anybody to pick up Herrick, who had inadvertently knocked down and killed a probably careless pedestrian.

The clerk put on his glasses and looked at the register. 'Mr. L. C. Herrick, yes, two-thirteen.' This was an old hotel, but still quiet and fairly respectable, if cheap.

'Thanks,' said Hackett, and turned to the stairs to climb the one flight. Faint dust rose from the thin carpet as he trudged upstairs. Two-oh-one to his right, two hundred to his left. He walked down the hall unhurriedly.

He came to two-thirteen, and rapped on the door. Hackett had been a cop for a long time, but it just never occurred to him to get out his gun, ready, just as it hadn't occurred to him to demand the key to two-thirteen. Herrick was hardly an important or dangerous man.

The door opened. 'Mr. Herrick?' said Hackett.

'Yeah?' Herrick was a lithe, middle-sized young man, dark. He needed a shave.

Hackett produced his badge. 'We've been asked to bring you in by the police back in—' He also had a warrant, which he was in the act of reaching for when he suddenly found himself looking down the barrel of a revolver which was twin to the one unfortunately reposing in his shoulder holster.

'Get in here, cop!' said Herrick.

Having no choice, and feeling immense surprise and not much else, Hackett moved to obey. Herrick stepped aside to let him in, and at that moment Mendoza shouted, 'Hold it, Herrick!' from the far end of the corridor at the stair head. Hackett saw the gun begin to turn in Herrick's hand and flung himself at Herrick, but Herrick dodged back and sent a couple of snap shots at the three men running up the corridor. Before they could return his fire, he whirled, aimed at Hackett and fired, ran into two-thirteen and banged the door. The slug took Hackett high up on one shoulder, and being a .38 slug, slammed him back against the opposite wall.

Doors began to open and the citizenry to come out. People ran up the stairs from below and down the stairs from above, asking excited questions.

'Art?' panted Mendoza.

'I'm O.K., I don't think the slug went in, just hit the top of my shoulder—' He was bleeding some, and damn it, this was almost a new suit. He had his gun out by now. 'What the hell is all this?'

'Herrick!' called Mendoza. 'Come out here, Herrick, and without the cannon! We're four to one and there's no other way out—for God's sake. I hope not,' he added in an undertone. 'John, go and find out if he can reach a fire escape—call up some more men—*Herrick!* Do you hear me?'

The answer came in a fusillade of shots through the door of two-thirteen. All three of them promptly opened fire in return. The coughing shots re-echoed down the corridor; the citizenry yelped in alarm and began to scatter. Somewhere a woman screamed.

'Herrick!'

Silence from two-thirteen. 'Did we get him?' wondered Grace.

Palliser came racing up the corridor, scattering the crowd further. 'He's right alongside a fire escape! His window—'

Mendoza and Grace surged forward and hit the door together. It shuddered but didn't give. They hit it again and the lock gave. They all ran across the room to the open window.

Herrick had got halfway down the fire escape. In a moment he would step onto a landing halfway down; from there he'd have to step onto the straight steel ladder hanging below the landing, which would slowly pay out under his weight and take him twelve feet down to the sidewalk. The hotel was on the corner of Grand and Pico, and this was the Pico Boulevard side—the sidewalk down there wasn't exactly thronged, but there were enough people passing that a shot would be risky, and already a small crowd was gathering to watch the man on the fire escape.

Mendoza snapped a shot down from the window and fell back as Herrick fired blindly up at them. 'Jase—'

Grace leaned out the window. Herrick was riding the ladder down; the crowd was yelling and scattering in all directions at the gunfire. 'People, people,' said Grace, and shot Herrick neatly through the right shoulder. Herrick let go of the ladder and fell, turning in the air, and landed heavily.

Of course, Herrick couldn't have been expected to know that Detective Jason Grace was a top marksman.

★   ★   ★

It was a couple of hours before the excitement was all over. Hackett went to the hospital with Herrick, where the interns cleaned up a deep crease on top of his shoulder, bandaged it, and told him he could go. The doctors said they couldn't question Herrick until tomorrow, he had a compound fracture of one leg and a broken shoulder, but would probably recover in time. Hackett carrying his ruined jacket, went back to the office with the rest of them and called Chief of Police Sparrow, while Mendoza complained that he was getting too old to stand shocks like this.

211

'If those damned rural so-called cops back there hadn't sat around for three weeks before finding out they had a couple of murders on their hands—¡Caray!'

'Yes, we've got him,' Hackett was saying ... 'Well, he's in the hospital, we had to take a shot at him, but—Yes, sure. Well, he may waive extradition, we'll see ... What? ... Oh, yes, sure ... Not at all, Chief. Any time. Any time at all. Always glad to co-operate.' He put the phone down with a rueful grin, wincing. 'Boys,' he said, 'it's after one-thirty and getting shot hasn't stopped me getting hungry. Let's go have something to eat and relax a little.'

'One of these days,' said Mendoza, looking at his watch in surprise, 'something like this will happen and I'll damn well have a heart attack. My God, what a day. All right, come on. You're looking thoughtful, Jase.'

'I was just thinking,' said Grace, 'I wonder what else we're going to clear up today. We've got two already, and they do say, "Never two without three."'

*   *   *

Alison was feeling so exasperated with Janet Brown that she could have screamed. Was the woman mentally retarded, or what?

Because, as she'd told Mendoza, she didn't believe in the random lunatic murderer for

212

one minute. Somebody must have had a good reason to want May Tate dead, and that meant someone who knew her. So, fired with confidence that anyway a woman could probably get more out of a woman, she had come to this dreary little florist's shop to see Mrs. Janet Brown and carry her off to lunch and an intimate talk.

That had been a fiasco. Mrs. Brown couldn't seem to understand exactly who Alison was or why she was here. She always, she said flatly, brought her own lunch and ate it in the back room.

'Well, I thought today you could let me take you out.' Alison smiled at her persuasively. 'I really do want to ask you several things about Mrs. Tate—after all, I was the one who—'

'Oh, I don't think I could do that. *What* did you say your name was?'

So Alison had just hung on in the shop—fortunately the owner wasn't there; he didn't come in until one, said Mrs. Brown—and gone on asking questions, between customers. There weren't many customers. After a while Mrs. Brown, maybe getting used to her or maybe just wanting to get rid of her, began to open up a little.

'Mrs. Tate told someone where she worked—or rather implied it—that she was thinking of getting married again. Do you know anything about that, or who—'

Janet Brown leaned on the counter. 'Well, *she* was thinking about it,' she said dispassionately. 'Whether she ever would have got him, I don't know. It was a man named Barrington, I never met him, she said he had a little money. I didn't blame her, mind you. A person our age gets awfully tired, standing on your feet all day, barely enough to get along on.'

'You don't think the Barrington man wanted to marry her?'

'Well, you said you met her. May was a good enough sort, but not much for looks, and she could be sort of—well, like wanting a finger in every pie, you know. Men don't like that.'

'Did she—er—go out with Mr. Barrington?'

'Oh, she never said. I guess she would have, if she did. Say, I mean. She used to know his wife before she died. The wife, I mean. I think it was more like, well, she used to call him on the phone, ask him over for dinner—' Janet Brown looked at Alison a little wearily. 'You know how it goes, pretending she was trying to cheer him up, do for him, on account she'd known his wife, when she was really out to get him herself.'

'Yes. Did she—'

'I told the cops about this funny guy comes in, she talked to here once. I don't mean to say I think she—you know—took up with

214

him. May wouldn't, perfect stranger. But I think he's a nut of some kind, and it must've been a nut who—who did that to May.' Janet Brown shivered. 'A woman alone, she's not hardly safe anywhere, big city these days. I been thinking of packing up and going home. I'm from up in Flournoy, California—way up north. I've got an aunt there. What I thought was, about this nut comes in, it could be he followed May or something. I wouldn't know why, but then who knows why nuts do things? I guess they don't know themselves. Imagine, right there in her own house!'

'Yes. What's this man like, Mrs. Brown? How is he funny?' Alison didn't believe at all that the funny man entered into the picture.

'Well, I don't know. He comes in and buys flowers. About twice a week, five-thirty, six o'clock. He smiles too much. It's not natural, you know? And he's got funny eyes. The first time he came in, he bought some daffodils and then he recited a lot of poetry about daffodils being like the Milky Way, and then he just stood there and said, "Wadsworth." Well—'

'Wordsworth,' said Alison involuntarily.

'It was crazy, I mean. I don't *know* he was the one killed May that awful way, but he *could* have been. Anyway, I'm just scared stiff to do it, but I told the cops I would, I said when he came in again I'd make an excuse and go call them.' She paused and added

215

reflectively, 'I wouldn't have, but that one cop was so nice about asking, saying how important it might be. Not the colored one, he was kind of nice too, but this other one with the mustache. I kind of go for men with mustaches. He was Italian or something, I don't remember his name.'

Alison nearly told her. 'Did she—'

'No, I figured May would never 've got that Barrington to come across. Didn't sound likely, for all she talked about it. Besides, there was somebody else after him, too—Edna Manning. She and May both used to know the wife. I only met her—Mrs. Manning, I mean—once, but she's a little younger than May and lots better-looking, she keeps herself up better—know what I mean?—and dresses nice.'

'She wanted to marry Mr. Barrington too?'

'I figure.' The door opened. 'I guess that's all I could tell you really. I got to wait on people.' She moved toward the man who'd just come in.

Well, thought Alison, disappointed.

★　　★　　★

It was getting on for four o'clock when Higgins came into the office. 'Understand you had a little excitement here this morning. Jimmy said Art's all right?'

Mendoza looked up. 'He's O.K., swearing

216

over a perfectly good suit ruined. What are you doing here on your day off?'

'Well, I tell you,' said Higgins, 'it's a dead case, so maybe that evens it up with my day off. I just had a little thought about that Gonzales thing, Luis. It sticks in my mind, you know. We never got any really definite evidence that Gonzales was serious in threatening suicide. Just drunken remorse.'

Mendoza looked at him. 'You always thought his wife did it, didn't you?'

'There was just something about it—So all right, he goes on periodic drunks, she was used to it, maybe she didn't like him so much any more, I still say it was unnatural for her not to go in and *look* at him that morning until after she'd worked around getting breakfast and seeing the kids off to school.'

'I don't know. She'd be used to him sleeping it off on the living room couch.'

'Maybe. The blanket was pulled up over him—his right arm outside it, so he *could* have thrown the razor across the room—and the kids didn't notice anything when they passed through on their way out.'

'Did you talk to the kids?'

'No,' said Higgins, 'and I'm thinking now maybe I should have. I haven't told you yet what brought me in. I just remembered what Mrs. Gonzales had been talking about when she quoted that proverb. Something else'—for some reason he flushed a little,

217

suddenly—'just put it in my mind. She said that—*evil-minded*—about her husband. And then I asked her if she had a job and she said she'd got one before he killed himself. I'd asked about her children, too, none of them old enough to help out, and she said no, the oldest was María, fourteen. And *that* was when she quoted that proverb about the opportunity creating the thief, and also said *evil-minded* again.'

'Oh,' said Mendoza.

Higgins passed a hand over his Neanderthal jaw. 'They weren't all Gonzales' own kids,' he said. 'And if I read that proverb right, it doesn't just mean thievery, but wrongdoing of any kind. Well, women—most women—I guess the one thing might set them off would be somebody mistreating their kids. I just sort of put one thing together with another, and hell, I might be adding one and one and getting twelve, but I thought it could be that because she had a job and had to leave the kids alone, she'd found Gonzales was maybe—'

'*El pensamiento*,' said Mendoza. 'I see what you mean.'

'I'd just like to talk to her again,' said Higgins. 'And I thought maybe if you went along—'

Mendoza looked up at him. 'I wonder if Jase was right. Very strong hunch, George?'

'I guess so.'

'Let's go see her.'

*　　*　　*

They found Mrs. Gonzales at home; her three-year-old boy was ill and she was off her job. She eyed them sullenly. 'Why you are back?' she asked Higgins suspiciously.

Mendoza wasted no time. He sized her up; he knew the type. She'd be Mexican-born, some little village off the beaten path. She hadn't much Spanish blood, mostly Indian, and on account of various factors, social, economic, she'd distrust the law, authority of any kind. Trying to question her, leading her step by step in logical progression, intuition, and habit, would close her up like a clam, and all you'd get would be *No sé, No sé,* I don't know. The stolid Indian face blank of expression.

There were two children at home; the sick boy in the bedroom wasn't visible, but the four-year-old girl playing on the bare living room floor was going to be pretty: much lighter skin than her mother's, fine regular features; Gonzales mostly Spanish.

Mendoza thought about blood lines, and felt tired. So many people read so much into that sort of thing, when it didn't mean a damn, this way or that way. Very probably in his own pedigree, look back far enough, there

219

were a few of those bloodthirsty old Aztecs as well as the aristocratic *caballeros* who'd come pillaging them. Any cross section of humanity, any color or creed, you got the good and the bad, the smart and the stupid, which the fanatics on both sides would never admit.

But the Mrs. Gonzaleses he knew, so he didn't waste any time.

'How was he bad to your children, Mrs. Gonzales?' he asked sharply in Spanish.

She stared at him. 'You speak of Alfredo? He was not—'

'Did he beat them? Was that why you killed him? It was easy, wasn't it? He was drunk, asleep, passed out. You came up behind him with the razor—his own razor—'

'No, no, he has killed himself. He has killed himself.'

'And he never knew what was happening to him, did he? Why did you, Mrs. Gonzales? How had he been bad to the children? *Your* children?'

'No—no—the disgrace of it—they said it was finished—You cannot come now—I must raise the children decently—María—'

Mendoza's eyes sharpened on her. 'Your *child*! What did he do? You did kill him, didn't you? You took his razor—he was an evil-minded man—and you—'

'No. No. María—' She was confused.

'I know! I tell you! You will tell me! You

go to the church, Mrs. Gonzales? You believe in what the church tells you?'

'I believe, I believe—I have sinned, but what else might I do?' She shook and gasped. 'What else might I do for my child? You—how do you know? I see you know—But he is an evil man, it is the drink puts the evil in his heart—I have not been to the church, I have not confessed, I think I believe, but there is an older law, policeman. There is an older law for women! I do not feel it is wrong, a mother must do what she can for her child. He is the sinner, not I, not I! I must be away from my children at work, for the money for the rent, the food—And so my child is alone, my María, and she is innocent, she begins to be a woman but she is innocent, and he comes at her, the sly, the secret, the evil, he assaults her, she is afraid to tell me, her mother, how this evil man uses her—A mother must protect her children! Yes, yes, so you know! At last, you know! You punish me that I protect my daughter, my innocent—' She stopped, her full breasts heaving.

'What's she saying? asked Higgins.

'An old sad story,' said Mendoza. 'About human nature, George. That's the trouble with people. Human nature.' He said to Mrs. Gonzales, 'You must come with us now. You know this.'

'My children,' she said dully. 'What will
221

become of my children? My María—my little son, he is sick—'

'Your children will be cared for,' said Mendoza. After a fashion, he thought. The compromises society made with itself...

He wondered how the vast, impersonal body of the law would deal with Mrs. Gonzales. He hadn't anything to do with that; his job was to find them and hand them over to the law. Quite often he didn't agree with what the bench decided.

'A mother has a right,' said the woman. 'A mother must guard her child.'

'What's she *saying?*' asked Higgins urgently.

'That you had a hunch, George,' said Mendoza.

CHAPTER FIFTEEN

'She didn't get much but junk mail,' said Edmund Whittaker. He was a young man and not bad-looking in his blue-gray postal uniform. 'You get to know the people on your route, you know, notice if they maybe have correspondents abroad, subscribe to a lot of magazines. Mrs Tate didn't.'

'I see,' said Palliser. They'd sent a routine inquiry to the post office about the regular carrier for Mrs. Tate's address. It wasn't at all

222

important; now that it added up pretty much for certain that it had been the random thing, her friends, her work, her routine, her past, didn't look interesting in the case. But at the same time they had to be thorough, and Palliser had come over here to the nearest branch post office to talk to Edmund Whittaker.

'I will say,' said Whittaker, 'she never left letters in her box to be mailed.' He shook his head. 'People will do, as if we didn't have enough to carry as it is. But Mrs. Tate didn't. What a thing, though—imagine her getting murdered, and right there where I—Say, I do remember one thing, Officer, don't know if it means anything, because I guess whoever murdered her was a nut and maybe never even knew her before, but—'

'Hm?' Palliser was feeling a lot better, more cheerful. His mother was better, seemed to be getting well at last, and the doctor said probably she wouldn't need the nurse much longer. And though he didn't like the idea, well, Roberta could go on teaching for a year or two after they—

'Well, she didn't get quite as many Christmas cards as a family would, of course, but some. And I noticed that all of them, both last Christmas and the one before—only two holidays she'd been on my route—were from right around here, postmarks, you know, except one. That one was from a town in Iowa. It's right on the tip of my tongue, damn it, I can't say it but—Now, damn it, what *was* it? Only thing I remember, it was the same exact name as this local dairy-you know—'

'Which—Oh, like Adohr?' asked Palliser.

'No, not that one. What are some others?'

Palliser conjured up a mental vision of the refrigerator case at the market where he often shopped for his mother. 'Wouldn't be Golden State? Or Gold Medal?'

'No, no. But it was exactly the same—'

'Knudsen.'

'Yeah,' said Whittaker. 'I think that was it. Knudsen, Iowa. It was a regular name. I mean, a man's name.'

'Well, thanks very much, Mr. Whittaker,' said Palliser.

'Welcome. Imagine, somebody on my route—Well, sure hope you get him. We don't need one like that running loose!'

Palliser agreed and left the post office. All this sort of thing was largely wasted effort, he thought. In fact, they'd put out a lot of wasted effort lately, but that was how routine went. They all felt that the routine likeliest to turn up the X on May Tate was the hunting and asking they were doing up in the neighborhood where she'd lived, around the places nearby where she had shopped. They'd widen that area of search if that didn't turn up anything. None of her friends, her co-workers, anybody she had known seemed to know anything or look at all suspicious; long odds and no takers, it had been the nut spotting her casually. And that was a very tough sort of thing to break.

What the hell had he done with the head and missing arms and legs? None of them thought they were in the lake, though they could be. Might turn up by accident any day—or never. They could be anywhere in the county, buried, or in another lake—Palliser thought suddenly, what about MacArthur Park? X had left the body in one lake, maybe he'd thrown the rest of it into another, and MacArthur Park with its larger lake wasn't so far away from Echo Park. He'd suggest it to Mendoza, anyway.

Their other case was looking dead and unpromising. They had finally picked up Clarissa Jones, the tough pro, and it had turned out she had a nice alibi for both the Friday night when Marion Stromberg had been killed and the Sunday night when Mr. Coleman's apartment had been broken into. She had been in the drunk tank from nine o'clock on the Friday night, and visibly in a downtown bar with several other people on the Sunday. That kind of thing was discouraging.

They had also, last night, found Janet Brown's funny man. He had come into the shop, Janet Brown had excused herself and

225

called them, and they'd chased a patrol car over *pronto* to pick him up. Mendoza, Hackett, and Palliser had then called their respective homes to announce that they'd be late, and waited expectantly—and hopefully—to question a murderous lunatic. But Mr. Bartholomew Barnes *was* just a funny man. A smiling, blond, rotund man who might be a little eccentric but was certainly not very likely to have gone berserk and committed a murder—and *such* a murder.

Mr. Barnes, who was fifty-two, lived with his mother, and they both had a good deal of money. Mr. Barnes, in lieu of a regular job, had numerous hobbies—photography, bird-watching, bowling, films, and so on. He had never been married. On the Saturday when Mrs. Tate could have been killed, he had been at the local public library, and home the rest of the day; on the Sunday when she could also have been killed, he had taken his mother out to see a film and have dinner; they had been in bed, he said, by ten o'clock. His mother said so too.

Mr. Barnes was discouraging also.

Now Palliser drove back downtown and found Mendoza and Hackett, with all sorts of other things to do, having their time wasted for them by Mr. George Barrington. Mr. Barrington had arrived home this morning—he had been over in Las Vegas—and on hearing the exciting news that somebody he knew had been murdered and dismembered, had come hotfoot down to headquarters to tell them what he'd known about her. None of it was of any use to them, little of it was news, but Mr. Barrington was quite impervious to gentle hints.

He was sitting alongside Mendoza's desk polluting the atmosphere with a very large black cigar, and he was having the best time he'd had in years, enjoying himself.

'Yessir, you gotta be careful of these widows, boys! Out for a man like a hungry shark—plenty of 'em after me, knowing I got a little money salted away. Never mind how much, but I done pretty good—pretty good. May, she was all out to get to be Mrs. George Barrington, just like that Mrs. Hoff down the street from me—any time I turn around, it's a pie or a cake, and "Don't you get awful lonely, Mr. Barrington, since your dear wife passed away?"' Mr. Barrington grinned knowingly. He was a great tall lank beanpole of a man, with long arms and legs, and he moved jerkily, like a badly handled marionette. Palliser found it impossible to conceive of the man standing on a chair to hang a picture without tumbling off, but according to the cleaning woman, this was the fellow who ran along girders twelve stories up and never turned a hair. 'Pretty good pie she makes, too. But I tell you, when I lost Milly, well, I made up my mind I wouldn't try again. Not that Milly wasn't a good sort, though not the cook my second wife was. If I *had* been thinkin' of trying it again—I may be seventy-two but the doctors say good as a fellow of forty-five, and I'm here to tell you, boys, many a good tune played on an old fiddle!' Mr. Barrington gestured exuberantly with one of his long awkward arms and knocked the lighter off the desk. 'Yessirree—if I *had* been thinkin' of it, I guess May might have been somewhere in the running, all right, because she was a very damn good cook—only there's Edna, too, Edna Manning. Them two, they been chasing me like a brace o' coonhounds after fleas, I tell you! Tickle you to death—first one thinkin' she's got an edge over t'other, and then vicey versey, like they say. Well, now, life in the old dog yet, and I got to admit I maybe give Edna the impression she's been gettin' to me. Hell, if I'd come right out and said I wasn't intendin' to take the plunge again, Edna'd go looking for some other fish in the sea—Why shouldn't she, hey?'

'Mr. Barrington—' said Hackett.

The tide rolled over him. 'Widow of a railroad man, Edna is. Nice-lookin' woman. And she's a hell of a good dancer, and me, I like to dance a lot—'

Palliser tried to picture Mr. Barrington throwing his arms and legs about on a dance floor without menacing his partner and

228

everyone else.

'—and Edna bein' the best dancer I know, I like to keep her sweet, jolly her along a bit, see. It don't hurt to let folks see you can still get hold of a pretty darn good-lookin' woman yet—for her age, acourse, she's no chicken, maybe forty-five. So that's why. But a man's got to be careful, they're cunning as foxes, these widows. I just wonder, did May get tired o' tryin' to get me and maybe take up with somebody else—but why'd any feller want to kill her? Don't seem very likely somehow. Not as if she'd been any kind of a looker.'

'Mr. Barrington—'

He chuckled. 'Oh, it was ding-dong between them two, all right. You might think seventy-two's pretty far up there but I ain't about to get senile yet. See that?' He flung out a hand and knocked the desk blotter flying. 'Steady as a rock! Why, I don't think no more of walkin' along a scaffold couple of hundred feet up than I did when I was *twenty*-two! Some people just born like that, don't mind heights. Never think about it. I earn thirty bucks a day when I fancy takin' a job—'

Palliser looked at him enviously.

'But I don't *have* to. Feel like it, I quit, take off over to Vegas. Like this time. Did myself some good, too—got into a hot poker game and won four hundred and some. Say, you boys got any idea who *did* murder May?

229

Seems about the *un*likeliest thing I could imagine—May letting somebody murder her!'

'Mr. Barrington—'

They got rid of him finally, and Palliser told them what the mail carrier had said. 'Damn all,' said Mendoza. 'What's the use of contacting Knudsen, Iowa, to be told sure, she was born there and still gets a Christmas card from an old friend?'

'¡*Animo*!' said Hackett. 'One thing I'll take a bet on, Luis, no nut quite as nutty as this one must be—even if he's never done anything before—doesn't look a little odd or act a little odd. Sooner or later, at that market, or the bakery, or around the neighborhood—somewhere—we're going to hear about some character who stares at women or makes funny remarks or something like that, and we'll be on our way.'

'Maybe. Did you get anywhere locating the brother-in-law?'

'Yes. He's dead. Failed in another business and shot himself four years ago.'

'Also helpful. Do you realize we haven't even got a formal identification yet?'

'I know, I know,' said Hackett, feeling his bandaged shoulder.

'I think,' said Mendoza suddenly, 'I must be losing my grip. Why in hell didn't I think of that before?' He reached for the inside phone.

'What?' asked Palliser through a yawn.

230

'Well, tit for tat, if Henry Kinger pulled a little violence in that neighborhood a couple of years back—Jimmy, get me O'Brien in Records—then so did the two younger kids who were with him, didn't they? It was just Henry's description that—' Mendoza broke off and said hello to O'Brien, asked him to check back on that case and let him know anything he could about the two other boys. 'Also, they might both still be living there. It's just possible—'

'Well, nothing really says—'

'No, but maybe. I still say,' said Mendoza, 'that that smells like a juvenile to me. You said to me, Art, that a lot of pros are just naturally lacking in empathy, in human feeling. *De veras*. But not all of them. We've all known the pros who looked on burglary or armed robbery as just another kind of job, and felt just like any normal citizen about their wives and kids and old grandmothers. And of course not all juveniles are lacking in empathy—we all know, too, that it's only two per cent of all juveniles who *do* get into trouble, and what I'm saying is that I don't think I ever ran across one of those who didn't have that very rudimentary lack of empathy, of the ability to put himself in somebody else's place. And it seems to me that only somebody like that could conceive of picking out frail, elderly people to rob because it'd be so easy.'

'That's kind of highfalutin' reasoning,' said Hackett. 'It confuses me.'

'For a man who majored in psychology at college,' said Mendoza, 'you confuse easy, *amigo*.' The phone rang; he picked it up. 'Well, quick work.' He reached for a pen. 'Yes? ... Yes, I've got that ... Oh ... Oh, I see. Yes. Addresses? ... O.K., thanks, O'Brien.'

'Look interesting?' asked Grace.

'Might be. The other two were Dave Durham and Emery Young. Both just under eighteen now. Young was picked up two days ago on a mugging charge in MacArthur Park, and is currently being held at Juvenile Hall for sentencing. He's still on probation for the other thing, too. Go on slapping him on the wrist until he turns eighteen, you're going to cure him afterwards by getting tough? *¡Vaya por Dios!*'

'Don't tell me you're coming to agree with those soft-hearted citizens who don't think punishment of any kind is a deterrent to crime,' said Hackett.

'Softheaded,' said Mendoza succinctly. 'Deterrent, hell, the main purpose of prison is to keep the wild animals shut up where they can't victimize the citizens. Dave Durham is still at large, still living down on Cortes Street in that area, still on probation. He's a school dropout, supposedly has a job at a gas station on Venice Boulevard—here's the address.' He

232

handed it to Grace. 'Suppose you go talk to him, if you can find him. Art, let's you and I go see Emery Young.' He got up and reached for his hat. 'John—Tom, you can chase up to Hollywood and join George asking questions around the Tate neighborhood.'

Palliser and Landers got up resignedly.

*   *   *

Emery Young had acquired some bulk since he'd been picked up and put on file—if without prints—two years ago. He would weigh in at around two hundred, and he was only an inch or so shorter than Hackett. Mendoza looked at Emery Young interestedly, a big lout of a kid, with a sullen and stupid look about him. Emery Young wore his sandy-red hair long in front, combed back into a high pompadour. In a struggle that pompadour might fall loose and lead to the long hair in their description. Here in the interrogation room at Juvenile Hall, Young faced them in a pair of institutional tan pants and a short-sleeved white shirt, and on his right arm were a couple of tattoos. Not on both arms, as one witness had insisted; but it was something.

'Where'd you get the tattoos, Emery?' he asked.

'What's it to you, cop?'

'Sit down, Emery,' said Hackett gently.

'And let's not waste time. Get that tone out of your voice. Where'd you get the tattoos?'

'At a tattoo parlor in San Pedro. You want the address? Maybe you like to get some like them?'

'Let's see them, Emery.' There were two; one on his upper arm, a coiled rattlesnake with its mouth open, and on the forearm an ace of spades. 'Why tattoos?' asked Mendoza.

'Why not? They're the thing. Lots of fellas get tattoos. It's the latest.'

'All right, Emery.' There wasn't any sense wasting time on this kind either; Mendoza looked at him. At seventeen, Emery's pattern was set. He wouldn't change. After a long time of being a cop Mendoza didn't know the answer, and maybe there wasn't one, even any set of answers; maybe it was just how people were—any cross section, good and bad. They'd apparently made a cure of Henry Kinger, who'd just got in with bad company once and was a little too suggestible, but the Emerys were something else again.

'All right, Emery,' he said. 'Short and sweet. Somebody down in your part of town has found a nice easy lay—breaking in on the old folks who can't put up a fight. We've got a description, and it could fit you. Very nicely it could fit you. How about it?'

Sudden fright glinted in the boy's eyes. 'That!' he said. He licked his lips. 'What the hell, you try to mix me up in *that*—I

234

never—that's murder! I never did no *murders*—'

'How did you think it might work out when you mugged that fifty-year-old woman in MacArthur Park on Tuesday night? She was walking with a cane, I understand—she's just getting over an automobile accident. You think it did her any good to be knocked down and half strangled? You think it couldn't have turned into murder?'

Emery looked bewildered, 'I didn't go to kill her. What you mean, cop?'

'Yes,' said Mendoza. 'Exactly the kind, Art—*¿Cómo no?* He doesn't know what I mean, he can't look two minutes ahead. Well, how about it, Emery?'

'How about what? I never did those break-ins, I wouldn't—'

'So prove it to us. Where were you a week ago last Friday night, and last Sunday night?'

'Jesus, who knows? Is that when—I got to think. God damn, who remembers a week ago Friday, that's—Lemme think, I didn't do those—' He licked his lips continually; he shot a furtive look between them. 'Dave—' he muttered, and then, 'I never done nothing like that.'

'What about Dave? Dave Durham?'

'Nothing. Nothing.'

'Did Dave pull those jobs?'

'No, acourse not. Jesus, lemme *think*. Sunday—' His face cleared. 'Yeah, yeah, I was with Dave—Dave Durham, yeah—up till about midnight, we was with two dames, we went to a movie and then a bar, it's Angelo's on Fourth—'

'For Cokes?'

'What's with C—Oh, yeah, yeah, Cokes,' said Emery quickly. Mendoza made a mental note to speak to Reynolds in Juvenile about checking on Angelo's for serving minors. Hell, they wanted it, they always found it somewhere.

'And after that?'

'Well, you know—'

'No, we don't know. What did you do?'

'Well, this dame—Well, hell, *you* know. I just—kind of—went home with her.'

And they wanted that, they always found it somewhere. So what? And in this section of the big town, or maybe almost anywhere, what seventeen-year-old male was an innocent? 'Girl's name?'

'Uh—June. June Small.'

'Where?'

'Uh—rooming house on Twelfth Street.' He added the address.

'All right. What about a week ago Friday?'

'Jesus, I dunno—why the hell you think—Well, I work Friday nights, I quit school, I got a job as a loader at a Sears warehouse—Olympic Boulevard—I worked till nine. I think maybe I went bowling after, maybe that was Thursday, I don't remember,

236

why the hell I remember? Or it coulda been the night I was in The Four Aces and met Dave—you could ask the barkeep, Mike his name is—'

'The Four Aces where?'

'Down on Figueroa. Yeah, yeah, I kind of think it was that night. We was there till about one A.M., I—'

'Drinking Cokes.'

'Yeah, yeah, Cokes, that's right, don't get Mike wrong. I kind of think—'

'All right, Emery, we'll check it,' said Mendoza dryly. As they came out he said to Hackett, 'Has any easy answer ever dawned on you?'

'For those?' said Hackett. 'I tell you, Luis, as an innocent idealistic young rookie I used to wonder hard. Thought about all the answers—broken homes, slum conditions, negligent parents, all the easy plausible answers the social workers bandy around. I've grown up since. I just figure that kind's there to be coped with, and there's no answer except some people are just that kind. Any class, any block in the big town, and slums be damned. Some very nice respectable people live in slums. I'd even say some nice respectable people have been divorced. And some others living in sin. And there are some real bastards making fifty thousand a year and living in Beverly Hills.'

Mendoza laughed. 'Facts of life,' he said.

They went back to the office. Piggott was there, bent over a typewriter laboriously typing up a report. The outside phone was ringing on Mendoza's desk.

'Mendoza.'

'Just me,' said Palliser. 'I forgot something. I had a little brain wave. Maybe. It just occurred to me, when he left the body in Echo Park Lake, could it be he put the missing parts into some other lake? I mean, sometimes they do use the same M.O., not having much imagination, you know. And MacArthur isn't far off. I just wondered.'

'It's an idea,' said Mendoza. 'We'll check it out, John. Thanks.' He put the phone down, sat down at his desk and reached for the county guide. 'Lakes. We've got quite a few around here. MacArthur, yes, and all the reservoirs—but most of them are fenced, not so easy to—'

'Lakes?' said Hackett.

'It won't do any harm to drag MacArthur,' said Mendoza and without any warning the door opened and Alison came in.

'What,' asked Mendoza, 'are you doing here?'

'What you should have been doing, detective,' said Alison. 'I thought you'd better hear about it right away. You know I've been going to see these people Mrs. Tate knew—because you can say all you please, it *was* a private, personal motive!—and—'

'I know. I do not approve,' said Mendoza. 'You—'

'Any time I let you dictate to me. Well, I went to see this Mrs. Manning, and she's disappeared too!'

'She wasn't at home. We haven't talked to her, no—we're not much interested. Apparently she's out a good deal, the manager of the apartment said—'

'You,' said Alison, 'didn't talk to the manager's wife. I did. You had better go and see her. The woman has gone. The manager doesn't think much of females, doesn't pay much attention to them, even his wife. She can tell you. The woman went without telling anybody where she was going, and she's taken most of her clothes and things. *And*—'

'What?' said Mendoza.

'*And*, by what Mrs. Kraus says,' said Alison triumphantly, 'she was Mrs. Tate's lunch guest that Saturday! So what about that, *querido*?'

CHAPTER SIXTEEN

Hackett went up to have a look, leaving Mendoza and Alison arguing about it; ten minutes after he got there he was calling Mendoza. 'You'd better come and take a look—and bring some lab boys with you.' He sounded utterly incredulous.

'I didn't rightly know what to do, no reason to call *cops*,' said Mrs. Kraus. She looked at them a little resentfully. Mrs. Kraus was the wife of the manager of the old apartment building on Mariposa Street, where Mrs. Edna Manning had lived. *Had lived* was the operative expression.

'When one of my men came and asked your husband about Mrs. Manning, he didn't say anything about her having moved,' said Mendoza.

'Well, we didn't know, then. I don't *know* she's moved now, she didn't take all her clothes, and she never said nothing. But I been thinking it's funny, the way I never laid eyes on her after that day about three weeks back, I usually do see her coming or going, few times a week, anyway. What it is, see, she'd told Fred the bathroom faucets was leaking, but that man—I been after him to go fix 'em, but he says he's got other jobs and Mrs. Manning hadn't spoke about it again—well, she hasn't *been* here, I guess now—and upshot is it wasn't till Monday he got up to her apartment on that. When he comes back, he says looks like as if she was moving out, things gone. I was surprised, I went up to look. And sure enough, them little framed flower prints as were hers were gone, and the little china figurines she had standin' around, and the books she had on a little

240

shelf, and all the things from her vanity table, and then I looked in the closet and most of her clothes are gone and the two suitcases she had. But she never *said* anything when she come to pay the rent first o' the month, and it seems funny. Why should she just pack up and go off like that, not *saying* anything? And what in time have you cops got to do with it, anyways? I don't—No, she didn't take any furniture, acourse, the places are furnished.'

'I'll be damned,' said Mendoza to Hackett. 'What is all this?'

'Wait until you hear,' said Hackett. 'Will you tell the Lieutenant what you told me about the last time you remember seeing Mrs. Manning, please, Mrs. Kraus?'

'Well,' she began obediently, 'when we found she was gone, and in such a funny kind of secret way—almost like she was running away!—I did think back, and I pinned down the last time I saw her because it was second Saturday in the month, that's the day some of us all meet up in the Whiteheads' apartment to play Canasta or something. Mrs. Manning, she used to go out a good deal—woman living alone, you know, she'd go out to the movies, or shopping, or just up in the park. I'd see her coming and going. Well, anyways, I met her going out that day, I remembered clear once I thought back, it'd be about eleven-thirty, quarter of twelve. It was in the front lobby and she was all dressed up, she had that real fancy hat on—she likes hats, Mrs. Manning, nearly always wears one. This one, it's got a lot of red and blue satin flowers all around it, and a kind of high crown. I said hello to her and wasn't it hot, and told her she looked nice, and she said back, thank you, way a person would, you know, and that she was going out to lunch at a friend's house.'

'Did she mention the friend's name?'

'No, but then I wouldn't have known it. Mrs. Manning, she lived here close to five years, since she lost her husband, and acourse we was friendly like, but I didn't know her so well as I know the Whiteheads or the Cassidys. So I was upstairs all afternoon and then I come home, we got the front ground floor'—they were, in fact, standing in the open doorway of it now—'and I got supper, and I never thought of Mrs. Manning again until along about eight o'clock that night. Mrs. Mapps called, that's the apartment right next to Mrs. Manning's, and I went up—catch Fred, laziest man in seven counties—on account her Venetian blind cord got broke, and I fixed it up for her kind of makeshift, and it was just before I left there I heard Mrs. Manning's door open and shut, so I just think, well, she's home a bit late for her. But when I come out to go downstairs again, it seems she'd got home before and now she was going out again, because she was walking downstairs ahead of me. I was

242

surprised because she don't generally go out alone at night, except when she goes with this old gentleman takes her dancing, or some of her friends. But for all I knew, somebody was waiting for her downstairs. Anyways, I'm a bit slow on stairs, accounta my eyes, and by the time I get down to the lobby she'd gone—I heard the front door shut.'

'How was she dressed?' asked Hackett.

'Well, I couldn't see if she'd changed her clothes, but she had the same hat on. And now I think back—it's dark on those stairs—she could've been carrying the suitcases, in front of her like. Anyways, that's the last time I laid eyes on her, and I been asking everybody lives here, I can't find anybody did see her since about then. And what in time she should go and do such a thing for—'

Mendoza said, 'Two suitcases? In front of her—so you shouldn't see them, you mean? Did she know you were behind her on the stairs?'

'Sure, I called out and said, "Well, going out again tonight?" or some such thing, but she never answered. I thought then she didn't hear me.'

'But two loaded suitcases—rather an awkward—'

'I don't say she had suitcases; besides, it'd be just one big one and a little case, what she had when she come here—but she's a strong woman, Mrs. Manning is, stronger than a lot of men, you know. It'd surprise you, she isn't a big woman, maybe five feet seven or so, and not, you know, fat—but she used to be—what do they call it now, mass something?—where they massage people.'

'A masseuse?' asked Mendoza.

'That's right. When I had the flu last year she give me one after, said it could help a lot, and it did, but my, the strength she has in her hands! Wouldn't believe it. Now why do you suppose she's gone off like that? You don't think something's happened to her? Is that why you're here—cops?'

'I don't know,' said Mendoza. 'We'll want to look at her apartment.'

As they went upstairs, Hackett said, 'Are you thinking what I'm thinking, or are we both crazy?'

'*Loco*,' said Mendoza. '*Loco, absolutamente.* Why? Do we say she killed Tate? It's fantastic. Dismembered the body? The whole idea in that is usually to prevent identification. We've said here it could also have been blood lust. But—a woman? And she carts the body around—Why should she run out? Why—'

'Got cold feet. Realized we were bound to identify Tate eventually, and would find out she was Tate's luncheon guest.'

'We don't know that. She just said a friend.'

'Well, it looks fairly significant, doesn't it?'

'A *woman*,' said Mendoza. 'For all we know, this could be a different case entirely, damn it.'

'When she and Tate were old friends?'

'So why the hell would she—'

'Let's look.'

They looked at the apartment. It was an inexpensive old furnished apartment, the furniture cheap and shabby but looking well cared for except for a film of dust. And to trained eyes, the apartment told a story. Eventually they turned the lab boys loose in the apartment and found out more of the story. Somebody had evidently done a very hasty job of packing things up in the apartment: there was still the faint impress of a large rectangle on the neatly made bed where a suitcase had probably rested, a little shower of face powder had spilled on the bed and the carpet beneath, a bottle of Listerine had been dropped and broken in the bowl in the bathroom as articles were taken out of the medicine cabinet, and the things that were left were all the sort of things a woman wouldn't bother with on a sudden flight—a couple of mended cotton dresses, worn old underwear, stockings with runs, an old pair of bedroom slippers. In the refrigerator were a bowl half full of hamburger, some stale milk, half a loaf of bread, three eggs, half a pound of bacon, and a cube of margarine.

The kitchen shelves held a sparse supply of canned goods, breakfast cereals.

Then the lab boys came in, and the first thing they turned up was some blood. Not much, but enough to type. There was a little on the carpet in the bedroom, an elongated smudge, and another spot on a straight bedroom chair. It turned out to be Type O.

'If you want an educated guess, Lieutenant,' said Duke, who was one of the smartest lab boys, 'I'd say this. I don't think it's very likely she'd still have had any blood on the soles of her shoes after coming home from Tate's place ... My God, what a thing! What a hell of a queer—What it could be is that she still had some on one of the upper parts of her shoes and took them off there, or just stepped out of them, and the shoe fell over on its side. And she might also have had a little blood on something she took off and dropped into the chair.'

'For God's sake!' said Mendoza. 'I don't know that I buy this.' They were sitting around the office looking at the lab report; Duke had just come in with it.

'It doesn't look as if you've got any choice,' Duke pointed out. 'You've now got, I understand from Sergeant Hackett, a confirmation that Manning was going to have lunch with Tate—'

'Yes, yes.' Mrs. Tillinghurst had unexpectedly confirmed that, after a reporter with a nose for news had worked Mrs. Manning's disappearance into the Tate story. Mrs. Tate had mentioned to Mrs. Tillinghurst, that Saturday morning the art lovers met up in Barnsdall Park, that an old friend named Mrs. Manning was coming to lunch with her.

'And,' said Hackett, 'we haven't a witness who saw her arrive at Tate's, but she probably did. And we don't know what time she got back here, but—'

'Wet blood?' said Mendoza. 'That long after the murder? How long would it take her to get back here from Tate's?'

'Depends on the buses. It's about, what, twenty, twenty-five blocks.' Hackett considered. 'Half an hour at least.'

'I don't believe it,' said Mendoza. 'What I'd be more inclined to believe—and that's almost as implausible—is that she was a witness to the murder, lost her head, hurried back here, and ran on for fear the murderer would come after her.'

'You're woolgathering,' said Hackett impatiently. 'The killer let her run out? I don't care how far she'd lost her head, she wasn't out in the wilderness someplace, she'd have run for the nearest phone and called the cops.'

'If she was somehow involved in the murder, not as the killer but—Or with the murderer? Damnation, what possible

247

reason—'

'She has to be somehow involved, because there's the blood,' said Duke. 'I told you about the prints. Same confused mess we found at Tate's, and the Manning woman had never been printed anywhere either, evidently. So that's that. A lot of smudges on the furniture, and Fred Kraus's in the bathroom and Mrs. Kraus's in the living room and on the closet door.'

Palliser and Higgins came in looking excited and grim. They'd all done a lot of work on this incredible thing since it had turned up yesterday—they still were—and of course it was a bastard to work, nearly three weeks afterward.

'Got some more,' said Higgins, 'with that snapshot.' It had been Palliser's brain wave to ask everyone who had known Mrs. Manning whether anyone had a snapshot, and a woman named Marsten had, and furthermore, in it Mrs. Manning was wearing the same beflowered hat. The hat, which had a medium-narrow brim turned down, partly hid her face, but otherwise the snapshot was very clear and detailed—and it was a color snapshot. Mrs. Marsten had even been able to give them the negative. It showed a woman not young, but still attractive, brown-haired, a tallish slender woman, very good figure, with plastic-framed glasses and a pleasant smile. She was nice-looking but unspectacular: well dressed but not with glaring smartness. In other words, nobody would look at her twice.

'What?' asked Mendoza.

'A couple of people who remember seeing her that day. Five people on the block who saw her in this hat, but aren't sure of the day or time. One who is this fellow who has a little market a block away from the apartment, he marks the day and time—that Saturday—because it was the day he got his dog back. Dog had been missing a couple of days and he was worried as hell about it. Dog finally turned up at the pound, and the owner's name is on his collar, so they called him—'

'Dogs!' said Mendoza.

'Well, he says he knows what time it was because he was just closing the market, it was a few minutes after six. He saw Mrs. Manning—he knows her, she shops in his place—get off the bus at the corner, other side of the street, and start up toward the apartment building. It was practically dark, but he says he saw her pass under the street light there, he knew her. Went on to say he's been wondering if she was sick, as she's usually in sometime during the week and he hasn't seen her since. He didn't speak to her, she was across the street, but that must have been when she came home.'

'Came home after having committed

murder! With wet blood still on her—in a lighted bus! *¡Pues hombre!*'

'Just a little unnoticeable blood,' said Duke, who was enjoying all this. Talk about offbeat ones. If this was what it looked like, it was a dilly.

'Take it easy,' said Higgins. 'A woman named Pfeiffer who lives in a furnished room on the ground floor front, two doors down from the apartment building, apparently hasn't anything better to do than sit and watch the street. One of those nosy old harridans who knows everybody and their business. Her I just came to an hour ago. She saw Mrs. Manning leave the second time—and she says she had the suitcases. All right, swear. The old harridan claims she saw her clear, and the time fits with what Mrs. Kraus says—it was about eight, a few minutes past. She pointed out that there's a street light in the middle of the block, and she clearly saw Mrs. Manning—she knew her, too, she'd lived there for five years, after all—walk past, carrying one large and one small suitcase.'

Palliser said, 'We don't know what the ins and outs are, but it builds up, doesn't it? We can say for almost sure now Mrs. Tate was killed that Saturday afternoon. Because when Mrs. Manning came back to her apartment she left those bloodstains—'

'You'll never make a detective, John. We

250

don't know that. We don't know it was Mrs. Tate's blood. Manning could have been in her apartment on Sunday and it just happened nobody saw her.'

'You're dragging your heels, *compadre*,' said Hackett. 'It adds up like—Now, look, let's just take it step by step, how it *could* have happened. I talked to that Marsten woman, for instance. It seemed that Mrs. Tate, in Mrs. Manning's life, dated from when both their husbands were alive. Mrs. Manning had moved away from her old neighborhood to this apartment and lost touch with a lot of her old acquaintances. I sort of get the picture of an active, extroverted woman who kept herself busy, made new friends, and so on. She had a pension from the railroad of about three hundred a month, and her husband had left her some invested savings which bring in another hundred or so—'

'I got the same picture,' nodded Higgins. 'She liked to dance, had a lot of casual friends, no relatives here or any really close friends. And only a couple of those people knew Mrs. Tate, had ever met her or heard Manning mention her name.'

'All right, yes,' said Hackett, 'because Tate dated from another period in Manning's life. The Marsten woman is the only one I found who'd ever met Tate. Met her in Manning's apartment about six months ago—card party.

251

I asked what about the relations between them. She said it was hard to say, just one evening, but they called each other by their first names. She's a pretty shrewd woman, and she also said she thought it was one of those long-time friendships which was pretty much on the surface, though they were friendly—called each other "dear" and "darling" and—'

'Oh,' said Mendoza.

'Yes?'

'*Nada*. Go on, build it. I like to see an exhibition of making bricks without straw.'

'*Pues no*. All right, Manning goes to Tate's for lunch. They get to arguing over something—who knows what women argue over—'

'Men. George Barrington,' said Palliser. He grinned.

'It could be,' said Hackett. 'But he wasn't intending to marry either of them.'

'They didn't know that,' said Mendoza. 'I got the distinct impression from Mr. Barrington that he gets a great kick out of all these eager widows chasing him, and deliberately keeps them all on the string, just enough encouragement to keep them hoping.' He lit a cigarette. 'I thought I had a little inspiration a minute ago, but on second thought—this is *the* damnedest thing we've ever had since I've been sitting at this desk. I swear to God. A woman dismembering—'

252

'Inspiration?' said Hackett.

'When you said they called each other "dear." I don't know about Mrs. Manning, but that doesn't sound like Mrs. Tate to me. I just faintly wondered if there could be a Lesbian flavor to this. It would in a kind of way bring it into focus for me,' said Mendoza plaintively. 'Because the queers of either sex can get mixed into violence and generally offbeat situations rather easily.'

'There's not a smell of such a thing about either of them,' said Hackett. 'All right. I don't say they had a physical fight, but say they got excited and were tending that way, and Manning shoved at Tate, something like that, and Tate falls and hits her head on that heavy coffee table, *kaput*. And Manning panics when she finds Tate's dead. First off, knowing she can probably be placed there, all she can think of is to run. She comes home, packs up her stuff, sneaks out. Maybe takes a hotel room somewhere—we're looking—and then she gets to thinking, hell, what you said yourself at the start of this. Who's Mrs. Tate? Unimportant woman, no relatives, no close friends—If she can dispose of the body, hide identification, it may never be connected with Tate. Robinson's will think she just walked off the job, the Bessemers will think she just went away—irresponsible, sure, a few people will talk about it and then forget her, nobody's going to be all that interested in chasing her down. Manning must have done her planning in her own apartment, come to think, because after all, you can't get away from it, Luis—there is the meat cleaver.'

There was indeed the meat cleaver. Found in Mrs. Tate's house, and very definitely one of the tools used to dismember her body, and positively identified by Mrs. Kraus as a meat cleaver belonging to Mrs. Manning's apartment, while Mrs. Bessemer had said they supplied no meat cleaver in Mrs. Tate's house.

It did add up. And for oddities in homicide, it should take some sort of prize.

'So she parked her things somewhere and went back to Tate's house.'

'The plastic bags,' said Higgins sleepily.

'Yes, yes, I know,' said Mendoza. 'I just—'

The plastic bags had been brought in by Mrs. Marsten. She'd been asked, as a close friend of Mrs. Manning, to try to estimate what clothes were missing from the apartment; she had divulged the information that Mrs. Manning had been very meticulous about her clothes and always kept dresses, suits, skirts, in zippered plastic containers fitted over hangers. And such plastic containers would, of course, have been eminently suitable for transporting such items as chopped-off arms and legs and the head.

'... Took the meat cleaver with her and spent the rest of Saturday dismembering the

254

body and getting it into the car. We know she knew how to drive a car, though she hadn't owned one since her husband died. She lay low all Sunday, and on Sunday night she used Tate's car to dispose of the body. What odds do you give, when and if we find the rest of it, it won't be in plastic bags? Maybe when we drag the lake in MacArthur Park tomorrow—'

'I'm offering no odds at all. I don't think I'm so old-fashioned,' said Mendoza, 'as to cling to the foolish idea that all females are nice, sentimental, gentle creatures a hundred percent less subject to the ordinary lusts and temptations than the gross male, but somehow I still can't see—A meat cleaver, for God's sake.'

'I don't know, Luis,' said Hackett. 'You know, at one point in the Black Dahlia thing, there was this and that to suggest a woman did it. And you know what *that* corpse looked like—details we never released to the public—how the whole body was completely drained of blood, and severed right at the waist, and washed clean. My God.'

'Well. And after that, what? Why, when she'd gone to all this trouble, and for a woman it must have been the hell of a job—'

'She's a trained masseuse. A lot of developed strength in her hands. She'd also worked as a practical nurse.'

'All right. Why did she go on running

255

away? She couldn't know she wouldn't be missed right away. I see that, of course—everybody who phoned her, called on her, just assumed she was out temporarily. But why—'

'I'll tell you why. I think she's a canny one, and she meant to lie low until we'd given up on it, or picked up some nut who could have done it, or definitely failed to identify Tate—until time had passed. And then she'd have walked back, from an impulsive vacation trip somewhere, all wide-eyed and innocent, "What, poor May murdered? How terrible!" And I think now we've identified Tate and hooked Manning into it—maybe just by the fluke that Alison—'

'I'll never hear the *end* of it,' said Mendoza.

'—That she's taken off, and—'

'Abandoning,' said Mendoza, 'her nice steady pension and the other income. For good.'

'For God's sake, she'd have to! *El que gana, pierde*—who wins, loses,' said Hackett. 'You can see that.'

'I see it,' said Mendoza. 'I just don't like it, boys.'

He didn't like it worth a damn, but there was evidence staring them in the face, they had to start the routine on it. They put out a pick-up-and-hold on Edna Manning; early to get out a warrant for her. They traced her back; she'd been born in Chicago, had come

256

to California in 1941 and married John L. Manning in 1945. Her parents were dead; she'd been an only child. Her only relative was a female first cousin living in Galena, Illinois. They asked the police there to check, but she hadn't showed there and the cousin said they exchanged Christmas cards, that was all, she hadn't seen her in years.

By Sunday they had checked every hotel in the county (with the help of other forces) and hadn't turned her up or any smell of her.

They had, discouragingly, a very tentative identification of Edna Manning from a Greyhound Bus clerk at the main station on Spring Street. He said he had waited on a woman who looked something like that on a Monday morning about three weeks back. He wasn't definite about the week, or the time, but he did remember it was a Monday because, he said frankly, he'd had one hell of a hangover at the time. He didn't remember at all where she'd bought a ticket to.

So that could be, or it couldn't be. Of course, in a place this size—

It looked as if their cut-up-corpse thing had solved itself—after a fashion. It also looked as if Edna Manning wasn't going to be found very soon or easy.

And Mendoza went on not liking it.

Everything about it was logical, everything about it fit. You could imagine any two women having a quarrel and a fight. Over

257

anything. And true enough, needs must when the devil drives, and faced with the prospect of being tagged for murder, Manning would indeed have forfeited her modest income, changed her name, and run—to save her life, or at least her freedom. She could earn a living at her old job somewhere, or as a practical nurse. She could have run anywhere.

All they could do was put out a general call on her, nationwide, and wait.

They could also drag the lake in MacArthur Park. They did, and got nothing at all. They started dragging every body of water in the county, leaving the reservoirs until last, as practically all of those were heavily fenced in.

They hadn't got anything at all up to Tuesday morning.

★   ★   ★

'What with all this excitement over our female butcher,' said Jason Grace dolefully, 'I don't suppose you're too interested in my research on Emery Young?'

'I'm interested,' said Mendoza. 'I'd like to get that one, too, God knows. Have you heard that the woman who had the stroke died? Yesterday. That—*hombrate*, whoever he is, is morally responsible for three deaths if legally for only one. Was it Emery Young?'

'I couldn't say,' said Grace. He sat down and lit a cigarette. 'I'll just say that Emery's so-called alibis don't stand up so very well, Lieutenant. That girl he says he was with, the night Coleman died'—Grace smiled—'June Small, nothing against her, orphan, works at a Woolworth's on Hill, about nineteen—she says indignantly she's a respectable girl, she'd never let a boy come home with her. So—'

'She look as if?'

'I don't care to guess about females,' said Grace, still smiling. 'With these crazy hair-dos and all the eye make-up, even the respectable ones can look like whores. Who knows? Dave Durham backs up Emery a hundred percent, but that doesn't cover the relevant times, and besides who wants to take Davy's word for it? Birds of a feather—The bartenders are kind of vague on dates and times. So what do you think?'

'I think,' said Mendoza energetically, 'by God, we'll get one case cleaned up at least! I think, Jase, that Emery Young sounds like a very hot prospect for our boy who had the brain wave about burglarizing the pensioners. Where is he, still at Juvenile Hall? . . . O.K., let's bring him in and do some questioning in depth!'

'Earn our keep on one case,' said Grace. 'Let's.'

CHAPTER SEVENTEEN

'When did you first get the idea of breaking in on the old people, Emery?' Grace.

'I never got that idea. I didn't do that. I told you where I was them times you asked—'

'So where were you really, Emery?' Mendoza. 'Your alibis don't stand up just so well. The girl you said you were with that Friday night says no. Says she never let a boy come home with her. What about it?'

'She's lyin' to you—that bitch—she puts out for any guy in town, I swear!'

'Do you remember back to Halloween, Emery? That was when you pulled the first one, wasn't it?' Palliser. Back to the old routine, the heavy questioning, to confuse and cow the suspect. This was about the fourth time around for all these questions; it was all very damn tedious, and it was after twelve o'clock and they were all getting hungry. But Emery wasn't talking up defiantly and insolently, as he had at first. He was running scared, he licked his lips and shuffled his feet and looked at them one after the other fearfully, and now he was answering with the same words in a hopeless sort of way, as if he knew they weren't believing him, they were hardly listening to him. They had given him glasses of water and cigarettes, and nobody had laid a finger on him, but he was wearing a look that said he had strayed into a nightmare and didn't expect ever to wake up.

'When did you decide to pull the first one, Emery?' Mendoza

'I didn't. I didn't do none of those. Why won't you guys believe me? It wasn't me, it wasn't me.' He wasn't even bothering to swear any more; his head was down.

'We've got a description of who pulled all those break-ins, Emery, and it sounds a lot like you. We've got his prints. Suppose we compare them with yours.' Palliser.

'You can do whatever you want, it wasn't me.' As a matter of fact, the prints were undergoing comparison right now; all most illegally, they'd got Emery's off one of the glasses of water. 'It wasn't me! I don't dare—I don't dare—*It wasn't me!*'

The first little break. Something new added. 'You don't dare what?' asked Mendoza quickly.

'Nothin'. Nothin'. Why can't you leave me alone, you guys? Jesus, I'm not gonna say I did something when I didn't. Ain't I in enough trouble already?'

'Do you know who pulled those jobs?' Palliser.

'No. No, I don't know nothin' about it. Leave me alone, I got nothin' to tell you.'

'Do you know who it was?' Grace.

'No!' It was half a sob. 'Jesus, how long

261

you gonna keep me here? I didn't do it!'

'Was it Dave Durham?' Mendoza.

'No, it wasn't Dave.'

'Then who was it?'

'It wasn't me. I didn't do them jobs. I didn't kill that old lady. I didn't—'

'But you know who did!' Mendoza pounced on him. 'Is that what you're telling us?'

'I ain't telling you a thing,' muttered Emery Young. He huddled miserably on the straight chair, with the detectives grouped around him standing. Emery's white shirt was stained with sweat; the men were tense and tired. But maybe they were getting somewhere. They didn't let Emery see any surprise at this new twist; they just kept pounding at it.

'Who did it? Was it somebody you know around where you live?' Mendoza.

'No. I don't know.'

'Do you know his name? How do you know he did those jobs—he tell you?' Grace asked.

'I don't know, I don't know, I don't know.' And suddenly Emery Young put his face in his hands and began sobbing. They watched him in silence. When he blew his nose and looked up, Grace moved in a little.

'Was it one of your pals down there—you don't want to give him away? Take your choice, Emery. If you don't put a label on him, we'd just as soon take you for it. You match the description.' Maybe Emery wouldn't know they hadn't enough evidence to charge him on that. He was only one of the just-possibles.

'You can't do that! I *told* you where I was—Why can't you leave me alone, damn you? Why can't—'

'Because we've got a job to do, you stupid lout!' said Mendoza hardly. 'Do you know who pulled those jobs? Don't lie to me or I'll—'

'*Do you think I wanna get killed?*' screamed the boy suddenly. And then he put a hand across his mouth. 'I never—' But he had said it.

'All right, who was it?'

'What's his name?'

Emery was silent.

'Who was it?'

Quite suddenly and oddly, as if they were the only two present in the room, the boy turned to Jason Grace. 'What—what will I likely get for that mugging, you think?'

'Well, it's a second count and you're on probation,' said Grace easily, 'I should think you'll get put away. Until you turn eighteen, and then come up before the bench again.'

'Where'd I get sent?'

'Probably the Sheriff's Honor Farm.'

'Oh. Oh. And—and—whoever you get—for them jobs he wouldn't be—the same place?'

None of them smiled. 'Not by a long shot, Emery,' said Grace. 'You know who he is?'

Emery nodded in a subdued way. 'It was Olly Fisher—Oliver Fisher,' he whispered. 'Dave and I both knew that—on account—we run into him one night long while back last summer, at Angelo's it was—he's a guy to stay away from, Olly, but some reason, he was a little high, he was acting friendly that night. He sat with us awhile, at a booth. He was talkin' about maybe pullin' some jobs, like boasting in front o' the girls, you know. And he said—he said he'd thought up a real smart way to do it, pick on real old people who wouldn't show any fight. Just in and out, he said, real easy, and a lot of old folks are like misers, you know, maybe got a lot hid away. When—when that first thing happened, I and Dave both knew it was Olly. But he's nobody to cross, Jesus, no, he's a mean one, Olly is. He find out I ever told you, I be dead, no lie.' He looked at them anxiously.

'We won't tell him, Emery. Do you know where he lives?'

'Somewhere on Union Place, I think.'

'All right,' said Mendoza. He straightened up tiredly; he never enjoyed these sessions, and he thought maybe age—or this other crazy case bugging them—was turning him short-tempered. It was all pretty stupid, but

264

you couldn't expect much else from the Emerys. 'All right, Emery,' he said. 'Don't worry about Olly, we'll take care of him.'

'Yeah,' said Emery. 'You gonna send me back Juvenile Hall now? I don't wanna be anywhere here when you bring him in.'

'Sure,' Mendoza went out to see if anybody else was there; Piggott had just come in. 'Matt, we've had a little session in here and we're all starving to death. You like to ferry this kid back to Juvenile Hall for us?'

'Sure,' said Piggott obligingly. 'Do us any good?'

'We broke the case,' said Mendoza. They turned Emery over to Piggott and he took him out. 'Let's go have lunch before we tackle Olly, boys. He sounds as if he's a little proposition.'

'Well, at least it'll be three to one,' said Grace.

* * *

Contrary to Emery's predictions, they picked up Olly Fisher without any trouble. They found him at home watching TV.

Certainly Olly Fisher matched their description nicely, right down to the tattoos on both arms. He also matched the private description Mendoza had built up on him; his I.Q. was probably under eighty, and he had a naturally mean disposition. He was seventeen years old and he lived with his divorced mother, who earned a living cleaning offices at night.

All his mother said, dully, was, 'He's allus gettin' into trouble, bullying the younger kids. I dunno why he does. I dunno why he's got to get into trouble all the time. What's he done now?'

It wasn't any trouble at all, breaking Olly Fisher down. He was too surprised they'd ever dropped on him for it, he'd thought he was too smart. Hadn't even known enough (*anybody* ought to know that, said Grace plaintively) to wear gloves, and now they had some hands to compare the prints with—When they told him the prints off those various screens turned out to be his, Olly agreed that that kind of proved he'd been the one. First he asked if that little bastard Dave Durham had steered them onto him, and when they said no, he sat thinking painfully for a moment and then smiled.

'Anyways,' he said, 'you can't do much to me for it. I'm not eighteen yet. You can't send me anywheres like San Quentin.'

'As you'll find out,' said Mendoza, 'they can do plenty, Olly. Plenty.'

'I can't figure how you got to me,' said Olly. 'Oh, yeah, yeah, the prints. But how'd you *know*?'

'We saw it in a vision, Olly,' said Grace solemnly. 'Don't you know the odds are

266

always on the side of the do-gooders?'

They charged him and took him over to Juvenile Hall. Then Mendoza called Robbery, asked for Goldberg, and told him his victimizer of the pensioners was under lock and key at last.

Goldberg sneezed and said, 'What? . . . Oh, that. Take you all this time to catch him, Luis?'

'You are so tactful,' said Mendoza.

* * *

That day most of the papers had run that snapshot of Edna Manning and announced that she was wanted urgently by the police for questioning in the Tate murder case.

About four o'clock Hackett took a phone call: a man said, said Sergeant Lake, he had seen the woman. The man turned out to be, of all people, little Mr. Parker, who had seen Mrs. Tate in the bakery at eleven-thirty that Saturday morning. He now said that, having seen the picture in the papers, he recognized this other woman. Having done his own shopping that morning, he had walked back up the block at about twelve-twenty, and seen that woman, 'in the hat all over flowers,' walking on the other side of the street.

'Toward the Bessemers' and Mrs. Tate's?' said Hackett. 'Well, why on earth didn't you say so before, Mr. Parker?'

267

'Nobody,' said Mr. Parker with dignity, 'asked me about this other woman before.'

So that really tied in Manning.

★　　★　　★

Palliser was just about to leave the office, at six o'clock, when Sergeant Farrell, who had just relieved Sergeant Lake, said somebody was asking for him on the phone.

'Palliser.'

'Oh, I'm glad I caught you, sir. This is Edmund Whittaker.'

'Who?' said Palliser. The name was vaguely familiar, but he couldn't—

'Whittaker—I'm the mail carrier you talked to.'

'Oh! Oh, yes—how are you, Mr. Whittaker?'

'Fine, I just called to tell you—in case it *is* important—it worried me, you know, silly little thing, but I've just got the kind of mind, I like to get things *right*. You know I told you that Tate woman got a Christmas card from someplace in Iowa, and the town's name was just exactly the same as one of the dairies around here, only I couldn't—'

'Yes?' Palliser yawned. It had been a tiring day.

'Well, you said Knudsen and I said it was. But the more I thought about it, the more I thought it wasn't. And I tried to sort of look

268

back and *see* the postmark, but it wasn't any good until today one happened to pass me on the street, one of the dairy trucks, I mean, and just like a flash I remembered *that's* what it was, sure.'

'What was?' Palliser yawned again.

'It wasn't Knudsen at all, it was Jessup. Just the same as that big Roger Jessup dairy over in Glendale, you know, Jessup, Iowa.'

'Oh,' said Palliser. 'Well, thanks very much for letting us know, Mr. Whittaker.'

'Not at all,' said Whittaker. 'I'd like to get things *right*.'

★   ★   ★

Higgins had dinner out and went home. Tomorrow, thank God, he'd be off. At seven-thirty he called Mary Dwyer and asked cautiously about the piano teacher.

'Oh, she's fine—a very nice woman, Laura liked her right away, and she listened to Laura play and said definitely she'd take her at a reduced rate. I really can't thank you enough—'

'Just—er—coincidence, running across her,' said Higgins. 'Any little thing I can do for you tomorrow? I'm off.'

'I know, I thought—well, we all thought—maybe you'd like to come to dinner, Sergeant? It was so thoughtful of you to remember Laura—it'll just be pot luck,

I'm afraid—'

Higgins quite suddenly felt as if he'd won the Irish Sweepstakes. He managed to say, 'Thanks very much, Mrs. Dwyer—that's very nice of you. What time?'

*   *   *

Mendoza went home and found the twins still up, still absorbed in their race-course gambols and distracting Mrs. MacTaggart, who was supervising dinner. He helped Alison corral them; she told him distractedly that Bast had disappeared. 'She's *always* in by three, for good, but I've called and called and—'

'¡*Porvida!*' said Mendoza, alarmed, and went out hunting. He searched all her favorite spots, up and down the block, calling; his darling Bast was the senior cat, the only one before her *mésalliance* with the Siamese tom, and this was Crisis as much as if one of the twins had been missing. At eight o'clock he found her, stuck firmly at the top of a Douglas spruce some *condenable* moron had planted at the corner of the next block. To all blandishments and coaxings she was impervious; she only kept announcing plaintively in her soft Abyssinian voice that she was Simply Too Terrified.

Mendoza called the Fire Department. They came and put up a ladder. 'Be careful,' he said anxiously. 'She's very timid, she won't—'

'Mister,' said the fireman cynically, 'I got cats outta trees before.'

Eventually he backed down the ladder clutching Bast, outrageously, by the scruff of the neck, and Mendoza received her tenderly.

'*¡Pobrecita!*How long have you been up there, you little *idiota*? Thanks very much—I'm sorry you—'

'Mister,' said the fireman, contemplating a series of long red scratches on one arm, 'I got cats outta trees before.'

Bast rode home in Mendoza's arms, was exclaimed over and scolded, ate an enormous meal of fresh-cooked chicken livers, and curled up on Mendoza's discarded jacket. Unprecedentedly, she was not disturbed to have the jacket removed for tidy hanging.

His household intact, Mendoza brooded over Edna Manning.

★   ★   ★

On Wednesday morning, the twenty-seventh of January, at about eleven o'clock, Mr. Sidney Shaw climbed stiffly out of his ten-year-old Pontiac at the gate of the Ockwood Cemetery in Charsworth and started out to visit his wife's grave. He had with him a large untidy bunch of mixed garden flowers from his own yard, some his wife had planted herself. He was a

271

sentimental man, Mr. Shaw, and January twenty-seventh had been his wife's birthday. He also had with him the miniature Schnauzer, Fritzie.

He and Fritzie walked into the quiet cemetery. The grave was at the far end. He let Fritzie off his leash; this was an isolated place. Maybe some people—some people had funny ideas—wouldn't have approved of Mr. Shaw bringing Fritzie to the cemetery, but his wife had loved Fritzie and Mr. Shaw figured he had as much right to come visiting her grave as he had. He knew Gertrude wasn't *here*, but it was just—well, maybe, sentiment.

So he found the grave and laid the flowers on it, and he didn't especially feel like praying because he knew Gertrude was still somewhere and he figured all that was best left up to God, but he stood over the grave a minute, remembering Gertrude and being thankful he'd had her, and the kids turning out so well and all, the years of his life, he was sixty-nine and still doing pretty well—And then he turned away and called Fritzie.

Fritzie was digging energetically, and into what looked like a newish grave. 'Hey, boy,' said Mr. Shaw, 'no! Bad! Come here!'

'Woof!' said Fritzie, and went on frantically digging.

Mr. Shaw went to get him. Just as he came

up, Fritzie stopped digging and nosed at something there interestedly.

Mr. Shaw glanced at it, fastening Fritzie's leash, and then looked again. The hairs rose on his neck; he looked hastily away. This was a grave, for sure—new headstone, could see it'd just been put up—*Margaret Elsa Campbell, 1899-1965*. But Fritzie hadn't dug more than six inches, a bit more—and besides, a coffin—

Mr. Shaw looked again at the object Fritzie had uncovered. 'My Lord Almighty!' he said suddenly, remembering that thing in the papers. And then he started in a hurry for the cemetery custodian's little building.

CHAPTER EIGHTEEN

At about noon, just as Mendoza was beginning to think about lunch, Sergeant Lake said somebody at the Van Nuys station wanted to talk to him. He picked up the phone.

'Mendoza here ... What? ... Found a—¡Vaya por Dios!—Art! John! As you were, we're heading somewhere besides Federico's ... Yes, Sergeant ... Where? ... I will be damned! ... Yes, I see. Listen, for God's sake, don't touch it, just post some men there and we'll be right out ... What? ... Well,

273

that's not very damn likely, is it? Even in a metropolis as big as this, to get two dismembered corpses at once—I refuse to think of such a thing ... No, it's got to be hers—we'll be right out.' He slammed down the phone. 'No lunch,' he said to Hackett and Palliser, 'or sandwiches to take with us. Dog turned up Tate's head out in a cemetery in Chatsworth.'

'Well, I'll be damned,' said Hackett mildly. 'Nice relevant spot for it. Why the hell Chatsworth? It's at the other end of the county.'

'Maybe why,' said Palliser. 'About as far from Echo Park as she could get—disposing of the corpse overnight.' They were already on the way. Mendoza swore, turned back, and told Lake to dispatch an ambulance and a lab man.

'Could be. It was evidently a new grave, soil loose and easy to dig in.'

'I wonder if the rest of her is there too.'

'That's what we're going to find out,' said Mendoza.

'Hell, we'd better take two cars. I've got to be in court at three—that Gonzales woman is being arraigned and I told George I'd stand in for him, his day off. Damn.'

They took the Ferrari and Hackett's car, the new Barracuda. Hackett had, three months back when he got out of the hospital, had to buy a new car because the Ford had been a total loss after rolling off that cliff; he'd intended sensibly to buy a family sedan, at a price he could afford; but the first thing that had hit his eye in the show room was that Martian-looking Barracuda, with its rear wall of glass, and half an hour later, somewhat dazedly, he had parted with the insurance check and a personal check for more than he should have spent, and next day come and collected the car. Its spectacular features were enhanced by the fact that it happened to be a screaming scarlet. Angel had not been amused, even when he pointed out how conveniently the collapsible rear seat folded down to make a platform for the children.

Mendoza, looking at it where it was sitting next to the long black Ferrari, said, 'Keep behind me. I don't want to be blinded. It's the Ockwood Cemetery on Andora Avenue.'

The Ockwood Cemetery was almost on the county line, way out at the end of the San Fernando Valley. There were two squad cars parked outside the gates and a man waiting to guide them—it was a fairly large cemetery. The ambulance pulled up as they started in, and another car with Duke in it. They all walked up to Margaret Campbell's grave. With the three uniformed men there stood a tall lanky old man in tan work clothes, who was introduced as Ben Watts, the chief custodian.

'Hell of a thing,' said one of the Van Nuys

275

men. 'Give you the creeps. And I don't think you'll get much from it. It's—pretty far gone.'

'This here part o' the grounds,' said Watts, 'you mightn't think so, but it's damp. I figure there's maybe a couple natural springs down there.'

'Mm.' They squatted and looked at the head. It was badly decomposed; it looked as if it had been buried much longer than nearly three weeks or so, but Mendoza refused to believe in a second, as yet unfound, dismembered body. It just wasn't reasonable. Edna Manning—or whoever—had had a car available, and could just as well have driven out here that night. Why here? Well, first things first. He said, 'We'll get plenty from it. First thing we'll get, at last, thank God, is formal identification. You did say you'd seen her dentist, John?'

'I did.' Palliser stood up; let the technicians who were used to it deal with *that* sort of thing. 'Had a little trouble—finally Mrs. Bessemer remembered recommending the one they go to. He gave me a dental chart, Bainbridge has it.'

'Good.' The head was not a very nice sort of thing to look at, even half covered with dirt; they stood back and let Duke and the ambulance men at it. 'Now—Mr. Watts? Do you remember when this grave was dug and filled in?'

'Sure. Funeral was on the eighth, a Friday it was. Not a very big funeral, wasn't more 'n ten people at the graveside. I understand she was an old maiden lady, no relatives. It was a lawyer gave orders to put up the headstone, men only come and put that up last week.'

'I see.' So there'd probably have been nobody interested enough to revisit the grave since the funeral, and the men who put up the stone wouldn't have touched the actual grave. The soil had been seeded and patches of grass were starting to spring up, but it wasn't nearly covered. 'Well,' said Mendoza, 'we're really going to search this place, because it's just possible the rest of the body's here too. I want some more men. Be quicker and easier to get them from your station—' He looked at the Van Nuys men. 'Unless you're too busy.'

'I'll call in. Probably they can chase a few cruisers over, Lieutenant. This is a big place to search, and trees and bushes, too—' But obviously the blond young man, young enough to be a rookie, was excited at being in on a big case.

They got, in the end, seventeen men and started combing the entire cemetery methodically. It was a newish one, but a landscape artist had come in and planted grown bushes and shrubs, a few trees: there were plenty of places to hide a pair of arms and legs. The first place they looked, of course, was in Miss Campbell's grave. They

277

dug it up almost down to the coffin, and found nothing. Ben Watts remarked that that would sure set back that grass, and he'd better reseed it.

At two o'clock Mendoza left them still hunting and drove back downtown to offer the police evidence at Mrs. Gonzales' arraignment for murder. That was part of the nuisance of police work too; after a thing was all done from their point of view, the paper work filed away, when they were busy on something else, they had to drop everything and go to court on a dead one, wasting time. The procedure, when the judge finally got to it at three-thirty, took exactly twelve minutes. The court-appointed public defender offered a plea of Not Guilty by reason of mental incompetence, and the bench ordered her held for trial, and Mendoza went and had a sandwich. He debated whether it was worthwhile driving out to Chatsworth again and decided it wasn't; by the time he got there, there'd be only about an hour of daylight left.

He called Bainbridge. 'Oh,' said Bainbridge, 'the head. Well, I'm afraid I can't get to it for a while, Luis. Tomorrow sometime. I've got that stabbing victim from last night to post, pure formality but it's got to be done, and a suicide Hollywood sent down, and that fellow the Harbor Patrol found on the beach. Besides, that head—well,

278

for God's sake, we know whose it's got to be, don't we? Pure formality too. I mean, I know the crime rate is going up, but even in L.A. we don't get dismembered corpses every day—or every year ... Yes, I've got her dental chart. I'll send you a formal report when I've checked it. After all, there's no particular hurry—you don't seem to be catching up to the Manning woman very soon.'

'You're so encouraging,' said Mendoza.

Hackett and Palliser came in at six-thirty. 'Nothing,' said Palliser. 'We're going to do it all over again tomorrow, just in case we missed something, but I don't think we did. What about the head?'

'We don't know yet. Bainbridge is busy, and as he so rightly says, there's no hurry. I had an acknowledgment from the Chicago boys, they said they'd check the neighborhood where Manning lived there before, ask around, but—'

Mendoza passed a hand over his jaw, which was showing black stubble at this hour of the day, and said, 'I'm still dragging my heels on this, but even I can see that at least we want Manning to question. We—'

'With the body identified by the head, I think we've got enough to charge her,' said Hackett.

'I want to hear the D.A.'s opinion on that. But let's think now, Manning couldn't have

279

had much money on her—¡*media vuelta!*—she had that two-fifty in cash Tate had meant to buy the car with, my God. Of course. That would have taken her anywhere across the country. But the woman's got to support herself. Masseuse. Practical nurse. More likely nursing, because I think a masseuse would have to show credentials, and even in New York or somewhere somebody might recognise the name—'

'So where's to look? My God,' said Palliser, 'don't I know, any woman these days who puts an ad in the classified saying she's a practical nurse, she'd get fifty jobs offered her inside twelve hours. I had to keep my mother in the hospital an extra week, till I found one. By scouring the county.'

'They dragged Hansen Dam today,' said Mendoza irrelevantly. 'Nothing.'

'Well, I'm going home,' said Palliser. He looked down at himself; his suit was rumpled and earth-stained where he'd been crawling around under bushes, and he'd torn his shirt on some thorns. 'My God, the things we have to do.' He added good night and marched out.

'Have you grown to that chair?' asked Hackett.

Mendoza yawned. 'I can't,' he said, 'get a picture of the woman, that's all. I think I'll go and call on a couple of her friends tonight. You said that Mrs. Marsten seemed to know

280

her pretty well.'

'I thought so.'

'Mmh. Well, I suppose we'd both better go home,' said Mendoza. They sat on of inertia a minute and then both stood up. 'How do you like that—that poor man's racing model?' Mendoza asked as they waited for the elevator.

'Oh, very nice, very nice indeed. I have to watch the speed, you know, I'm not used to acceleration yet. You've certainly got it when you want it. And look who's talking.'

'I operate on the principle,' said Mendoza, 'of buying the very best on the market and driving it until it falls to pieces.'

'Yeah, but you can afford to buy gas for a twelve-cylinder engine,' said Hackett.

*　　*　　*

Mendoza cornered Alison in the living room after dinner and took her book away from her. The twin monsters were peacefully asleep, the cats were disposed here and there about the room, and Mrs. MacTaggart—who had taken over the household as well as the twins—was busy at something in the kitchen, singing to herself in soft Gaelic.

'I cannot,' said Mendoza, 'understand the emotions behind this thing, that's all. I thought I knew quite a lot about women—'

'Entirely too much,' said Alison.

281

'But these two baffle me. Now, you are a woman.'

'*Innegable*,' said Alison. 'True.'

'So explain these two to me.'

Alison was silent a moment and then said, 'What you mean is, you don't understand the relationship between them. That's not surprising, *amante*. You understand women—any given woman—from your viewpoint, and while—well, let's go back and qualify that, you see through a woman *as* a man, and while you're a very perceptive man, my darling, you *are* a man. Again *innegable*.'

'Do I read a double meaning—'

'We are talking about women. Relationships between women,' said Alison thoughtfully, 'can be awfully funny. And run the gamut of feelings. Men, well, you like a man or you don't, and unless he happens to be actually rivaling you for a girl or a better job or something, you don't *automatically* regard him as a rival. But that's the premise women start from, though it can be quite unconscious. We are still—*both* sexes, no funny ideas!—fairly uncivilized socially, when it comes to the basic things. Take a couple of pretty girls—'

'I'd prefer them one at a time,' said Mendoza, admiring the copper gleam of her hair where the lamplight fell on it.

'You asked a serious question—¡atención! A couple of pretty girls, they may be good

282

friends but unconsciously they are rivals for any attractive man who may come along. They might stop being good friends then, or quite likely they'd go on pretending like mad on the surface they *were* friends, while going all out to get the man first. Or suppose one of them gets married. Well, the other one might think the husband was dull as ditchwater, the last man on earth *she'd* ever want to marry, but the fact remains that a nice safe marriage is a major goal to a woman, and the married friend has thus automatically moved a step farther up the ladder and is now superior to her friend, and don't think both of them don't know it! It's never mentioned, they're the same friends on the surface they always were, but it's there. And on the other hand, especially in this year of grace of relaxed morals, if you want to get fancy, the minute a woman acquires a husband she's got property to protect, and any unmarried woman who is fairly attractive and fairly young is immediately suspect, because there's no way of knowing what the state of her morals may be. She may look as respectable as can be, and be playing around in her off time with one man or a dozen—in which case she may not care whether the men happen to be husbands.'

'This is all no news to me.'

'No. The point is,' said Alison, 'if I can explain it—Well, you take Angel and me.

We're good friends, I think. But it's a lot more *complex* relationship than the one between you and Art. You don't think about Art's emotions, or he about yours, you know each other so well you just take each other for granted as being *there. And* that relationship wouldn't ever change. Whatever happened.'

'Whereas yours with Angel could.'

'Oh, my, yes,' said Alison. 'Oh, yes. Let's suppose that tomorrow morning on your way to the office you meet a drunk driver and get killed.'

'*¡Dios me libre!*'

'Yes,' said Alison. 'Well, I get all sorts of sympathy and because Art was such a close friend, from him especially. Angel, too, of course. And because he'd feel sorry for a woman alone—even with all the money, you know—he might easily drop in occasionally to ask how things were going. Well, I've turned into a lone woman again. I'm a potential menace to Angel. We'd act the same to each other on the surface, but there'd be a big difference. Or suppose Art has the accident on the freeway—knock on wood—there's Angel with the kids to bring up, we're sorry, we know it's no fun being alone, we ask her up to dinner—and the first thing you know, I'm looking at her and thinking she's really a very pretty girl *and* nearly four years younger than me, and you and I have been married three years and a bit and you're getting rather

284

used to me and maybe it'd be just as well if I didn't ask Angel to dinner quite so often after all.'

'Females,' said Mendoza. 'She's a nice girl, *cara*, but—'

'But you never do know about men,' said Alison. 'And then, something else—going back to marriage. It's not so easy for a middle-aged woman alone. Any way. Most of them want desperately to marry again. Not just for a man, not just for the prestige, though that's a big factor, but money, money, money, and I don't mean they're all greedy. They want the *security*. Stability—and somebody around to talk to when they're feeling low, and somebody to have their meals with instead of a book. And they haven't got much more time before any chance will be behind them, and they'll be old women without anything new to hope for. And I don't suppose even a man would subscribe to the—mmh—TV-fostered notion that a woman like Mrs. Tate, just because she was in her forties and not very pretty, and so on, couldn't possibly be at all interested in S blank X.'

'Not even me. In fact, they do say—'

'Yes. I can very, very easily see,' said Alison, 'those two women quarreling violently, even having a physical fight, over some man. If matters really came to a head between them. It was about the last chance for both of them—especially Mrs. Tate. Neither of them had much money. They'd both been after this Barrington man—there could easily have been another, more attractive man on the horizon—Tate had actually said she expected to remarry soon. And at the same time—being women—they could *easily* have still been on such surface friendly terms that Mrs. Tate would invite Mrs. Manning to lunch and Mrs. Manning would accept. For all we know—if there's another man, he could be leery of getting involved and lying low—for all we know, Mrs. Tate invited Mrs. Manning just in *order* to gloat over her, tell her she *had* captured a man. Which would be nothing flagrant, all girls together, "I'm so happy for you, dear." Women,' said Alison in an even more thoughtful tone, 'often aren't very nice people. I sometimes think.'

'Well, that's all very enlightening,' said Mendoza. 'You can see her cutting up that corpse?'

'That,' said Alison, 'would have been sheer self-preservation. At the risk of disillusioning you—if that's possible—I'd say, too, that the average woman can be about fifty times more cold-bloodedly logical, when it comes to a really important issue, than the average man.'

'Um—yes,' said Mendoza, thinking of Mrs. Gonzales. 'Do you realize, *cara*, that nearly every case we've been sweating over in

286

the last month had its roots of motivation in a woman? Dangerous, these females. Maybe Milton was right. "This fair defect of nature"—mmh, yes. I am now off to visit a woman. Will you be worrying hard about my moral state while I'm gone?'

'Not,' said Alison, 'until we've been married about another two years. I understand that's the danger period. Though you could be unpredictable.'

Mendoza laughed and leaned to kiss her. Then he straightened and rubbed the back of his neck and said, 'You're right, Angel is a very pretty girl—now you put it in my head.'

'And Art Hackett has six years, five and a half inches, and forty pounds on you,' said Alison. 'Go and call on your middle-aged widow.'

*　　*　　*

Mrs Marsten was, unfortunately, a middle-aged wife. She was an attractive brown-haired woman, neat and slender, with a pleasant low voice. She had also a good deal of common sense, and there was a minimum of 'Isn't it terrible?' and 'I just can't believe it.'

And she told him this and that about Edna Manning. She would, she said, looking distressed, hate to think that Edna would—But it was, she thought, possible.

287

Edna was a woman of short temper, a very decisive woman—not at all mannish, but when you knew her, you knew she was, well, a strong personality.

'I see,' said Mendoza. He got a clearer picture of the woman they were hunting. One of those quietly strong women, passive on the surface until something aroused her, maybe. A woman who, in a suddenly awkward situation, was capable of the lightning decision, and could carry it through coolly. Awkward situation—¡caray!—stuck with a corpse, and the clear realization that the only way out of it, the only way to avoid total involvement and prison, was to burn her bridges behind her, forfeit the steady income, and vanish. Hackett was probably quite right there—if they hadn't identified Tate, linked Mrs. Manning in, she'd have come back with a plausible excuse, quietly taken up her ordinary life again.

Now—

A lone, on-the-surface ordinary, not young woman. Where and how to start looking for her?

On considering all the evidence—the meat cleaver especially—he thought in all probability the D.A.'s office would say there was enough evidence to charge her and issue a warrant.

Once they had the official identification, from the dental chart and the head.

'Thanks very much,' he said absently to Mrs. Marsten.

★ ★ ★

He got to the office at eight-ten on Thursday morning. Grace was in, and informed him cheerfully that Tolliver was being arraigned sometime tomorrow morning so they'd have to get along without Jason Grace's invaluable services for a couple of hours. 'I found another interesting one to try, by the way. Very appropriate. Called the Los Angeles.'

'An interesting what? Oh, out of your book of drinks.'

'Um. Whiskey, lemon juice, sugar, a raw egg, and sweet Vermouth,' said Grace. 'Should be good for warding off colds. Everybody else, by the way, has gone out to search that graveyard again.'

'Why not you?'

'Why, Lieutenant,' said Grace, 'didn't you know we black folk just mortally afeared o' graveyards? I thought somebody ought to stick around to mind the store.'

Mendoza laughed. Sergeant Lake swung around from his switchboard and said tersely, 'You've got a new one. Squad car just called in. Man and woman shot—both D.O.A.— over on Werdin Place. Baby-sitter found them—she had a key. Woman was in process of getting a divorce, she says, a Mrs. Ruth

Fearing—woman takes care of baby while she's at work. Walked into the apartment twenty minutes ago and found Mrs. Fearing dead in bed with a strange man, also dead.'

'¡Ca!' said Mendoza.

'What about the baby?' asked Grace.

'How do I know about the baby?'

'Well, let's go find out,' said Grace.

CHAPTER NINETEEN

The baby was perfectly all right, yelling lustily to add to the confusion in the hallway outside the apartment door. A couple of uniformed men were guarding the door; the ambulance had just arrived and the interns were in the apartment.

'Let us through, please,' said Mendoza. 'We'll want to talk to some of you in a few minutes, but—'

'Musta been shots I heard, all right!' a thin man in undershirt and tan pants was exclaiming excitedly. 'I figured it was backfires, hell, what else could it—'

The apartment was small, and cheap, and old, and very shabby. They went through into the bedroom. The interns gestured, and said they supposed it'd be some time before they could take the bodies. Mendoza agreed: a lab team was on the way.

The bodies were on the bed, a double bed. There was a man, there was a woman. The woman had been a pretty blonde; she looked about twenty-five; she'd been shot once in the right temple. She was lying perfectly straight and composed. The man had one leg half off the mattress, and was slumped to one side, away from the woman. He had been a good-looking dark man with curly hair. Both of them were naked.

'Well, well, they will do it,' said Mendoza. 'She was asleep when she was shot. And the shot woke up the man, and he was just starting to get out of bed when X leaned over and shot him. Took two shots to get him.' The man had been shot in the back, high up on the right shoulder, and also in the back of the head.

'Um-hum,' said Grace. 'Not much we can do here until the lab boys finish.' They went out to the hall again and started to sort things out.

Mrs. Kedler was the baby-sitter. She was a placid-looking elderly woman, very clean and neat in a blue cotton house dress, and when she started to talk she went on and on in a slow unemphatic voice. That little Mrs. Fearing always seemed like such a nice girl—and a strange man in bed with her! Getting a divorce from her husband, she was, but a nice girl for all that—'She had to work, of course, she works at a Manning's coffee

291

shop on Sixth, so I take care of the baby for her. I'm on pension, earns me a bit more, and there's not much to taking care of a baby, I ought to go see to her right now, but—'

'You don't know who the man in there is?'

'Never laid eyes on him before. Such a shock I had—'

'He's not Mrs. Fearing's husband?'

'Well, I don't know. Never laid eyes on him either. She moved here after she started getting the divorce.'

'Then it could be Fearing?'

'I guess so.' She shook her head. 'That'd be terrible, if they'd just made up again and then got murdered, wouldn't it?'

The thin man was still excitedly announcing that he'd heard the shots. They asked him when. He thought around 1 A.M. He'd never laid eyes on the dead man either. This was an old building, fairly solidly built; nobody else had heard the shots. Nobody else who lived there had ever seen the dead man with Mrs. Fearing.

The lab men brought them his wallet; his clothes had been hung over a straight chair in the bedroom. By all the papers in the wallet, the dead man was one Howard Redfern, twenty-seven, and he worked for a nationwide trucking outfit as a driver. He had lived at a hotel on Flower Street.

'Could even have been a casual pickup,' said Grace.

They looked at the lock on the apartment door. It was an old lock, and not a very good one; it was no good now; somebody had forced it with a tool of some kind.

The baby stopped yelling; Mrs. Kedler was seeing to her. They questioned a few more people. Nobody knew anything, Mrs. Fearing hadn't lived there very long, only about three months. Seemed like a nice quiet girl.

When they could search the place, after the lab men had gone and the bodies were tagged and carted off, they found the address of an attorney in the woman's address book, and nothing much else to suggest a lead. Beyond, of course, the obvious lead they had.

'Estranged husband,' said Mendoza. 'Want to bet?'

'Almost bound to be,' agreed Grace. 'All the signs. He may be mad about the divorce, and 've got madder when he discovered Ruthie was making it with somebody else. But where is he?'

'Maybe the lawyer knows.'

They went to see the lawyer. He didn't know much about her except what she'd told him in order for him to file for the divorce. He had the husband's address, yes; had, of course, needed it for the record. Fearing had moved in with a friend, an apartment on Congress Avenue in Hollywood.

They went up there. Nobody was home,

but the manager told them where the friend, Pat Glosser, worked—at a garage in downtown Hollywood; so they went there. 'Cops and cab drivers,' said Grace, sighing, 'we do get to know the city.'

Glosser seemed surprised to see them. He said Hugh Fearing hadn't showed up last night. Sure, Hugh'd been living with him since his wife left him—Hugh's wife, that was, Glosser wasn't married, catch him.

'Well, where do you think he was? He say where he was going?'

'No, why? I figured he was with some dame, he's been after this one at the place he worked last, so when he didn't show I figured—'

'Does Fearing own a gun?'

'A gun? A *gun*?' 'Say, what is this? What the hell would he want with a gun?'

'Do you own a gun?'

'*Me?* What the hell would *I* want with a gun? No, I don't.'

'Do you know anyplace where Fearing could have had access to a gun? Any friends?'

'No, I don't. Say, what *is* all this?'

They told him. Then they drove back downtown and put out a pick-up-and-hold on Fearing. They had a look in Records and he didn't have a pedigree, so then they asked the D.M.V. what his plate number was—Glosser had told them he was driving a 1959 Chevy. He'd be picked up some time, maybe soon.

This was probably a very routine one.

Grace left for court to offer the police evidence on Tolliver.

Ballistics called at one o'clock as Mendoza got back from lunch. 'These slugs the morgue sent down a while ago,' said the voice from Ballistics. 'Man and woman found shot this morning?'

'Yes?' said Mendoza.

'It's a .22, that Ivor-Johnson Supershot. Eight-shot double-action revolver. We think it's almost a new gun, very few individual markings.'

'Mmh,' said Mendoza, taking notes. 'But when, as, and if we do come across it, you can match it up with the slugs?'

'Oh, sure. We can always do that, provided we *get* the slugs more or less intact.'

'Well, thanks very much.'

Well, wait until they picked up Fearing, see what transpired.

At two o'clock Higgins, Glasser, Palliser, Landers, Piggott, and Hackett came in, all looking tired and rather dirty, from the Ockwood Cemetery.

'Find anything?' asked Mendoza.

'We did,' said Hackett. 'After we crawled over every inch of that damned cemetery'—he felt his still bandaged shoulder wearily— 'George here, who is slightly smarter than the rest of us dumb cops, asked if we hadn't looked for tire marks outside the gates, and at the other entrance in back. The rest of us gently pointed out to him that there have been about twenty funerals held there since the head was buried, cars coming and going, but when George gets an idea in his head, mules aren't in the running.'

'I only said,' said Higgins, looking amused, 'that she might, even at night, have parked a little way down on the shoulder, while she reconnoitered, before she got in, and if there were any tire marks left, well, hell, we've *got* the car, it'd be another link in evidence.'

'So it would. Don't tell me you found any?'

'No, but I found something else,' said Higgins. 'There's a lot of wild country all around there, it's right on the county line, out beyond Chatsworth proper, and along the road it's mostly brush, sage, and so on, wild grass, a few bushes. And pushed down under a big lantana bush there, growing wild right next to the road, I turned up a plastic bag. Kind women use to put over clothes on hangers. Kind we found out Mrs. Manning used. And it was stained all over inside with what is probably blood. We left it off at the lab.'

'Oh,' said Mendoza. 'Another little link.'

'Link hell,' said Hackett. 'Anonymous plastic bag, Luis. Anybody can buy a set of them, three for a dollar twenty-nine, or something like that, at any of about ten thousand stores through the county. Not even a maker's name on the thing itself, only on the outer wrapping. We can ask the lab if a chemical analysis can pinpoint the manufacturer, and then try to find out what make Manning bought—who'd know? I'll bet you,' he added meditatively, 'if I called Angel right now and asked her what brand she buys—she puts them over my suit jackets, and blouses—she couldn't tell me.'

'But it's something,' said Mendoza. He looked at his cigarette and added suddenly, 'How did she get in if it was after dark, as it must have been? Aren't the gates locked at night?'

'We even thought of that—belatedly,' said Palliser. 'We went and asked Watts. And he got very touchy and said who the hell would want to get into a graveyard at night, and he didn't damn well know whether the damn gates had been locked or not—'

'In fact,' said Higgins, 'he sounded so touchy that I had another little idea, and there being some men working around, mowing the lawn, and so on, we went and asked them some questions, and do you know what? It turns out that Watts, who is the last man out and first man in—supervises all the care of the place—is definitely supposed to lock the gates at night. But he hardly ever bothers. He was caught in it once, a while back—a minister came by early before he got there, and found the gates unlocked, and I gather he nearly got fired over it. Which does seem a little funny. Why be so strict about locking up a cemetery?'

'Wasn't there that case—years back it was—' started Hackett.

Mendoza nodded. 'Some kids, one Halloween. Just fooling around, but if they hadn't managed to get into the Hollywood Cemetery, all trying to scare themselves to death, you know, feeling adventurous as hell—well, it ended up by a little girl getting knocked down against a headstone and fatally concussed. Quite a little uproar over the place being left open.'

'Oh, I see,' said Higgins.

Grace thrust his head in and said, 'Conference? The D.M.V. just came through with that plate number. Has Ballistics looked at the slugs yet?'

'Yes, it's an Ivor-Johnson Supershot .22 revolver. Almost new.'

'Oh.'

'What's this, not a new one?' said Hackett, feeling his shoulder.

'What else?' Mendoza filled them in on it and they all said, 'Oh, the husband.'

The inside phone rang. It was the lab. 'This plastic—er—bag,' said Duke. 'You can tell the boys it's blood on it, all right.'

'Yes. What type?'

'You workhorses may think we're miracle workers but we really aren't,' said Duke. 'I've

298

only had it a little while. I'll tell you what type in about four hours.'

'Oh. Well, thanks.'

'Don't mention it,' said Duke.

Mendoza passed that on. Palliser said suddenly, 'Yes, but how did she know?'

They looked at him.

'Know what?' asked Mendoza. 'Oh, my God, yes, how did she? That the gates would probably not be locked? ¡Porvida! Either I'm going senile prematurely or—' He reached for the outside phone, groping at the stack of phone books. He got, finally, Ben Watts on the wire. Was there a record of all the people buried at the cemetery? Of course there was, said Watts testily, got to be orderly even about dead people. Could it be seen, and where? Right there. Mendoza hung up. 'One of you chase back and look, *pronto*. This could establish another link. We've got a lot of names of people Manning knew—look for those. Also look to see if her husband just maybe is there. She could have attended a funeral there, overheard something—could have known the minister who'd once caught Ben Watts leaving the gate unlocked—I don't quite see how, but if there's any connection to be found at all—'

Higgins got up and said he'd go, he didn't mind. Hackett said he'd better be the one, Higgins the brain, he might get another little idea. Higgins grinned and went out.

'George seems very cheerful today,' said Mendoza. 'I wonder—' They all wondered.

As a matter of fact, Higgins was feeling cheerful because (A) he'd discovered that Mary Dwyer was a very good cook, and (B) he'd at least got the children calling him by his first name. He felt he was making progress.

*　　*　　*

They picked up Hugh Fearing at three-thirty, when he came back to Glosser's apartment.

Grace and Palliser had gone over to Redfern's address and found that he'd lived there for years, everybody knew him and immediately supplied his sister's name and address, so reluctantly they went there and broke the news. When she finally stopped crying and asked questions, she burst out angrily, 'All those *girls*! Howie was always running after some girl, not *nice* girls, you know—I *knew* sooner or later he'd get in some trouble—but this!'

She couldn't tell them anything; didn't even know Ruth Fearing's name, Howie had never mentioned it. So Grace and Palliser went back to base, and found Fearing there, undergoing questioning.

Fearing was a big hefty fellow about thirty, dark and good-looking in a very virile way. He seemed dazed, and was still saying,

'*Ruthie* dead? Ruthie *dead*? I can't take it in—The baby? The baby's all right?'

They asked questions, and eventually they got answers. The answers sounded discouraging. Fearing acknowledged that he hadn't come back to Glosser's apartment, where he'd been living, last night. 'I was feeling kind of low, the divorce and all, hell, I guess I couldn't blame Ruthie, I ain't been much of a husband to her, but—oh, hell, I guess I got nine counts on me, only got past eighth grade and all—it's kind of hard to get a job, a guy like me—'

'Last night. Where were you?'

'Well, I got to admit I tied one on,' said Fearing. 'God, I still got the damnedest head—*Ruthie* dead! *Murdered*—' It hadn't apparently penetrated his mind that they had tagged him for that. He sagged his head into his hands. 'I ran into a guy I useta pal around with, hell of a nice guy, Ray Scott, he's out of a job too, we was both feeling low, but he was pretty well heeled on account he'd had some luck at a poker parlor down in Gardena. So we started out kind of—you know—drinking big. Last place I recall, before I guess I passed out, was a bar somewhere down on Fourth. I dunno; anyways, I woke up this morning in Ray's place, and it turns out this pal of Ray's brung us both home—damn nice of him—and—'

Hackett and Landers went out on it; there

was still the tail end of the working day left. They found Ray Scott. Well, he had been drunk: he wasn't such a hell of a good witness. But then they found his other pal, whose name was Neil Smith and who happened to be one of the bartenders at the bar on Fourth Street, a big tough-looking customer who eyed them with aloof interest and answered questions economically.

'Good Samaritan, me,' he said succinctly. 'Ray's a good guy, and he don't tie one on often. Didn't know the guy he was with from Adam, but they seemed to know each other pretty well, and what the hell, it ain't no fun, night in the drunk tank. It was quitting time anyways, two A.M. I—'

'Had they been there long?'

'Since about midnight. I scouted around for Ray's car, and drove 'em both back to his place, unloaded 'em on the bed. Good Samaritan, me.'

'Well,' said Hackett, feeling resigned. And maybe the man at the apartment building hadn't heard the shots at 1 A.M., but if he had, then Fearing couldn't very well have fired them if he'd been getting fried in a bar at the same time. 'They were both passed out? Completely?'

Smith eyed him dispassionately and said, 'Mister, drunks I have seen plenty of. They was both out cold. But cold, man. If either of 'em moved a muscle before ten A.M. this

302

morning, I ain't standin' here talkin' to you now.'

Outside, Landers looked at Hackett. 'Not the husband,' he said dismally. 'Who?'

'Guess,' said Hackett. 'One, another of Ruthie's boy friends. Two, the boy friend of some girl Redfern had led up the garden path. He seems to have been a regular love pirate—something of a chaser, what the sister said.'

'Um. We just seem to be *getting* them these days,' said Landers. 'The teasers. The offbeat ones. I'm tired. I want to go home.'

'It's only a quarter to five,' said Hackett.

★   ★   ★

Dr. Bainbridge called at a quarter to five. 'This head,' he said. 'Death was undoubtedly caused by a massive skull fracture of the anterior region of the skull. I would guess, warily, perhaps a two-by-four or something even heavier—there were a few tiny splinters of wood still in the wound. No special skill was shown in cutting the head from the body.'

'Oh,' said Mendoza. 'Well, we said when we got the head we'd probably get the cause of death. She could also have been knocked down and hit her head on a piece of furniture?'

'Possible. I have sent the splinters to the

lab. The head,' said Bainbridge, 'is the head of a woman without much doubt, of between forty and fifty years of age. She had dark hair. I can't tell you the color of her eyes.'

'Blue,' said Mendoza.

'I don't know. The eyes are decomposed. I would have a guess, judging from the sample of soil where it was found, which you so thoughtfully enclosed, that the head may have been deceased from between two to four weeks.'

'Well, we know—'

'Do we?' said Bainbridge maliciously. 'I trust you'll be passing this on to the Van Nuys station.'

'Well, why?'

'It seems,' said Bainbridge, 'to be their pigeon. The teeth, Luis, my boy, are not the teeth of Mrs. May Tate. There is no resemblance between the teeth and Mrs. Tate's dental chart.'

'¡Diez millón de demonios desde el infierno!' said Mendoza violently. 'I don't believe it! I don't—'

'I do wonder,' said Dr. Bainbridge, 'where the rest of *this* one is.'

*　　*　　*

'I do *not* believe it!' said Mendoza. '*Two* dismembered bodies? *¡Imposible!*' He paced the office rapidly, trailing smoke behind him like an angry dragon. It was five-thirty. Hackett, Palliser, and Landers sat watching him glumly.

Two men from the Van Nuys station arrived, Roberts and Woodson. 'Lieutenant Mendoza? Did I understand you right on the phone? That damn head—you don't mean to say—'

'I do not understand anything about this at all!' said Mendoza. 'It is simply impossible and I don't believe it!'

'*Not* your dismembered corpse?' said Woodson. 'Just another middle-aged woman? Out in our territory? I'll be damned. Say—' He looked at Roberts. 'Say,' he said, 'I wonder,' and in unison they said, 'Elizabeth Wayne!'

'Elizabeth Wayne?' said Palliser.

'Reported missing by her husband about six weeks ago. Well, what the hell, Bob? She's forty-six, dark-haired. Did we get a dental chart on her?'

'I think Clint went out on that, yes.'

'Well, we'd better check,' said Woodson. 'My God, what a thing. Set you back a little on your job, Lieutenant.'

'I do *not*—Oh, for God's sake,' said Mendoza, 'I'm going home. I'm going home and I'm going to forget all about bodies and dental charts and people killing people and why the hell they do. My God. I don't *believe* it.' He took up his black Homburg and stuck

305

it slantwise on his head. 'I don't think I'll come back. Ever. I can take just so much of the absolutely impossible. *¡Qué disparate!* And this goddamned Fearing business on top of—I am going home.'

'It's a bastard, all right,' said Hackett gloomily. 'I know how you feel.'

'Have lots of fun with your bodiless head, boys,' said Mendoza to Roberts and Woodson, and he marched out of the office, lighting another cigarette viciously.

★　　★　　★

'The thing is simply not reasonable,' he said violently to Alison. It was not the first time he had said it during the evening. He clipped his trousers tidily into a hanger and hung them up.

'I know, darling, it seems so wild—a head without a body, and a body without a—'

'It's impossible,' said Mendoza. He hung up his suit jacket neatly on a hanger, stripped off his tie and hung it on the tie rack, wadded up his shirt and put it in the hamper.

'Sooner or later you'll—'

Mendoza shed his underwear and socks, dropped them into the hamper, reached for clean pajamas, and said, 'I refuse to believe it! The dismembered bodies do not show up once in years! It's—'

'Look, *amante*,' said Alison patiently, 'I

306

know, I know. But these things—'

The phone rang. Mendoza charged out to the hall to answer it. 'Luis, for heaven's sake, you're—' Alison snatched up his dressing gown and chased after him.

'Lieutenant? . . . Farrell. Sorry as hell, I just caught this note Higgins left to be relayed—he called in about six-thirty. Don't know what it might mean, but he says there's no record at the cemetery of a Manning or any of the other names, but there is a Millicent Barrington, funeral July of 1963. Common name, he said, but might be worth checking. I'm sorry I—Lieutenant?'

'¡*Válgame Dios!*' said Mendoza softly, and simply dropped the phone.

'Luis, you're stark—For heaven's sake what—' Alison replaced the phone properly.

'But how very simple,' said Mendoza, staring raptly past her shoulder. 'Two middle-aged women. *Two*—Where the hell are my clothes? Let me—' He turned and ran for the bedroom.

*   *   *

'What?' said Palliser. He'd been tired; he was just getting into bed. 'What?'

'That mailman, goddamn it! Whitman, Whittaker, whatever. What did he *say*, that town in Iowa?'

'Oh,' said Palliser. He yawned. 'Jessup.

Like the dairy farm over in Glendale.
Anything up, Lieutenant? What—'

'Me,' said Mendoza. 'I don't know, boy. I
don't for God's sake know. It's one of my
longest shots, by God. Yes, I'm at the
office—because that's where the teletype
machine is. My God, it'll be one A.M. there,
but maybe—just maybe—'

CHAPTER TWENTY

'Talk about long shots!' said Hackett
incredulously at a quarter to ten on Saturday
morning. Higgins, Palliser, and Grace had all
studied the teletype and were looking as
stunned as Hackett.

'I kept hearing how you had a crystal ball,'
said Grace in an awed tone. 'But this was
reaching out into thin air, Lieutenant—
mighty thin air.'

Mendoza had, the night before, had to
contact the Iowa State troopers and go
roundabout to reach the Chief of Police of
Jessup, which was a very small town. This
morning's teletype, evidently dictated to the
teletype operator at a state barracks, even in
its terse language conveyed a definite
bewilderment on the part of Chief
Hunter—and in a way, of course, one could
understand why.

EUNICE MAY TATE NEE TANNER NATIVE THIS COMMUNITY UP TO 1934 ATTENDED LOCAL SCHOOLS ET CETERA ONE SISTER MRS. BELLA VERRIL STILL RESIDENT HERE MRS. TATE RETURNED JESSUP EARLY THIS MONTH TO TAKE UP RESIDENCE WITH SISTER WHO IS WIDOW WHOLE FAMILY EXCELLENT LOCAL REPUTATION WHY IS LOS ANGELES INTERESTED HUNTER CHIEF OF POLICE JESSUP.

'*Tate?*' said Hackett. '*Tate* killed *Manning?* When did this—this great light dawn and how did you get there, for God's sake, and just how in the name of all that is holy did you pick Jessup, Iowa, out of this very thin air?'

'The questions answered themselves, boys, once I looked at the thing right way up—'

Hackett said simply, 'If this was a couple of hundred years ago, Luis, you'd have been burned for a witch long ago—which I've said before.'

'Two middle-aged women,' said Mendoza dreamily through a haze of cigarette smoke. 'We heard from everybody who knew them this and that about both. We heard, incidentally, that they were about the same size, but in almost every other way they were different. Mrs. Tate was rather plain, not a smart dresser, aggressive in a very obvious way, and so on, while Edna Manning was younger, better-looking, dressed smartly, liked to dance, always wore hats. Mmh—that hat—yes, that played an important part in all this. Well, I dragged my heels on it, but there was some nice clear evidence, wasn't there? It was Mrs. Tate who had vanished, leaving all her possessions behind—who had arranged to buy a car next day and never showed up. And her car was used to transport the body. Whereas it was Mrs. Manning's meat cleaver which had been used to cut up the body, and Mrs. Manning had also vanished—but taking practically all her possessions with her, so she had obviously vanished voluntarily. The whole setup, by the time we'd got that far, looked obvious. I was only dragging my heels because it didn't seem like a woman's job—but of course Alison's right, females can be fairly cold-blooded, and when your neck's at stake *anybody* can be—The only thing I don't yet see is why she went to *such* trouble to cover up what might be a second-degree homicide, if it was more or less accidental—But I trust we'll find out about that.'

'I still don't see how you got there,' said Hackett.

'I didn't, consciously,' said Mendoza. 'It was my subconscious mind, or inspiration, or something. So we find the head at last, we all heave a sigh of relief and think, we're that

310

much further on, now we can at least get a
formal identification and go ask the D.A.
whether we've got enough evidence on
Manning to get out a warrant on her. And
then Bainbridge knocked us flat on our backs
by saying it wasn't Tate's head, entirely
different from the dental chart. First, that
seemed to shoot the head right back at the
Van Nuys boys, because—as we said at the
time—Chatsworth is the hell of a long way
from Echo Park. And second, it set us back
on our cut-up corpse with the hell of a thud.
And third, it violently offended my sense of
logic. We don't often get dismembered
corpses, as I've been monotonously pointing
out all along. And when we find the
dismembered body of a middle-aged woman
in Echo Park, and the head of a middle-aged
woman even thirty miles away in Chatsworth,
a simple logical expectation is that they
originally belonged together. When
Bainbridge told us yesterday that they
didn't—or rather that it wasn't Mrs. Tate's
head—I suffered a kind of spiritual
dissolution. Because that made it all *too*
untidy—completely without form and void,
as it were. I said I didn't believe it. My mind
refused to accept it. Damn it, the body and
the head had even been deceased about the
same time. I know L.A. has the reputation of
being home base for some very peculiar—and
violent—people, but by God, I refused to

believe that within a few days of each other *two* people—lunatic or sane or whatever—had made up their minds to murder two different middle-aged women and dismember the bodies. The thing was ridiculous.

'And having suffered this—this spiritual shock treatment, I went blind on it. My God, I should have seen it right away, as soon as Bainbridge told me that! *Anybody* should have seen it! But I'd been struck blind, and I went home muttering about not believing it, and kept on muttering until Rory Farrell happened to find that message you'd left for him to relay, George. To the effect that a Mrs. Barrington was buried at the Ockwood Cemetery. And I stood there woolgathering, wondering whether it was our Mr. Barrington's latest wife and if so what it might say, and all of a sudden the dawn broke, and from thinking that both Tate and Manning had known Mrs. Barrington, I realized what I should have realized hours before—Bainbridge hadn't told us that the head and body hadn't originally belonged together. All he told us was that it wasn't Mrs. Tate's head. And everything fell beautifully together with an audible click in my mind.

'Because, you take two very different middle-aged women, dead, take their clothes *and their heads* away, and who is going to say which was which? As it happened, Mrs.

Manning didn't have any birthmarks, but even if she had had, quite possibly nobody would have known it, far less what it looked like if it was in a spot usually covered. Her husband was dead. She was well past the age when the girls get together, all giggles, to try on each other's clothes. Very likely not a soul had seen her—mmh—in the altogether for years. I don't know whether Mrs. Tate has any birthmarks, but the same thing applies there in reverse. Probably she hasn't. Anyway, as I say, suddenly I saw the thing back to front, as it were, and saw what a really beautiful little scheme it was. I'm really looking forward to meeting Mrs. Tate. Because, provided you can permanently dispose of the head, really there couldn't be much better cover for a murderer than getting the body identified as her own. *¡Muy lindo!* And of course, if she simply cut off the head, even we dumb cops might have got to wondering about that, so she had to turn it into the standard dismemberment case.'

'But damn it, she was *seen* going back to her apartment—the Manning woman—'

'*Como sí.* After dark, and wearing that very noticeable hat which everybody knew was Edna Manning's. She took some chances there, but it had to be done and she got away with it. I do hope,' said Mendoza, 'she's going to tell us the whole story.'

'And did your subconscious mind whisper

313

the little words Jessup, Iowa, to you?' asked Grace curiously.

Mendoza grinned. 'No, that was John. You remember the other day, John, you just happened to mention how that mail carrier called you back—one of those conscientious people—and corrected the name of that town? The only place out of the county, aside from junk mail, that Mrs. Tate heard from—and at that only a Christmas card. And I saw it was at least a gambler's chance that, one, it was her original home town, and two, that she had relatives and/or friends there, and three, that that might be where she headed to go to ground.'

'Now that I don't see at all,' said Higgins, wrinkling his brow.

'And you're all supposed to be detectives! Look at your own billfold, George, all we have to carry around with us these days! And then think what she had to walk off without if she was going to get away with her illusion. She had to leave everything behind—the Social Security card, her driver's license, her credit cards, everything like that. And she wouldn't dare—remember this—she *couldn't*, in applying for another job somewhere, give Robinson's as a reference. May Tate was supposed to be dead. Murdered and dismembered. Well, it's true anybody can walk into a Social Security office and give the name of Lucious Guggenheimer and get a

314

card. Ditto a driver's license. But it was hard enough for her to get that job at Robinson's nine years ago—how much harder for her it would be now, that much older and having no references at all. I thought, if Jessup was the small town it sounded like, whether it was her home town or not, she knew somebody there, and in small Midwest towns you generally find a settled population who know each other. If it was her home town, how easy for her to go back there, even after all this time, say she'd got tired of city life and also say she'd lost all her documents by theft on the way, something like that—and so about then I started trying to contact Jessup. And we now see'—he nodded at the teletype—'that that's more or less what happened. She didn't correspond with the sister there except at Christmas, so the sister probably wouldn't have heard all this hopeful talk about getting married again, or anything about Mrs. Manning. And everybody in Jessup knew about May Tate out in California all these years. It now appears that she used her middle name here, probably liked it better, but in Jessup she'd be known as Eunice Tate. All right. She could and did coolly vanish from L.A., ostensibly as the corpse in the lake—it's been hitting headlines here, but I don't suppose it has in Jessup—and coolly reappear in Jessup as Eunice come home—get a new Social Security card, driver's license,

315

and so on, take a job in town—who'd ask references of her there?—and hey presto, the magic trick is accomplished. When we do go hunting, we go hunting Edna Manning, who is a very different woman.'

'Well, you pulled the rabbit out of the hat,' said Hackett. 'I see it, I see it. Of all the—And look, genius, hadn't we better take some steps to have an eye kept on her back there? That Chief of Police—these small towns!—probably went straight around to see her to ask her why the cops in L.A. are asking questions, and she might take off and—'

'I sent him a teletype,' said Mendoza, 'telling him what we want her for and asking him to hold her. I haven't heard from him—I should imagine he was so dumbfounded he couldn't think what to say—but I also wired the state boys, and they'll be there too.' He lit a new cigarette and contemplated them. 'Which adventurous pair of you would like to fly back to the corn country and get her extradited?'

While the due process of law was going on, they found Mrs. Manning's dentist, got a dental chart, and formally identified the head.

In the end, Mrs. Tate waived extradition, Palliser and a policewoman flew back to escort her home.

She faced them there in Mendoza's office that next Tuesday afternoon, a plain, no-nonsense woman unblinking behind plain plastic-framed glasses. Her square face, with its rather thick brows and straight nose, was a little thin-lipped, but she'd be not unattractive at all if she'd taken more interest in her make-up, her clothes, her hair. Her sturdy body was clothed in a neat beige dress which did nothing for her, and she wore plain brown oxfords.

'Are you the one in charge?' she asked Mendoza abruptly.

'Mrs. Tate wants to talk,' said Palliser. 'Yes, this is Lieutenant Mendoza.'

'We'd like to hear what you have to say,' said Mendoza interestedly. Higgins and Hackett were the only others there—the Fearing thing was dragging on with no leads and probably would go dead on them eventually, but they were still working it; Mendoza called the other two in.

She looked at them, sitting very erect in a straight chair. 'Well, I lost my gamble,' she said in her rather harsh, uncompromising voice. 'That's all. I'm sorry about it, but there it is. I never thought you'd get onto me.'

'We'd like to hear all about it, in detail, Mrs. Tate, if you'd care to tell us,' said Mendoza. He offered her a cigarette, which she refused.

'It was really an accident,' she began, and then looked down at her clasped hands. 'No,

I don't suppose I can really say that either. I lost my temper and I hit her deliberately, and then—and then I was stuck with her, of course. It was the baseball bat I hit her with.'

'A *baseball* bat?' said Hackett involuntarily.

'Yes, that's right. It was right there on the chair, you see. It was a present I'd got for Joey, my great-nephew—Bella's daughter's little boy—for his birthday. I'd been up to Barnsdall Park that morning—that Amateur Artists group I belonged to—Goodness, it seems a long time ago I ever took any interest in that. And Edna was coming to lunch.' She was silent, and then went on, 'I don't suppose you could say there was ever any real friendship between us, but, well, you know people, you've got to mix with them, have some social life, or sit home and twiddle your thumbs all the time. As a matter of fact, that was really why I had—had to do something desperate to cover up that—that she was dead. After it happened and she *was* dead. You see, I'd written her some anonymous letters.'

'You had—'

'It was a fool sort of thing to do, I admit it,' said Mrs. Tate forthrightly. 'She always seemed so quiet and all, I thought maybe it would scare her off. But it didn't. And I hadn't a notion whether she'd kept them, or maybe even taken them to the police, and I wrote them on my own typewriter. That first

318

minute I saw she was dead, all I could think of was those letters. Because I do know something about how the law reads, and I had made threats in them, and if they were traced to me, as they very easily could be, you'd say it had been premeditated murder. You get the gas chamber for that in this state. It wasn't premeditated, but—'

'Why the letters? Scare her off what?'

Mrs. Tate looked angry. 'Off George Barrington,' she said. 'Why, *I* introduced her to the Barringtons before Milly died! He was my friend first, and he'd been—he'd been very nice to me, George may be a little odd some ways but he's really a very nice man—'

And reputed to have quite a bit of money, thought Mendoza.

'And just lately he'd dropped several remarks and really I did think he was going to ask me to marry him—You don't know, a person gets tired.' She shook her head. 'A woman gets tired, my age, having to work all day. I was getting that fed up with it. With everything. You don't know how it is. Alone and all. George has got a nice house, and even before Milly got sick he had a woman come in once a week, help her clean, and he likes a good table, he wouldn't be stingy that way. You might think it sounds funny, me wanting to marry him—*or* her—but I did, and so did she. I don't suppose you need telling that there are more women than there are men to

go around. At our ages we couldn't be picky.'
She looked defiant. 'And I really thought
George *was*—Edna'd been going around some
with another man. I forget his name, a
widower he was—that was last fall. And then
George began taking her out to those dances,
and, well, I didn't like it. Who would? She
was younger than me, and if I'd take George
for all his funny ways because I like the man,
she'd put up with him for his money. And
men will be such fools—fall for her smarmy
ways and let her trick him into a wedding
ring. Well, I knew George first, and before
she came around he *would* have asked me to
marry him—' She stopped on a little gasp.
'Well, anyway, I wrote her those letters. That
was before Christmas. And then George gave
me quite a nice Christmas present, a silk
scarf, and I began to think maybe I could
bring him around—But meanwhile I'd met
Edna here and there, and a couple of things
she said, I don't know, I began to be worried
she guessed it was me who'd written those
letters.'

'What did they say, Mrs. Tate? We didn't
find any of them.'

'You *didn't* have them?' she said slowly.
'Oh. I didn't find them there, and that was all
the more reason for—going on with it, I
didn't know but what you had them, you see.
As a matter of fact, that was half why I'd
asked her to lunch that day, to sort of sound

her out. And if she came right out and accused me, well, I meant to tell her plainly what I thought. What was in them, well, I'd written that lots of people knew she was just after George for his money and if she didn't stop chasing him his friends would see he knew too and she'd better watch out or something might happen to her. You can see how they'd have looked. And I know you can tell which typewriter—'

'Yes,' said Mendoza. He made a steeple of his hands and watched her over them. He thought, incipient violence in this woman to start with, born of frustration, of desperation.

'Well, she came. We had lunch and she actually insisted on helping me wash the dishes. She was nice as pie, sitting there in a chair chatting. Just small talk, you know. She never said a word about the letters, so I thought then she *didn't* suspect, and George had phoned me just the night before and sounded—so I thought—'

The old fox, thought Mendoza, keeping them all sweet, the eager widows chasing him. He grinned into his clasped hands. George Barrington would get a big charge out of this the rest of his life, one woman killing another over him when he was seventy-two. And it probably wouldn't teach him any lessons, the old reprobate.

'And then she said, out of the blue, had I seen George lately, and I said no, and she

321

said, all casual—oh, *such* a lady she was, all dressed up to the nines, and her toenails painted, I could see—she said, "We're going to be married, you know." And I didn't say anything, and after a minute she went on and said it was practically settled, nothing definite at all but they were, and I didn't know whether to believe her because he hadn't said a word on the phone the night before, but she—'

'It wasn't true,' said Mendoza. 'There was nothing definite.'

'Oh,' she said. 'Then—yes, I see—She deserved all she got, that sly bitch! She was trying it on with me, she *did* know about those letters, she was trying to get me mad enough so I'd—'

'And did you get mad enough, then?'

Mrs. Tate bent her head, looking back to her moment of truth. 'You get so tired,' she said in a low voice. 'You get so tired. All of a sudden, when she said that—I supposed she *was* sure of him or she'd never have dared say it—all I could see was me going on like that till I died, work every day, come home, fix dinner and watch some fool TV show while I ate, it's no picnic living alone, for anybody, and single women don't get invited places, and then do the mending or watch more TV and go to bed and go to work next day, come home—And I'm not getting any younger, and maybe after a while getting to where I can't
322

work, and what do I do then? If that stupid fool of a husband of mine hadn't gone and lost all his money—And there'd be Edna, that *I'd* introduced to George, more fool me, living like a princess and no work to do at all. She sat there preening herself like a—like a peacock or something, those jangly bracelets she always wore and—dressed up like a *tart*—And all I could think was it wasn't fair, it wasn't fair, and I hated her so hard and before I knew what I was going to do I walked over and picked up that baseball bat and hit her as hard as I could on the back of the head, and she fell out of the chair, against the coffee table. That was how it happened.'

'And then,' said Mendoza, 'you began to think about the consequences.'

'I thought about those letters, yes. First I thought, well, her keys'd be in her bag, I could go to her place and look for them. But suppose she'd taken them to the police? The minute she was found dead they'd—And she was dead in *my* living room! I stood there looking at her, and you know, I still hated her, and—it was funny how it happened—I remembered hearing her say once—she was always boasting, in little ways, you know—how she didn't have a single birthmark, and I thought, well, neither do I, and the whole plan came to me in a flash. I saw just how I could do. We were about the same size and general build. It'd be a lot of work, but then,' she said grimly, 'I had a lot at stake, didn't I?'

'So you did. Why'd you pick the cemetery to bury the head, and how'd you know you could probably get in there?'

'I went to Milly's funeral there. I don't know how George knew, but he said something about the custodian being in trouble for not locking the gates at night. I saw the old man then. Well, the head was the one thing that mustn't ever be found, and I thought burying it in a grave was a very clever idea, I thought probably there'd be one recently dug, so nobody'd notice if the soil was disturbed—and if there wasn't, or the gates were locked, I thought it might do just as well to just go off the road into that wild country and bury it there. So I drove out to the cemetery on Sunday morning and I saw the same old man in the grounds, so I took a chance I could get in and I did. I'd gone back to Edna's after dark Saturday—oh, I took good care nobody in *my* neighborhood saw me after Saturday—I wore her hat, and—'

'Yes, we know about that. You spent Saturday night cutting up the body?'

'It had to be done, so I did it,' she said shortly. 'Yes.' They were listening to her, fascinated. 'I didn't mind it so much as I thought I would. I can't say I've ever been squeamish. I brought the meat cleaver back with me from Edna's. I didn't try to—clean up any, the house I mean, because I wanted it to be obvious, when you—And I took care to leave some blood in Edna's apartment, too. And I put all the—pieces in the car—'

'In Mrs. Manning's plastic clothes protectors?'

'Well, the arms and legs and head, yes. I thought the park was a nice public place where the body'd be found soon—And next morning, very early, before it got light, I got away from the house. It was lucky about the money, I had that two hundred and fifty dollars I'd meant to buy the car with, you see. And Edna had almost fifteen in her bag, I took that, too. And I tore the page out of my address book that had my sister's name; naturally I didn't want you asking around there. I'm not a great one for talking about the past and I was sure nobody here knew I still had relations back East, or where.

'It kind of worried me about Nicky, leaving him all that time, but he's a very healthy dog, and besides, if he did get too hungry and raise a fuss, the neighbors would find out I was gone even sooner. I knew the Bessemers'd be back the next week, and I left out a whole lot of dry kibbled food for him, on newspapers against the house, and I left the hose turned on just a little so he'd have water—'

That Düsseldorf monster, hadn't they called him, killing some fifty-odd people and weeping over his pet canary, thought

325

Mendoza.

'And I don't know as there was anything here I regretted leaving,' she said. 'I didn't especially care about going back to Jessup, but it was the one safe place I *could* go—get a job without any questions asked. Like I had, at Wallace's drugstore. Everybody always called me Eunice there, and I could—'

'Mrs. Tate,' said Mendoza gently, 'where did you leave the arms and legs?'

She looked at him and smiled very faintly. 'They're in the Monteria Lake Reservoir in Chatsworth,' she said. 'There's no fence around that one.'

And Higgins said involuntarily, 'Jesus H. Christ! That's going to put the hell of a lot of people off their breakfast coffee tomorrow morning!'

       ★   ★   ★

They started dragging the reservoir.

And at lunch on Wednesday, when Mendoza ordered a drink, Detective Grace said to him, 'What you ought to order, Lieutenant, is a thing I came across last night. Called a Brainstorm. Irish whiskey, dry Vermouth, Benedictine and orange peel. Talk about a brainstorm.'

'God,' said Mendoza, 'what a mixture. Well, we do get the oddities once in a while, don't we?'

'But what a *thing*,' said Angel. 'How any woman—'

'Well, it all followed sort of logical, once she *had* killed the other one,' said Hackett. 'You can see that. And me saying females aren't logical. Talk about cold-blooded—'

'Um, yes,' said Angel. 'When you come down to it, Art, not many people are that logical, period.'

'I guess not, but most females—Well, for God's sake, you having Sheila all formally christened when we're not members of any—'

'And you,' said Angel, 'walking into that agency, an innocent lamb, and letting them con you into buying that—that *sports* car—'

'¡*Perdón*!' said Hackett. 'I guess you've got me, girl.' He ruminated, and added, 'But she does handle very nice. Very nice indeed.'

Angel made a face at him and said, 'Men.'

★ ★ ★

'Brother,' said Grace. 'And I sometimes think I'm halfway smart. Little education working for him. I'd heard about the crystal ball, but he was really *on* this one. Very smart boy, that Mendoza.'

'He seems to be,' said Virginia. 'You're shaking down there, Jase? Liking it?'

'Nice bunch of fellows,' said Grace. 'Sure. I usually get along with people, honey.'

'So you do,' said Virginia. 'So you do.'

★　　★　　★

'It was really *my* murder,' said Alison, brushing her hair. 'Why, if I hadn't happened to have met Mrs. Tate, you'd probably never have *connected* her, Luis. It might have been ages—or never—before she was reported missing. And the same with the Manning woman, you said so yourself, you weren't interested in her any more, you wouldn't have gone back unless I'd—'

'All right, I said I'd never hear the last of it, your very own murder.' Mendoza looked at her. 'Are you coming to bed?'

'In a minute. What a very funny business it was. In a way, you can understand it—passions of youth and all that maybe not quite as passionate as the yearning of middle age for security. But that *woman*—Really you could say I gave you all the leads on it, *amante*—'

'So you did. You like to come down to the office with me tomorrow and try your hand at solving this damn Fearing thing?'

'No, thank you,' said Alison with dignity. 'I might spoil my record. Turn your new brain, Detective Grace, onto it.'

Mendoza laughed. 'And I do wonder if

328

something new will turn up tomorrow. Probably, probably. About due for it. We do get them.'

'That *woman*. But then who was it said, "The female of the species—"'

'I have heard the quotation. *De veras*. Are you coming to bed at all?'

'I'm coming, I'm coming,' said Alison hastily. And came.

Photoset, printed and bound in Great Britain by REDWOOD PRESS LIMITED, Melksham, Wiltshire